The Layers of
Human Suffering

Martin Garcia

authorHOUSE®

AuthorHouse™
1663 Liberty Drive
Bloomington, IN 47403
www.authorhouse.com
Phone: 833-262-8899

Published by AuthorHouse 06/21/2021

ISBN: 978-1-6655-2995-2 (sc)
ISBN: 978-1-6655-2996-9 (hc)
ISBN: 978-1-6655-3006-4 (e)

Library of Congress Control Number: 2021912691

Contents

CHAPTER 1

MICHAEL JAYDEN MANFORD

September 11, 2001, was a day that shaped the lives of not only many Americans but also many people around the world. The event awakened many Americans to the horrors of terrorism. As a naïve child who weighed scarcely eighty-five pounds and stood four feet eight, Michael Jayden Manford was awkward, as many children are at the age of nine.

Michael had started to discover his independence at an early age, when his mother informed him she made an appointment with their dentist to straighten his tooth. Michael quickly rejected the idea by saying, "No," it is different than children in my class, and I like it." When Michael was not quite five years old, he received an earth-shattering jolt the loss of his father, and now he was about to learn the realities of life.

In the early morning hours of September 11, Michael was about to turn nine, and his only thoughts up to that moment were about pulling stunts on his family, mainly his mother and his aunt, Jayda Manford.

His stunts, or tricks, were not harmful or malicious, yet his antics were more sophisticated than any child well over his age could imagine. His number one goal was opening presents on Christmas and birthdays. Michael never liked being surprised with gifts, which his family learned early in his life but did not fully understand.

Yes, Michael had an unconventional way of dealing with the loss of his father. He became more interested in reading, writing, and solving mathematics, which made him smarter than many older children. Early in the morning, Michael acted as if he had just at that moment woken up and was still sleepy. He rubbed his eyes to make it look like he had just stumbled out of bed and was walking into the bedroom where his mother was sleeping soundly. It was seconds before 3:00 a.m.

Michael was attempting to hoodwink his mother into allowing him to open his birthday presents; besides, he could not relax in anticipation of what he would be receiving.

Michael had figured that his mother would be too sleepy to realize what was going on and permit him to open his presents before she went right back to sleep. He had studied his mother in the morning just before her alarm clock went off; she reached to hit the snooze button before falling asleep again. He had done his homework on this assignment.

Michael Jayden Manford's father, Jayden Michael, was killed in a horrible car accident five years earlier. Michael believed his father was assassinated. This belief, which he never expressed to his mother, was a ticking time bomb that no one had noticed.

Now, Michael was reflecting on the right time to make his move. He quietly but quickly walked to the room and started the countdown in his mind: *Ten, nine, eight …* Michael had practiced for this moment all week. *Three, two, one … 3:00 a.m.* "Ma! Ma!" Michael called out his mother, almost shouting from the foot of her bed.

Michael contemplated the situation. *In the morning, when my mother questions me, I will say, Mommy, I asked you last night, and you said I could open my gifts. Do you not remember the conversation we had? Naturally, I will flash her my innocent smile, and I will then answer.* "Mother, you permitted me to open my presents last night. Have you already forgotten? I did not do anything wrong, honestly."

Mrs. Catherine Manford was so startled by the noise that she nearly jumped out of bed. Her son had a high-pitched voice that penetrated her ears; it was like a siren had gone off in her room. She sat up in the bed to see what was amiss, checking the clock.

At first she looked around trying to gather her bearings, until she saw that it was her son standing at the foot of her bed. Her first thought was that he had to be sick. She began feeling his forehead to see whether Michael was running a fever, and once she realized there was nothing, she asked, "What is wrong, Michael? Are you in pain?"

"No, Ma."

"Michael Jayden Manford!" Catherine exclaimed. She composed herself, realizing that he was trying to pull the wool over her eyes. "Young man, what are you doing up at this time in the morning? Is there something wrong?" she asked him again, glancing at her alarm clock on the nightstand.

"No, Mommy, I am all alright." He was disappointed to realize that his plan was not going according to schedule; his mother should be falling asleep by now. "Ma, I wanted to say it is my birthday. Remember you told me last week I was born at three in the morning? You also said that I would not be allowed to open my presents until I was nine. Well, it is three, and I am nine years old. I am ready to open my presents. You said I could." Then he flashed his innocent look, which always seemed to work on her.

"Michael, are you serious, waking me up at this time so I can permit you to open your gifts? Young man, march yourself right back to bed, or I will tan you for your first present. Michael, for your information, you will have to wait for your party tonight—as I am sure you are aware. You have school in the morning, which is more significant than any present you may obtain today or any other moment in your life. Understand? I will talk to you tomorrow; now, you need your sleep, because you have school tomorrow." Catherine could not disbelieve Michael would pull his stunts at this time in the morning to ask permission to open his gifts. She gave Michael a stern look.

Michael was confused by her pronouncement. In his mind, there was nothing more important than opening presents on his birthday or Christmas. "I think so, Ma." Michael did not understand, although he had learned to trust his mother in the past when she had made similar commentary.

"Michael, in time you will understand when you are older. Now, we both need to sleep; you have school tomorrow, and I have to work in the morning. We will continue this conversation tomorrow when I return from work. You will be able to open your presents at the birthday party, unless you prefer to prolong that opportunity until Saturday. Your choice."

Michael put his head down in disappointment that he would not be able to open his presents. Michael had been looking forward to the moment for several days. Nonetheless, he knew all too well the tone of voice of his mother when she meant it. His mother had never hit him but, Saturday was out of the question, and that threat was on the level.

He had to settle for waiting; in the meantime, he would have to study his notes and figure out what went wrong with his plan. "Okay, Ma, I will wait until tomorrow." Michael turned around and headed toward his bedroom; his whole world had crumbled around him.

Catherine was trying not to smile while he was in front of her. Michael reminded her of his father. "Michael, would you like to sleep here tonight?"

"Yeah, Ma!" he said excitedly. "You want me to sleep in here with you?" He had thought she would be upset at him for days after waking her up, especially after she told him that they would talk, which always meant after she returned home.

"Michael, as long as you do not ask me any questions or interrogate me about your gifts or to give you hints. One more thing: do not try to wake me up before my alarm goes off. Do I make myself clear?"

"Okay, I promise." Michael ran over to his mother and jumped into her arms, hugging and kissing his mother as hard as he could. After he settled in bed, he became curious. "Ma, how is tomorrow your first day of work? What about the three weeks you were going to their office?"

"Yes, it is; that was training. I will start working at the World Trade Center in the North Tower. I seem to remember that you wanted a tour of those buildings. Michael, if you are on your best behavior the rest of this week, on Saturday or Sunday, I will take you. How does that sound?"

Michael started meditating and then added, "That is great. Can we make it on Sunday, the sixteenth? The number six is a better number for us. Ma, what about the last three weeks you were in training. Did they pay you? What was …?"

Catherine interrupted Michael because if she let him continue, the alarm would go off without her having been able to sleep. "That was training, and now it is time I get at least a catnap. No more questions, understand?"

"Okay, Ma. I love you. Good night."

Catherine lay in bed, hugging Michael and thinking he always had to have the last word. She had received a letter the principal had written: it seems that they wanted to advance Michael to the seventh grade. Catherine knew Michael was an exceptional student.

Michael completed his homework assignments in his classroom while the teacher was still giving them the task. *Still, I have my reservations. Michael would be the youngest child in the class by three or four years, other children may start resenting him when he starts to outperform them—and he will. My fear is they may start picking on him; Michael has never responded well to being bullied and has his way of getting even.* This was when Catherine missed Jayden, who had died too young in that car accident.

Catherine continued thinking about the death of her husband. The driver was driving a stolen dump truck. The man steered head-on into Jayden. Nothing happened to the driver. It almost seemed as if the man maneuvered into the car on purpose, according to a witness. The driver was in the country illegally and had been deported several times; the man had escaped the judicial system. *I have not told Michael the truth about the*

5

death of Jayden. Knowing my son, he will mount his own investigation with mathematical formulas.

Later that morning, the alarm clock went off; Catherine figured this meant a ten-minute catnap. She went to hit the snooze button but then practically bounce out of bed. Catherine stared at the time in disbelief; the time seemed to be all wrong. She immediately looked around for Michael and said out loud, "Michael has to understand this cannot happen again. Tonight I will have to have a serious conversation with that boy. Michael, up at this time? That is unbelievable."

Catherine composed herself. There was only one place he could be at this time. She tiptoed out of her bedroom and went into the spare room as she slowly opened the door. Michael was at the edge of the bed and seemed to be measuring the boxes of his presents. "What in the world are you doing now?"

Michael was startled. He needed to think of something quick. "Good morning, Ma! How did you sleep last night? I want to thank you for letting me sleep in your bed."

"I guess you want me to cancel your party tonight? I see you want to wait until Saturday to open those presents. Forget the Twin Towers trip. That is good, because I will get some much-needed rest this weekend, which I will require after your stunt last night."

Michael looked at his mother. She was about to give him a long lecture. "It is not what you think. Ma! I was looking around for my shoes." That was the only words he could think of on the spot.

"You mean the ones you have on your feet?" Catherine gave him a long, hard stare.

He quickly went into defense mode. "Ma, honestly, I was not trying to open my presents. Look: the wrapping on the packages are still intact."

"Go on, Michael. You have thirty seconds to explain yourself, and it had better be good."

He looked at his mother, and that stare meant she was very serious. He knew that he had to come clean, or she would know it.

"Honest, Ma! I was not trying to open my presents. I was weighing and measuring the boxes to have an idea of what I may be receiving for my birthday. I already know where you bought the presents, and it is not clothing or shoes."

"And why did my alarm go off one hour late?"

Michael was caught off guard. "You went to bed late last night. I wanted to give you an extra hour of sleep." The answer was more like a question.

"You mean because you woke me up at three in the morning."

"Ma, I am sorry and will never wake you up like that again. I promise."

She looked at him in disbelief. "Go to your room and finish dressing. Mrs. Wilson will be here before you know it, and she is always in a hurry. I want you to be ready when she arrives, and I want you to complete your chores."

"I have already brushed my teeth, made the bed, cleaned my room, and had breakfast, Ma. Is my party off? I was not trying to open my presents, honestly." Michael had a look of sadness on his face.

"Michael, I am going to give you the benefit this time of doubt this time." Catherine was upset. However, when Michael turned around and headed toward his room, she could not help but smile.

Catherine thought, *He has completed all his chores without me having to repeat myself at least a dozen times. That has to be a world record.* Michael always seemed to know what presents he is receiving.

Catherine checked the time. *Oh, boy, now I am running behind schedule. I do not want to be late.*

At 11:30 that morning, Michael found it strange that all the children were being let out of school this early. The teachers were acting unusually quiet, and their eyes seem to be red. The parents and nannies were mostly outside waiting. His aunt Jayda was waiting for him across the street, and her eyes were bloodshot. Mrs. Wilson was nowhere in sight.

On second thought, he contemplated, *Jayda may let the cat out of the bag.* She may at least give him a hint as to what his mother had purchased. She had already informed him of what she had bought for him for his birthday.

Jayda ran up to her nephew and hugged him hard, tears streaming down her eyes. She had never been able to hide her feelings when it came to her family.

"Michael, we have to talk." She looked down at him with bloodshot eyes and trembling hands. She thought about how to break the news to Michael. She was trying to collect her thoughts as they walked toward her car.

Michael started crying. Although he did not know why at the moment, he did not want to hear what his Auntie Jayda was about to say. The last time he saw Jayda crying like that was when his father had gone to heaven. "Auntie, where am I going to live?" The words seem to flow out of his mouth. There was a fear in his tone of voice as his hold body started quivering.

Jayda was startled. She had not expected Michael to ask such a question. How could he know Catherine was dead? She looked down at him, "Oh, baby, you know that I love you. You are a son to me. You will live with me for as long as you want." They hugged each other and cried in the middle of the street. Finally, Jayda mustered up the strength to speak again. "Let us go to the apartment and pick up some things that you will need for the next couple of days. You can even open your presents. Catherine was telling me how anxious you are to see what you received for your birthday. How does that sound?"

"Auntie." Michael always referred to Jayda as Auntie. "I will never open those gifts."

Jayda was too preoccupied to hear what Michael said; there were too many things on her mind and another funeral to plan. Jayda had to make arrangements for Catherine; she could not believe that in less than five years, there were two burials.

Catherine named Jayda the executor of the estate and to have custody of Michael. Catherine had changed her will two weeks ago but never explained as to why. Furthermore, Catherine had explained, "Jayden and I want to draw up the will. We talked about it, and after his death, I never seemed to have time. This is the right thing to do. One day, I will sit down with you and clarify why it was essential."

Once inside the condominium, Michael looked at Jayda and said, "Auntie, I want to keep some things from my mother. Could you pack some of my clothing?"

Jayda found the request unusual, especially because Michael was choosy regarding his clothing; he never allowed anyone to select his clothing. He had always chosen his apparel and matched all his outfits. *It has to be the loss of his mother.* "Michael, take all the time you need, and if you need my help, call me; I will be right here." Jayda needed to recover documents from the safe in the bedroom.

Michael needed time to grieve the death of his mother in his own way.

Michael and Jayda never again talked about the death of Catherine. Jayda would never detail the conversation she had had with Catherine minutes before her death.

The funeral was held six weeks after her death without her remains; the authorities had informed Jayda recovering the remains for precise identification was questionable. *Catherine was on the phone with me from inside the building, and she wanted to notify me. She was inside without an escape route. The plane crashed floors below Catherine. I stayed on the phone with her until there was one final horrifying scream from Catherine, and the line went dead. I watched on TV as the tower collapsed at that moment.*

The psychologist informed Jayda, "Michael seems to be adjusting to the loss of his parents remarkably well." However, Jayda was not sure; there was something in his demeanor that concerned her.

In the following years, Jayda kept reading books on children and adolescents losing both their parents. Jayda never noticed anything unusual in his behavior; to her, it did seem that Michael was blaming himself. The psychologist said, "That is normal. He is coming around. Yes, at first Michael had felt that if he had let his mother sleep, she would have been able to escape."

However, Jayda had become convinced there something was stirring within Michael, embedded within his subconscious. Jayda kept reading books on children losing their parents early in their life even after Michael went off to college.

Michael breezed through junior high and high school. For college, he wanted to complete the four years in two. *I do not see why he is in such a hurry,* Jayda thought.

On Saturday, May 3, 2008, Michael was a college sophomore at the age of sixteen, preparing himself for several midterm exams he had come up and at DePaul University in Chicago, Illinois. He was studying management science.

In the same city, a seven-year-old child was crying. Her mother was leading her down a dark street by the hand, almost to the point of dragging her. "Monica, you need to walk faster; I do not want to be late."

"Mommy, I am afraid because it is dark. Can we go home now? I am hungry; are we going to eat today?"

"After tonight, Monica, you will never be hungry ever again," Cheryl commented as two men approach them from out of the shadows.

One of the men stepped up closer to them while the other man stayed in the background. "Hey, Cheryl, is this your beautiful daughter? Hi, honey. What is your name? You are pretty." Bruce Williams, known as the Demon of Chicago, kneeled next to Monica while trying to befriend her. "Here, this is for you." Bruce Williams held a candy bar for her in his left hand.

Monica was terrified of these men. She had never seen these men before and was trying to hide behind her mother. "Where is my daddy? Mommy, you said that he was going to meet us here. I want my daddy!"

Monica was hungry, however her father had always said never to accept candy from strangers, and she had never seen this man before. On the other hand, the pain in her stomach was overtaking her sense of logic. Her hand was shaking as Monica started to lean toward Bruce, and her hand started reaching almost to the point of taking the candy bar.

"Monica, say thanks to the nice man and take the candy. Monica, you were complaining about being hungry. Well, Mr. Bruce Williams is giving you food." Cheryl then turned her attention to Bruce. "Do we have a deal? I need one now, and I want all the money upfront."

"Cheryl, what are you going to do with one thousand dollars and three free fixes? I will tell you what I will do for you, because I am a very generous man. You are a preferred customer, and I will always look out for your well-being. I will give you five free fixes that you can ask for whenever you want. I can see you require your medication now, plus one hundred dollars now." He held a hypodermic in his right hand but hid the needle from Monica's view. "Cheryl, this is take it or leave it."

Bruce said to the man with him, "Bill, take Monica to the car. We will take her out to get some real food. How does that sound to you?" He directed his question to Monica.

Bill practically started dragging Monica away. Monica cried, dropped her chocolate bar, and started calling out for her father.

"Do not drag her," Bruce said, "Picked Monica up and carried her the way you would your child." Bruce was annoyed with Bill.

"Bruce, I thought we had a deal. I know you need Monica, and I want my money—or should I take her to someone else?" Cheryl tried to plead her case, however, her body was shaking, and she needed a fix.

Bruce waited before saying another word. He made sure that Monica could not see or hear their conversation. "You sold your daughter for a few fixes. What are you going to deal with now? I have your daughter; what kind of mother sells her child for one thousand dollars and three free fixes?"

Bruce then tossed a hypodermic needle at her feet as he started walking away. He stopped to turn around as Cheryl was injecting herself and threw a crumbled bill at her face.

Cheryl picked up the bill as the drug took effect. "Hey Bruce, this is a one-hundred-dollar bill. When do I get the rest of the money?" As Cheryl spoke, the words were slurred and incoherent. Her eyes were droopy, and she had trouble keeping herself awake. Cheryl was losing control of her bodily functions.

"Cheryl! Are you entitled to thirty gold pieces for selling your daughter? File a complaint with the Better Business Bureau—that is if you are still alive tomorrow." Bruce looked at Cherly with disgust.

The next morning an unidentified man called 911 and claimed, "There is the body of a woman lying at the corner of South Maplewood Ave and West Thirty-Fifth Street." The man would not identify himself.

An hour and a half after the call to 911, Detective Nelson Carter, assigned to the Twelfth District, asked the officers on the scene, "Anyone here know who she is or have seen her around before?" The police identified the body as Mrs. Cheryl Arrowood, according to documents found on her person.

Detective Carter sensed something wrong. The situation did not seem to add up. At first glance, it was an overdosed, but nothing added up. *A hundred-dollar bill? A Junkie does not have that kind of money. She would have spent the money on the drugs.* He hoped an officer knew her.

Officer Merkerson, who had just arrived on the scene, took a closer look at her. There was some hesitation in from Merkerson before he said, "Detective, I have never seen her in this area, but that is Cheryl Arrowood. She is an addict and has needle tracks between her toes. Was there a small girl with her? The girl's name is Monica; she cannot be more than six or seven years old." Officer Merkerson became concerned as he checked his notes. "I hope her father has Monica, otherwise we could have a missing child."

"Officer Merkerson, you said this is not where she hangs out. Did you filled a report to the Department of Social Services? I hope that the department has the girl," Detective Carter said.

"Detective, I reported the incident to Social Services three times," Officer Merkerson said while reading from his notes.

"Sir, this would be the first time in my career the Social Services Department would have taken action. I am hoping for her loser father to be touring around town with Monica. Cheryl is the type of mother who would sell her daughter for a fix." Officer Merkerson had never had much respect for the Social Services Department.

"Officer Merkerson, I want you to follow up with the Department of Social Services; let us hope that they have custody of Monica. Then find the whereabouts of her father on the chance he is babysitting." Carter's own irritation with Social Services was apparent. The incompetence of the department may have cost the life of this girl. His only priority now was to find Monica. He called all the officers together and informed them to spread out and start checking the neighborhood. There was a railroad yard nearby, so Carter would need additional officers to check the area.

Carter's investigation revealed that Cheryl Arrowood had been homeless for over a month. Monica had been living on the street with her mother. Monica's father was in jail, being held on armed robbery and attempted murder. He refused to be interview by Officer Merkerson until his lawyer was present, even though Merkerson made it clear that this was about his daughter, who was missing; the officer was not there to inquire about the criminal's latest exploits. Furthermore, Merkerson informed Mr. Luis Arrowood that they needed a picture of his daughter.

They wanted to file an Amber Alert with a photograph of Monica Cindy Arrowood, seven years old. They had to settle for a description from

Officer Merkerson of the minor without her picture for the first twenty-four hours.

Once his lawyer arrived, Mr. Arrowood had one question: Could they make a deal for his cooperation? His concern for his daughter was lacking.

Detective Carter was no stranger to these types of abuse or missing children cases after his thirty-two years in the police department. He had never heard that request. Nevertheless, Carter's only concern was for Monica, and knowing the dangers existing for children that went missing are chilling, he reflected on all that he had learned about missing children throughout the years.

One in six runaways will likely become a victim of child sex trafficking. Traffickers are looking for the vulnerable, run away, or children in a difficult situation are often a primary target. In this case, we have a mother who may have sold her daughter for drugs? That is the question. Runaway and homeless children; are sold into survival which is another form of child exploitation. Monica never had a chance; not this time I will find her——one way or another.

Detective Carter was tired of seeing this script play out over and over again in his career.

CHAPTER 2

BARBARA WHITMORE

On Thursday, June 20, 2008, Barbara Whitmore was riding her bicycle in the middle of the street, and she was so upset that her eyes welled up with tears. Her vision clouded as she went down Church Street and headed toward Diberville Avenue in Ontario, Canada. Barbara wanted to disappear from shame after learning her girlfriends had received their acceptance letters from the colleges of their choice.

Students in school were starting to harass Barbara for over a week and selected her to deliver the graduation speech—until they learned Barbara had not received an acceptance letter from any college. She nearly missed her turn and so made an abrupt turn; a van barely missed hitting her. "That is just what I need to end a horrible week," she mumbled as she arrived home. "I should inform my teacher that I will not be giving a graduation speech."

She checked the mail, but there was nothing for her. Then there was a knock at the front door; her next-door neighbor, Mrs. Couture, was at the front porch.

"How can I help you?" Barbara asked. As she was attending to Mrs. Couture, a vehicle drove past the front of her house. It looked like the same vehicle that had just missed hitting her moments earlier.

"Barbie, dear, these letters were delivered to my mailbox by accident. My husband just found them mix with the mail that we received while on vacation. It must have been the new postal carrier." Mrs. Couture gave her a pack of letters and then turned around and went home without saying another word.

"Thank you, Mrs. Couture," Barbara replied. *She always insists on calling me Barbie. I've reminded her in the past that I want to be addressed by my name. That was a nickname as a child.* She looked at the letters, which were mostly junk. Halfway through the pack, there was an envelope, and Barbara started sweating profusely. It was a letter from Harvard Law School. She was apprehensive about opening the envelope; the other correspondence slid from her trembling hands.

After a few minutes of a blank stare, she made up her mind to open the envelope and could only focus on one word: *Acceptance.* She cried, but this time with tears of joy.

Four hours after contacting her girlfriends, Barbara was celebrating with Nicky and Terrie. They were at a bar and grill on Cambridge Avenue, just minutes from their homes.

"May I ask what is it that you ladies are celebrating?" said a man in his midthirties. He was well dressed with a thick mustache, and he had a heavy French accent.

Nicky responded, "You are looking at a future *Cour Suprême du Canada.*" It was the equivalent to a Supreme Court judge of the United States, and she stressed that part in French. "Barbara will be attending Harvard Law School on a full scholarship."

"Congratulations! Barbara, may I buy you, Nicky, and Terry a drink to help you celebrate?"

Before Nicky or Terrie could answer, Barbara said, "No, thank you for the kind offer." She had a pleasant smile on her face while rejecting him. *There is something about a man his age who wants to hang around teenagers.* Barbara was bothered. *The only way he could know our names is by listening in on our conversation? Why is he so interested in us? That is creepy.*

"How rude of me for not introducing myself. My name is Arthur

Charpentier. Are you sure there are no strings attached?" After a few seconds, he realized Barbara had rejected his offer. Barbara was controlling their conversation. He smiled at them, said, "Perhaps next time," and walked out of the establishment.

"Are you crazy? He is kind of cute in a disgusting sort of way for a man his age—and he has eyes for only you?" Terrie commented.

Nicky added, "Besides, the drinks would have been free." She laughed at her own remark.

Once the celebration was over, they were ready to go home. Barbara started leading Nicky and Terry out of the establishment and turned to Nicky. "Okay, hand me the keys. I am doing the driving. You guys can stay over at my house—or should I drive you home? Tomorrow, I will return your precious car to your house." Barbara was not an alcoholic drinker and was the designated driver of the group.

Nicky reached into her purse and held the keys over her head in a joking manner. "Okay, Mother Dear. On the condition that we have a slumber party at your home."

"Yes, let us have a slumber party!" Terrie agreed with her sister.

They were all hugging and laughing with each other. They started dancing and singing while walking toward the vehicle.

When Barbara turned the corner and headed toward the parking lot, a black van with the hood up was blocking their car, and two men were carrying on a conversation. They did not seem to be in a hurry to move the vehicle while smoking cigarettes and leaning against the side of the van.

"Excuse me, gentleman, how long will it take before you can fix your vehicle? It is blocking our car." Barbara thought that if they were waiting for a tow truck, she would call her father, who was minutes away.

"I do not know—I am not in charge," one of the men answered as he rapped on the side of the van. The door slid open.

Barbara founded herself sharing down the barrel of an automatic weapon being held by Mr. Arthur Charpentier, who was standing inside the van. "Barbara, why did you reject my generous offer? I was trying to be kind to you."

Before Terrie and Nicky could move, Mr. Charpentier aimed his automatic weapon at them.

Terrie and Nicky focused on the weapon Mr. Charpentier aimed at them, so they did not notice the two men moving behind them. These men had quickly maneuvered themselves behind them and injected them with a hypodermic needle into the side of their necks.

Nicky and Terrie were carried as tears rolled down their eyes; they seemed like zombies.

"Barbara, I am not letting you escape a second time, and it will not be healthy for your girlfriends." While Mr. Arthur Charpentier spoke, he aimed his weapon at Nicky. "Besides, I want to make you an offer you will not be able to refuse." His facial expression was of pure evil, and he gave Barbara a murderous stare.

Barbara Whitmore and Terrie and Nicky Muller had been missing since Friday, June 20, 2008. The Royal Mounted Police, Missing Persons Unit, mounted an investigation of their disappearance, and foul play was suspected.

Two weeks after Barbara, Terrie, and Nicky disappeared, the police discovered the vehicle belonging to Nicky burned in the woods fifteen miles from their last known location.

The pressure that mounted on these two families was overwhelming. On Saturday, September 4, 2010, on Nicky and Terry Muller's twentieth birthday—two years and three months after their disappearance—Mrs. Muller walked into the living room and threw a rope over the chandelier. Mr. Muller found his wife hanging at the entrance of their home that evening. Three years after Barbara's disappearance, Mr. and Mrs. Whitmore filed for divorce. They had been married for over twenty-six years.

Authorities believed that because they had disappeared together, it was under suspicious circumstances.

Mrs. Whitmore was asked by her colleagues to become a spoke person on human trafficking.

Mrs. Whitmore rejected the offer, however she privately informed her friends, "If I become vocal, I fear that the kidnappers will retaliate against my daughter—if Barbara is still alive." She wanted to work in the background.

What Mrs. Whitmore learned about human trafficking horrified her.

The victims, mostly women, and children were deprived of their human rights. Hard labor or prostitution through intimidation, force, sexual assault, and threats of violence to themselves or their families.

On Friday, December 22, 2017, Michael was returning home from active military duty—at least, that was what he had told his aunt Jayda. After completing seven years of active military duty in the US Navy, he had not seen his aunt for almost three years. "Auntie, I am home! Hey, where is my favorite gal in the whole world?"

"Hay is for horses, young man. You have not learned that by now? I thought you knew better than that, with all that education you received. Has the money been a total waste? So I am your favorite gal in the world? Liar, liar, pants on fire." As Jayda spoke, she came out of her bedroom in a rush and gave Michael a big hug. There were tears of joy in her eyes. "Are you ever going to give me grandchildren?"

"Grandchildren! You know that I am not married, and that is not in my immediate plans. On the other hand, you have never given me the brother or sister I have always asked you for. On second thought, at this stage in my life, I prefer a sister. By the way, is there anything cooking in your oven?" Michael rubbed her stomach playfully.

"Hey, buster, show me some respect! I am your aunt. You think you must be married before you have offspring, but it is okay for me to have children out of wedlock?" Jayda punched him in the stomach. However, she broke a fingernail in the process and checked the rest of her nails. "What do you have under there?"

"That is my six-pack," Michael said as he gently held her hand and kissed it with a smile on his face. "Besides, Auntie, you don't want me to charge you with child abuse, do you?"

Jayda and Michael had a private joke between them when a fifteen-year-old called 911 claiming her phone was stolen by her parents.

The police officer responding to the call discovered the following. The previous night, the girl had informed her parents she had to study for an exam and had gone into her room. At 4:40 a.m. the next morning, her mother caught her trying to sneak back into the house through her bedroom window.

They were both laughing, and Jayda held Michael by the hand as she led him into the kitchen. "Come on, tell me about your adventures in the navy—and do not leave out any of the juicy details. Do not think I have forgiven you for not calling or writing in the last three years. Since when do we send postcards to each other? I am still feeling hurt."

Jayda studied Michael; something was not right with him. She scrutinized Michael from the minute she saw him standing in the living room. He was well dressed, however that was not his style. Michael never wore turtleneck shirts, sweats, or scarves, yet he was wearing a turtleneck shirt with a sports jacket. Jayda stared at his neck and then added, "Michael, I missed you so much." She moved in to hug Michael again, reached around his neck, and quickly pulled down on his turtleneck shirt. "How long did you think you were going to keep that from me?"

"Auntie, I did not want you to worry. This is nothing, just a small scar."

"Michael, if the injury is small and nothing to worry about, why are you hiding it? I see you had plastic surgery. I can recommend someone who is an expert, and it will look like nothing happened—if you are interested." Jayda changed the subject because she could tell the conversation was making him uncomfortable. "Are you hungry?"

"No, Auntie, I am taking you out for dinner. But first I want to ask you a few questions about my mother and father."

"Michael, what is on your mind? This sounds serious." Jayda started to boil water for their tea. Then she asked him, "Do you have a list of restaurants that you want me to select from, or have you changed your ways?"

Michael gave Jayda a piece of paper with a list of three of the top restaurants in New York City. He knew she liked to patronize those three restaurants. They were three of the finest in Manhattan for her.

"Michael, I see that now you are resorting to bribery; this is a good start. However, you have not changed your ways."

Michael ignored the remark; he had heard similar comments many times in the past.

"Auntie, today I visited the gravesite of my parents." Michael had not returned to their graves since the remains of his mother were buried. That was almost one year after her funeral. "I need to ask you a few questions about them. The memory of my parents seemed to be fading, especially my father; I do not remember him. The only things I remember about him are starting to become blurred, and I am having trouble picturing him in my mind; if it were not for the stories you have related to me about him, I wouldn't have anything. I have better memories of my mother."

Jayda had been wondering for a long time when Michael would start asking questions about his father. Jayden and Jayda were twins. She knew that this date was just around the corner. He had at no time asked any questions about him before. Why now? What had changed? Jayden's death was a complete mystery, and the person responsible for his demise had avoided justice.

"Michael, what do you want to know about your father? I will tell you everything you want to know about Jayden and then some; he was not a perfect man. He was working hard to be a good husband to your mother and loved you very much.

"Jayden and Catherine were married for a short time, and they were happy in their brief relationship. He was a good and honest man. Catherine and I became good friends from the moment we met; she had a personality that attracted the attention of everyone in a room."

Jayda though to herself, *Michael used to pepper Catherine and me with all types of inquiries about the death of his father. When Catherine died, Michael never spoke of the subject again. I feel he is investigating the car accident one more time.* She answered all of his questions about his father; these were not the types of questions she had anticipated. *Those inquiries appeared more like a blistering cross-examination; I am surprised he did not pull out a lie detector. I hope Michael will drop this or run into a dead-end.*

At dinner, Jayda thought this was nothing new for Michael. He had always learned to compartmentalize his life events since his ninth birthday, or maybe after the death of Jayden. He became so interested in numbers and reading, and now this seemed more of an obsession.

In the past, Michael never withheld any information from me, no matter how painful or embarrassing. The last three years ago, Michael stopped all corresponding with family and friends. I asked Michael why he cut off communication with the family or where he had been station, and Michael changed the subject. When he joined the Navy SEALs, I did my research. It did not surprise me that Michael joined one of the most arduous units in the military.

Jayda finally realized why he was asking all those questions. *Oh, no—Michael is out for revenge. What has Michael learned about his father's death? What makes him suspect someone within the family could be involved?*

Jayda learned for the first time what Michael had to experience throughout his training; this reminded her when Michael learned he could skip three grades in school. *Michael pleaded with me until I agreed, and he handled it without showing effects in school.* Jayda felt for some time that Michael showed no impact in his behavior or education. Jayda was now having second thoughts. Michael may have been fooling her and his psychiatrist.

Presently, Michael was extraordinarily quiet in thought, contemplating his journey to Texas. "Auntie, how is your apple pie?"

"It is good," she commented while pointing at the apple pie. She reached over and took ice cream from the plate. Jayda placed it on the pie. That was normal behavior between them. "Would you like some?"

"No, thank you, I will pass. It does look delicious."

During their conversation, Jayda learned what Michael had to endure to become a Navy SEAL: twenty-four weeks of basic underwater demolition SEAL school and twenty-eight weeks of the SEAL qualification training program. Only 1 percent of sailors who entered would complete the course, but that was not the end of training. Training could take up to thirty months before their first deployment, and he never said a word while going through the process. *I am sure the scar is why Michael does not want to discuss his deployments in his last three years. That was before his mission three years ago, when he cut all ties with the family just before the deployment.*

Michael was unusually quiet during dinner; his thoughts were elsewhere until after he ordered dessert. "Auntie, I have a friend who will be visiting me tomorrow around 6:00 p.m."

"Michael, is this a young lady friend you want me to meet?" To Jayda, this did not sound right; Michael was up to something, and she immediately knew she had been set up.

"No Auntie. Richard is in New York City visiting his sister. His niece is going to be married, and he wants to attend the wedding. While he is here, we will be taking care of business."

Jayda thought, *"Michael said, we will be taking care of business, not he will be."*

"Michael, are you by any chance trying to set me up on a blind date?" Jayda instantly started studying him for hints usually gave him away, such as a slight smile running across his face that would go unnoticed to all except her. That smile had been unmistakable since childhood.

"I am sure you will find him to be an interesting person. He is a nice guy. Richard is a former Navy SEAL."

"Michael, you said the divorce rate for Navy SEALs is over 90 percent. Do you want to see me become another statistic?"

"No, Auntie, it is not what you think. Richard was in the navy for over twenty-five years and was married over fifteen years."

Michael was not able to finish his statement, and Jayda cut him off anyway. "What? I am no longer your favorite gal, and now you are pawning me off to a stranger—a divorcee to boot—the way one would discard an old pair of shoes. Is this any way to treat your preferred aunt, or have you replaced me with someone else so I am no longer of any use to you? What is up with that?"

"Auntie, let me explain—"

Once again Jayda cut him off; she was enjoying herself watching Michael trying to figure out how to wiggle himself out of the dilemma. It reminded her of when Michael was a child. How was he going to talk myself out of this debacle? However, this was the first time Michael had ever tried to set her up on a blind date. "I am truly hurt."

"Auntie, it is not what you are thinking; Richard, his wife, died of bone cancer; she had something called sarcomas."

Jayda was smiling as she teased Michael the way she used to when he was a child, until she heard how Richard was by her side until his wife passed on; that was a rare quality in any person. Jayda knew how taxing those types of illnesses affected the families; ultimately, the sickness shredded them apart.

Surprisingly, few people had that type of determination to stay with their spouses until the end. She had statistics to back her theory, as a doctor who witnessed the outcome repeatedly. He had a strong spirit she admired.

"Does your friend know that he is coming here to meet me, or did you set him up too?" There it was—a slight grin with the blameless look on his face, saying, *I am innocent*, which Jayda enjoy seeing on his face. No words were necessary for her to know his response.

"May I ask what are you going to cook for us, or is it going to be a surprise with one of your pièce de résistance?" Jayda have Michael a long, piercing look as she asked him.

"What?" Michael was in the process of eating some ice cream, and he almost dropped it on his clothing. "Auntie, you know I do not know how to cook." He made his comment while checking his clothing.

"Well, Michael, you invited him for dinner without notifying me, and I have nothing in the refrigerator."

Michael had a dumbfounded look on his face and seemed speechless. "Auntie, I will buy whatever you want."

"Michael, do not worry; I will take care of it. Do you have an idea what Richard likes to eat?"

"No, but I once mentioned to Richard that you made a mean lasagna, and he said that sounded delicious."

Michael will get even with you––one way or another.

Michael paused for a few seconds to study Jayda's expression; there was her fragile smile while slightly biting her lower lip, which to him meant she was serious. "Michael, what is his last name?"

"His full name is Richard Livingstone."

"That is interesting; I was reading about a detective agency named Livingston that was going to open up a branch here in Manhattan."

"Richard is the owner of the company."

Jayda thought, *Impressive. Not that it changes anything.* "I was under the impression that he lived in Texas."

"Richard lives in Dallas and is opening a branch in Manhattan. He is so motivated, this could be just the beginning. The company mostly employs former military personnel. His mother suggested that his father has a heart condition and will not be able to take the pressure. Shortly after

Richard started running the company, his father had open-heart surgery, and he passed away last year in Houston."

"Michael, speaking of Texas, when you are going to visit your aunt Veronica Bishop? You know, the one you are always referring to as the wicked witch of the west. Or should I say the one you consider the incarnation of pure evil?" Jayda had previously become suspicious of why he was keeping a secret. "I have raised you to always be truthful with me." Jayda was contemplating asking him his true intentions for traveling to Texas, but a cold chill came over her, and she decided it was better not to know the truth. "Michael, you have never said a kind word concerning Veronica, but all of a sudden you are going to visit her."

"Auntie, I was an adolescent spewing offensive comments about Mrs. Veronica Bishop. I did not consider how harmful my expressions could be to her. I want the opportunity to apologize in person, to bury the hatchet between us. Children tend to speak out of turn, without knowing or considering the consequences of what they are saying."

Did Michael say he wanted to bury the hatchet? Now I know he is up to something. Unless he is talking about embedding the hatchet into her body. I know Michael better than he knows himself. The truth is he cannot stand her or even bring himself to call her by just her first name. I have continuously observed Michael, and his eyes have an expression has never decreased despite his attempts to persuade me.

Mrs. Veronica Bishop had tried to obtain custody of Michael; that was her biggest mistake. She presented a will and claimed that Catherine had informed her in case of her demise, Michael should be raised by Mrs. Bishop.

Before her death, Catherine confided with me she did not trust Veronica Bishop, and their relationship was nonexistent. Catherine informed me in confidence that there was no love between them. However, she never went into details of their conflict; I know at times Catherine went years without speaking to her.

When Mrs. Veronica Bishop presented the will and informed me she had legal custody of Michael, everything sounded suspicious if not downright nonsensical. I had my reservations about the documents she displayed; notwithstanding, it was not necessary for a long, drawn-out court struggle. There was no way she was going to take guardianship of Michael. The judge determined the will invalid because Catherine had drawn up a new testament.

Michael took the diary from the bedroom on the date terrorists killed Catherine in their suicide attack. I should not have allowed him to keep the journal, however because she wrote it in code, I thought he would not be able to read the details of her private life.

"Michael, do you still have the diary of your mother? Have you been able to break the code?"

"I have it in a safe-deposit box in one of the banks I deal with. Why are you asking? Do you know the code?"

The next day, Mr. Richard Livingstone was on time for dinner. He was a handsome man in his late forties, about 240 pounds and six feet two inches. He had salt-and-pepper hair and a black mustache and was well dressed. The first thing Jayda noticed when Richard entered the condominium was he handed Michael a brown envelope, though they were secretive about the exchange. Jayda watched from the kitchen.

While Jayda was in her home office attending a call from the hospital about one of her patients, Michael and Richard were in the living room, carrying on a conversation. Jayda was not sure whether she would be able to stay for the rest of the evening.

"Richard, I have read the report, although I find the facts compelling. How sure are you of the details?"

"I had one of our most experienced men in the company working on this. The report is accurate; in that I am sure. However, this is out of your league. Michael, you should leave this in the hands of the authorities. Furthermore, the story of us traveling together to Texas, and that story about visiting your aunt, is not going to fly. Your aunt Jayda is too smart. Michael, meaning no disrespect, you are treading on thin ice if you continue down this road—dangerous territory. On a different note, when are you going to let the cat out of the bag? That was a wonderful present you bought; are you planning to keep it in your pocket forever?"

"Richard, I want to wait for the right moment."

Jayda was in her home office, and she knew Richard and Michael were traveling together to San Antonio on a short vacation, although Richard lived in Dallas and Veronica resided in Houston. There was something unnatural concerning all this. *Michael has never been fond of long drives; whatever he is planning, he has drafted Richard to help him.*

CHAPTER 3

CONSUELO ROSA FONSECA

Six months earlier, before Michael Jayden Manford returned home from active duty from the military, Mr. Manuel Mendoza considered himself a gift from heaven to women. He was in his thirties and stocky, not fat or muscular.

Manuel had recently arrived in the dirt road town in Chiapa Providence, Mexico; today, he was in town on business. Chiapas was the most backward of any state in Mexico. Per-capita income was the lowest of the thirty-two federal entities, at barely 40 percent of the national median.

Manuel was on the phone. "What do you mean, you only have one? I needed at least two." He hung up without waiting for a response. Manuel received information on merchandise for sale in this town; he had hoped to purchase merchandise that would change the outlook of this trip.

The equipment he had surveyed would break down within a year, and this trip would be disastrous. Manuel had arrived a few days earlier and was feeling dejected.

He started reviewing his schedule while thinking there were two more cities to visit. Manuel only had four more days to complete his task, and felt he was producing at best minimal gains.

Then he spotted a beautiful young woman walking down the sidewalk toward a diner. "Well, there is nothing to say I cannot enjoy myself even if this business trip from hell," he said to himself. Manuel started his ritual as he parked the car, checking himself out on the rear-view mirror. He combed his hair, checked his smile, and reached for his wallet and sunglasses from the glove compartment.

Manuel hoped this young beauty was alone and did not work in the establishment. In the past he had tried to avoid incorporating business with pleasure, however for this gorgeous young woman, he would make an exception.

When Manuel walked in, he was disappointed she was working in the establishment. He waited a few seconds to see what area this young mermaid was attending.

"Oh, well, I can still enjoy myself while I am shopping," Manuel said in a low voice. He sat down in her section and made a phone call.

Consuelo Rosa Fonseca had started working at Margaritas Diner a week ago. She saw a man walk in and sit down in her area. She was meditating on another customer; this one has to be a better tipper than the others. So far this week, there was only a handful of them who were tipping. Their tips put together would not buy her a burrito with coffee.

Manuel was still on his cell phone when Consuelo approached him. He held up his right hand in a polite manner, suggesting she wait a minute. He then continued his conversation while being secretive about his communication.

"That is the merchandise. I am happy that you agree with me that you will work on helping me obtain the equipment. I am not a millionaire; you are asking for too much money. I will pay you what we have agreed on for high-quality equipment. I will even drop a little extra in your envelope. How does that sound to you? Great, so we have a deal? Once you deliver the merchandise, as always. Good, I will see you then."

He hung up the phone. "Sorry, I did not mean to be so long on the phone. I will have …" There was hesitation in the response. "Select for me?" Manuel turned the menu so that the waitress could read from the lunch section. Then he asked, "What do you suggest? I have never been to this town before; I do not know if the chef is a good cook." Manuel wanted to see her reaction.

Consuelo had been studying this handsome man with a pleasant smile. She looked at the menu and was uncertain how to respond. "Combos one and seven seem to be the favorite in this place since I have been working here."

Manuel studied the menu. "One and seven. I see. Huh." He turned back to Consuelo. "I am embarrassed to admit this, however I am allergic to eggs and strawberries." He looked around as if he was bothered to say the words and did not want anyone else to overhear their conversation. He pulled out a piece of paper with a list of items on it. "I have a medical condition, and these are the things that I cannot eat."

Consuelo was surprised that this man was ashamed to admit he had a medical condition. He seemed too bashful to be a businessman.

However, the conversation she had overheard was that of an entrepreneur. *On second thought, the conversation could have been for my benefit to impress me. The man is not a farmer or any of the other hard manual laborers.* "I am sorry, sir, I do not know how to read."

There was a sigh of relief as Manuel took a deep breath and smiled at her, making sure his dimples showed. All the women told him that was his best feature.

"I will be able to figure out what I can eat. Thank you for your honesty. That is a rare quality in people nowadays. What is your name?"

Consuelo started to point to her name tag as she had done with the other clients and caught herself. "I am sorry. My name is Consuelo, and this is my first week working here. I will leave you alone to make up your mind." Consuelo gave him a glass of water and then added, "Would you prefer something else to drink?"

"No, thank you. This will be fine for now."

"What brings you here? I do not mean to pry, however you did say this is your first time in this city."

31

Manuel had studied Consuelo from the minute he had laid eyes on her walking down the street. She moved around the room with elegance, and she had a killer smile and enchanting eyes. Consuelo seemed bashful that it was natural and not a put-on; she claimed to be illiterate. However, something told him Consuelo was smart and astute.

"My boss will be arriving here in a few days; I think he is contemplating expanding his business in this area. He will be hiring people from this region, and there will be many positions opening up for your parents or family members who need a job. I will recommend them to my boss; he values my word." Manuel has discovered everything he needed to know about Consuelo in their short conversation.

"I have been in this town for two days. I am an only child, and my parents have both passed away; I do not know anyone here. Manuel, I have no idea why the manager hired me. Every question he asked me about this job, I did not know."

Manuel thought to himself, *Bingo—what I wanted to hear. Consuelo meets all the requirements I need. I will wrap up my business in this region first, but I want to entertain myself afterward. My boss may be displeased with the equipment obtained on this trip, however I will enjoy myself.* "Once again, thank you. Please do not mention anything about my allergies or why I am in this city. My boss is the one who makes all the decisions." *I may salvage the business end of this trip in the next town. First, this beauty needs my attention.*

"Sir, do not worry. I understand."

"My name is Manuel Mendoza. Please call me Manuel."

Consuelo smiled at Manuel as she started to walk away.

Mr. Carlos Gonzalez was the manager of Margaritas Diner. He was a man who had seen his share of brawls and was five feet nine inches and 190 pounds. He was in his midforties, and his nose seemed to have been broken several times. A scare on the left side of his face ran from his cheek on a slight curve and downward to the neck. He walked over to his new waitress.

"Consuelo, you are new here, so I am going to say this once. When a customer is taking on his cell phone, do not waste my time in attempting to take their order. I am not paying you to stand around doing nothing. Now, get back to work." He patted Consuelo on her rear in a disrespectful manner.

Forty minutes had passed before Manuel signaled Consuelo over. Consuelo walked over to him and gave him the check "Will that be all, sir? You had a chicken quesadillas with a cup of coffee. Would you like anything else?"

Manuel smiled at her while slipping money into her hand. "No, thank you. This is for you." He had gone out of his way to be friendly to her.

Consuelo looked at the money and stated, "This is too much. I will be back with your change."

Manuel placed the money on the table. "This will cover my bill, and you can share that with your coworkers. I feel sorry for you and them. I hope that I do not get caught up in my work this afternoon because tomorrow will be impossible."

"Why are you so willing to give me such an opportunity?"

"To answer your question, you seem like an honest person. That is a rare quality in people nowadays. Your boss is mistreating all the waitresses here; I have seen him disrespectful toward all of you. I do not understand how you can accept these work conditions. I have observed you, and I can tell you are a hard-working person. I will put in a word to my boss, if you want." Manuel smiled when he added, "My boss demands hard work from his employees, however you will be treated with dignity and respect—not what you have here."

Consuelo thought, *Mr. Gonzalez gets like this when drinking heavily; he must have started earlier today. You do not know the hold story, Manuel; he also has the hands of an octopus.* Then she glanced at the money. "Sir, are you sure? You gave me too much money." She had been taught by her father never to backbite anyone, so she just smiled. She was curious about the employment proposal.

Then she tried to make a joke for some reason. Manuel was making her uneasy. Consuelo did not want to admit her faults; her mother had raised her to always be truthful, regardless of the consequences. "Sir, what does your company manufacture? I have never worked in a factory before. What job could I do for the company? I am unable to read or write. I do not even want to eat my cooking. Thank you for the tip; I will be careful around my coworkers."

"My boss has his ways of discovering hidden talent in different people. If you want, I can ask him to interview you. I believe he can help you, Consuelo. And it's more important to remember to always believe in yourself. Look at me; I am practically illiterate. I started sweeping floors and cleaning bathrooms, and then moved to being a chauffeur. Now, he has me driving around the country, buying merchandise for the company, and doing different jobs. I am learning the business from the ground up, and who knows, someday I may have my own business."

Consuelo was not convinced. "Your boss sounds like an angel. What is his name?"

Manuel hesitated; his boss did like his name tossed around. "Mr. Santos-Santos, and the man lives up to his last names." (The word *santos* in English means *saint*). "I will try to come back around dinner tonight, if I have the time. What time do you get off work? I will try to return."

"Today, I work until 8:00 p.m."

Manuel looked at his watch. "Eight, huh." An idea ran through his mind. "I will try to be back around 7:30, but I cannot guarantee anything. I have a hectic work schedule today; you could walk out now. I will assure you work—I give you my word. My boss has a way of discovering hidden talents."

"My schedule for this afternoon is intense, and tomorrow is out of the

34

question. I am leaving for Mexico City in the morning. If I recommend you, please do not embarrass me. Do the best you can."

"My parents always taught me to do my best when I am working. You do not have to worry about that. Why would you do that for me?"

"Consuelo, Mr. Santos gave me an opportunity for a job and believed in me when no one else did. He allowed me to move up in the company. He believes we all have hidden talents; it's simply a matter of exploring or allowing a person to grow intellectually. He hired me in the same manner, by giving me an opportunity."

The first instinct Consuelo had was that she should not trust Manuel; this job opportunity sounded too good to be true. Why would any person offer a stranger a job? Manuel had a cross around his neck, he had prayed before eating, and he seemed to be a good Christian. Nevertheless, something did not sound right. "Can I think it over?" she asked.

"Consuelo, I would have been disappointed if you did not think it over." He was not only discouraged but upset.

As Consuelo walked toward the cash register, thoughts ran wild in her mind.

Maria Montezuma, a waitress who had worked at the diner for two years, walked up to her. "Consuelo, you were conversing with that man for too long, do not let Mr. Gonzalez catch you chatting with clients; that is one of his rigorous rules. Especially today, it looks like he is on the warpath. I have seen that man around here before, and he is cute, however he looks shifty."

"I do not think so!" Consuelo caught herself now; she was not sure whom to trust. "I have never seen him before." She thought, *I am not lying to her.*

"Be careful of people like him in this place. I am sure I have seen him before, maybe around this area. He looks very familiar." After Maria spoke her piece, she turned around and went back to work.

Consuelo thought, *Manuel is not the only voucher around here; I will*

35

be on the lookout. From now on, I will keep a close eye on coworkers. Manuel was vague as to which of the personnel were stealing the tips.

At fifteen minutes to 8:00 p.m., Consuelo was anxious to get off work. She was dead on her feet, and the minutes seemed to pass by like days. All the customers seemed to be in a bad mood, and she was looking forward to a much-needed rest. Consuelo glanced at the time and then at the parking lot. Manuel had not returned to the diner. She knew Manuel had been feeding her a line; it seemed too fantastic to be true. On the other hand, maybe she had missed her opportunity to find a good job. *No, chances are Maria was correct.*

Mr. Gonzalez was on his cell phone when he walked up to Consuelo. "Go home. I will need you here tomorrow at 9:00 a.m. And Consuelo, for your first week of work anywhere, that was okay. I will need you for this weekend."

"Sir, it looks like you are going to be busy until closing. If you want, I could stay on an extra hour or so." Consuelo was hoping Manuel was running behind schedule. *Who knows? Maybe this is my last day working here.*

Mr. Gonzalez was about to answer Consuelo when his cell phone rang; he said into the receiver, "I will see you in ten minutes," and hung up without waiting for an answer. Then he turned his attention to Consuelo. "I require you to be here tomorrow at nine." Mr. Gonzalez was mumbling his speech; it was apparent he had been drinking heavily. "I have already made arrangements for a couple of waitresses to stay overtime. I will keep you in mind for the future." He added, "When you leave tonight, use the back exit."

Consuelo was about to object, but given the condition of Mr. Gonzalez, she felt it was better not to say a word. "Yes, sir."

A few minutes later, Maria saw Consuelo walking toward the kitchen exit. "Where are you going? No personnel go out there unless they are on a smoke break or are fired." There was a look of genuine concern from Maria.

"Did Gonzalez fired you? He is an asshole. Do not move—I am going to talk to him." Maria was the only waitress who had the nerve to stand up to the manager regardless of whether he was intoxicated.

"No, I am just going home for the day."

Maria had a glimpse of satisfaction on her face, and she grinned at Consuelo. "That is good news. Mr. Gonzalez is known to fire waitresses when he has been drinking, and today the man smells like a brewery. Wait for me. Consuelo, this is a dangerous neighborhood—you should not walk around here at night alone. There are stories about people disappearing around this place. Besides, I want to make you an offer."

Consuelo was about to say something, however before she could say a word, Maria had already grabbed her purse and started walking out with her.

Maria and Consuelo were outside of the diner in the parking lot, walking toward the main road. There were a few delivery trucks in the parking lot. Suddenly, the lights went out in the parking lot. "Do not worry—that happens frequently. Still, Consuelo, we should walk faster."

Consuelo started shaking. She felt a cold chill running down her spine even though it was a hot night. They both picked up their steps while heading toward the main road.

Suddenly, someone said, "Consuelo, why you are walking so fast? Let us talk awhile."

They were unable to identify who was talking to them or where the person was.

"Consuelo, who is that?

I can't recognize the voice. He sounds familiar, however I am not able to tell who it is." Consuelo turned her head in every direction, trying to identify the person while they practically ran toward the main road.

Maria said to Consuelo, "Be ready to run—something is wrong."

They thought about returning toward the dinner, however they were closer to the main road.

For a split second, Consuelo thought she recognized the voice. It had to be her nerves playing tricks on her. Consuelo was about to say something to Maria when a van pulled into the parking lot, interrupting her thoughts. Surely no one would try to harm them with witnesses in the area.

"Consuelo, stop walking so fast. It is Manuel. Have you forgotten me already? I am sorry for being so late." As he said that, he rushed up behind them.

Consuelo and Maria stopped walking and turn around to look at him. Manuel was accompanied by two men. The attire of the men looked like gangsters out of a B-movie.

Maria was worries now and was sure about seeing Manuel before. She said, "Let us keep walking." She grabbed Consuelo by the hand and pulled her away from Manuel while walking away. Maria was ready to start running, and her body trembled. Maria felt emboldened. There was a person in a van facing in their direction, and the engine was still running.

Manuel came up behind them and grabbed Consuelo by her shoulders. "Who do you think you, are walking away from me? You are an ungrateful bitch. I am offering you a job of a lifetime. I give you a chance to leave this sinking hellhole, and you repay me like this? How dare you turn away from me? I will teach you manners." Manuel slapped Consuelo across the face, and the force knocked her to the ground.

"Hey, Manuel, leave Consuelo alone. You are hurting her!" Maria wanted to be loud to call attention to the person in the van. She did not have a chance to finish her sentence.

One of the men grabbed Maria from her right side and punched her hard in the stomach, knocking the wind out of her. She collapsed to the ground, gasping for air.

The other man grabbed Consuelo, hastily pinning her hands firmly behind her back.

Manuel signaled the van that had just pulled into the parking lot with a flashlight. The driver in the van sped up and stopped next to the group.

Manuel opened the side door, and Maria and Consuelo were tied and gagged. They were picked up and propelled toward the back like sacks of potatoes.

Mr. Carlos Gonzalez ran up to Manuel. "Hold up, you are only supposed to grab Consuelo, not Maria. She is not part of the deal. Maria is one of my best waitresses. I will make sure she keeps her mouth shut."

Mr. Gonzalez had always been interested in Maria, who was his hardest worker. Nevertheless, his interest in her had nothing to do with her work skills, even though he trusted her to run the diner when he stepped out. Mr. Gonzalez's enthusiasm for Maria was purely physical, and up to this point, she had not given him the time of day. He hoped this would make her so grateful for saving her life she would be more receptive to his advances. Furthermore, she could help him recruit more girls for the El Fantasma business.

"Mr. Gonzalez, this is your fault. I have told you in the past not to allow anyone else to come out with my merchandise. Besides, no one is going to miss her; she is only a waitress. They are a dime a dozen. I cannot allow her to walk. Maria knows too much. Look, my merchandise on this trip lacked appeal, and she is somewhat pretty. I will pay you for both of them."

"I am still going to be a girl short tomorrow."

"Mr. Gonzalez, I understand there are two women, and they both meet my requirements for our clubs." Manuel took out more money and gave it to him. "You could have informed me about Maria a long time ago. I would compensate you for her and add a little extra."

"Manuel, this is not exactly what I call extra. You can still make it up to me. Maria here is my best worker; to replace her is going to be difficult. The fact is that I will be shorthanded tomorrow. It is never too late to do the right thing."

Manuel was annoyed at Mr. Gonzalez always begging for more money.

He pulled a white envelope from the inside of his jacket. "Here is what I promise you for Consuelo. I have paid you for Maria."

He changed the subject. "We are always shorthanded of young girls and boys. I will pay you good money for them. I am also interested in those who are fifteen or younger. Mr. Gonzalez, give me a call when you have about six or more children lined up. I will make the trip to pick up the merchandise separately. One more thing: make sure they are homeless or runaways."

"I will see what I can do." He secured the envelope and headed back toward the diner.

Manuel jumped into the passenger side of the van and signaled the driver to go. "Miguel, if you ever hit one of my girls like that again, I will bury you alive. We do not damage our merchandise, do you understand me? And you had better pray that Maria does not have any broken ribs. We need these women working on their backs. Do I make myself clear?"

Miguel swallowed hard as he took a deep breath to compose himself and answered, "Yes, sir."

As the van speed away, the lights in the back parking lot turned back on.

Consuelo and Maria leaned against each other, trying to comfort themselves. They lost track of time, but it was starting to turn daylight. They had been intimidated for hours after their abduction, and not knowing their fate, they had fallen asleep out of pure exhaustion. They were expecting to be raped and killed at any time. The confusing part to them the long drive.

Finally, the van came to a stop. "Get out," someone barked at them.

Consuelo and Maria stepped out of the van. A man helped them and informed them to stay right there while he untied their hands. He also removed their gags while instructing them to stand by the vehicle.

Maria was having problems seeing, and squinted. After a while, Maria caught a glimpse of a police car approaching them down an isolated dirt road. She tapped Consuelo on her left side in a discreet manner to call it to her attention.

Consuelo informed Maria to stay still; she had heard Manuel saying that they had many police officers on their payroll.

Maria disregarded the warning. In her mind, this was their chance to escape the clutches of these animals. She waited until the man by her side was distracted, and she broke loose by pushing him to the ground. She ran as fast as she could toward the patrol car, screaming, "Help!"

The police officer stopped the vehicle two feet from Maria. A man stepped out; he looked to be in his late fifties and about six feet one inch. He was thin with streaks of gray hair on each side of his head that made him look like a wannabe gangster out of *The Sopranos*. He had a thin mustache, a black Armani suit with pinstripes, a powder blue shirt, and a bright red tie.

The man held Maria at arm's length. He was more concerned that his suit would be soiled. Maria was trying to explain she had been kidnap.

Manuel walked up to the man and said, "Good morning, sir, how are you today?" He grabbed Maria by her hair and pushed her toward Miguel.

"Manuel, where is the woman you were rejoicing about over the telephone?" The man thought, *She looks to be older than I usually favor.* He seemed disappointed with the choice. *Not the usual woman Manuel chooses for me.*

Miguel ran up behind Maria, snatched her by the hair, and whirled her around to face him. He backhanded Maria hard across the face, knocking her to the ground.

Manuel quickly added, "No, sir, she is by the van," and he pointed to Consuelo.

As the man walked past Miguel and Maria, he looked at Miguel with disapproval.

He approached Consuelo and started to examine her as if he was buying steaks in a butcher shop. "Well done." Afterward, he took a closer look at Maria. "Well done on both ends. Prepare her." The man started walking away. After a few steps, he turned his head toward Manuel and added, "We need to make an example." He pointed to Maria. "Manuel, I am rushed today. You need to expedite all preparations." He then signaled Manuel over to him and whispered something to him.

Manuel walked over to Maria. "This is the second time you have tried to embarrass me. You have been nothing but trouble and have cost me money." He pulled out his automatic 9mm handgun and aimed it at Maria. Manuel paused for a second and added, "Miguel, you are standing too close to Maria. Blood tends to spatter."

Miguel quickly stepped back two feet away from her, watching Maria closely. There was a wicked smile on his face as he stared at Maria. Miguel kept a close eye on her gold chain with a locket, which had been overlooked in the original search. Miguel wanted to make sure no one else took it because he wanted the items for his wife.

Maria dropped to her knees, accepting her faith as she started praying.

Manuel patiently waited as Maria prayed with her eyes closed. Afterward, she made a sign of the cross with her hand. He shot three times, hitting his intended target in the chest.

Miguel had a look of shock on his face as he fell backward to the ground.

Manuel turned his attention to Maria. "You had better learn to accept your destination. This is your final warning." He looked at the police officer who had been driving the car and added, "You are now responsible for ensuring that they do not escape." Manuel had no apprehension about killing Miguel in front of a police officer.

Two days had passed since Maria and Consuelo had been kidnapped. They were being held captive in a small cage made of wood and barbed wire. They had just enough room to move around so they could relieve themselves in a bucket in one of the corners without the benefit of privacy. However, they did not have enough room to move around freely. There was a sliver of sunlight shining into their cramped space. Consuelo and Maria heard the cries from other people in other cages: children, women, and men.

They had learned their fate. Mr. Gonzalez had sold them into slavery.

Manuel phrased it differently. "You are going to be in the entertainment business. Learn how to be actresses." He added, "If you practice hard enough, one day you may be as good as Sassy Milly." Sassy was a porno star who had been rumored to have slept with a few former presidents. Manuel was mocking them as he ensured that they took a thorough shower.

Consuelo and Maria were tied to a bed, and the man forced himself on Maria and Consuelo. Manuel then went into the room and told them, "It's time you learn how a real lover satisfies a woman." He informed his men. "Consuelo and Maria are off-limits. If you feel the urge, take any of the other women who are being held captive." He turned to Maria and Consuelo. "Do not worry; you will learn to enjoy it after your first few hundred times."

After the ordeal was over, Consuelo remembered asking Maria, "Who is Sassy Milly?"

Maria responded, "Maybe his mother. After all, honorable women could not have given birth or raised animals like them."

"Maria, the only way to escape from this hellhole is to outsmart them. We will need to play along with them as if we have lost all hope of escaping, let them think they have dominated us. We need to learn how they operate—their ways and their schedule. Then we will be able to devise a plan to escape. Selecting the right moment is extremely important. You saw how they killed one of their own; that was a message for our benefit. We needed to learn and emulate their ways."

"Consuelo, I would prefer to be dead than to live like an animal."

"Maria, I agree with you; this is no way for anyone to live. Our only solution is to escape. Afterward, we can make them pay in the harshest form for what they have done to us and those other people over there."

Maria pointed in the direction the sound of human suffering was coming from.

"Consuelo, you are dreaming. They will use us until they are tired, and then they will kill us."

Consuelo looked at Maria, and what she saw in her eyes scared her. The eyes of Maria were lifeless as if she had given up. Consuelo remembered observing a similar stare in her uncle John, who a few days later committed suicide. John was a hardworking man dedicated to his family, and he was well on his way to becoming prosperous while helping Consuelo's father support us. One day, a drug lord cast his eyes on the land. The drug lord ordered him to sign over his farm to him.

Afterward, they forced John and his family into the barn; the men took turns forcing themselves on his wife and girls. Then they burned them alive. John barely escaped with his life, but he always felt guilty about not being able to save his wife and three girls.

"Yes, Maria, you are right. I am dreaming of one day escaping on my terms and punishing them one by one in the harshest manner. We need to be smarter than them, and afterward we can beat them at their own game." There were tears in her eyes and a growing hatred in her heart.

"Our best opportunity for escaping will be when we arrive in the United States, but not when they are transporting us because they will be watching us closely. Everywhere we are taken, they will have to be guarding us. Do not trust anyone. I am sure they have connections in the police departments. We cannot afford to make any mistakes. You need to bide your time, play along, and wait for the right opportunity."

Four hours after their conversation, Maria and Consuelo were transported across the Mexico–US border with a group of men. Armando Sebastian De La Rosa Santana, known as the Coyote, escorted Consuelo, Maria, and three men.

Consuelo quietly acquired several facts about Manuel. He used Armando for their specific trips across the border. Armando attempted to keep his name secret, yet one individual of the group knew his full surname. She discovered Manuel used Armando for specific details and referred to him as the Coyote. The three men accompanying Armando appeared to be transporting some heavy equipment in their rucksacks. Armando reminded them not to make loud noises, conserve their energy, and not drink their water all at once.

Consuelo was not sure whether these three men were working for Armando or were being forced to smuggle the contraband across the border. She noted that the loads are heavy, and she heard one man say there would be payments once they were safe across the border. Either way, she was not taking any chances and would deal with the man in charge.

Consuelo asked Armando, "Have we already crossed the border?"

"Yes." Then he reminded Consuelo to keep her voice down.

Consuelo learned that the three men were smuggling the drugs for their payment passage to the United States. *The men have to ensure we did not escape; they will be held responsible for our actions.* Consuelo deduced that they only crossed with Armando.

Armando made a call and then added, "Send them now," before he hung up. Afterward, he intensely observed the scene through binoculars, making sure they were all hidden. Minutes later, he mumbled something about, "That will keep Border Patrol busy."

After a long, arduous day of walking under the blistering sun, the group was running behind schedule. They were resting underneath a couple of trees, bushes, and ditches. Maria walked over to Consuelo and sat next to her. She started smiling to the point that she was almost laughing out loud. It was the first time Maria had smiled since their kidnapping, and Consuelo was inquisitive. "What is funny? Let me in on the joke."

"Consuelo, at the diner I was going to ask you if we could share an apartment. My concern was that you were going to say no. Now it looks like we are going to live together whether we want to or not."

Consuelo smiled as she held Maria and then said, "Maria, we will be all right. You will see. Remember, trust no one—they could be working for Manuel Mendoza."

"Manuel Mendoza? What are you talking about? He is not the boss. Manuel is working for El Fantasma; he is just a pawn in all this. Consuelo, you have a lot to learn if you want to survive. You are talking about how we will live through this nightmare? Then wise up. These people own us."

"El Fantasma! Who is El Fantasma? That sounds like the name of a bad horror movie."

Maria smiled at first but suddenly became solemn. "Consuelo, I remember saying something similar when I first heard the name. The fact is we are in the grips of one of the most infamous gangsters in Mexico with tentacles throughout Mexico and the United States. That is the animal in the fancy suit. He runs this whole operation—drugs, human trafficking, and whatever else he can smuggle across the border. To think that I ran into his arms like a damned fool. No one knows what his real name."

"I know his last name is Santos-Santos, however Manuel never told me his first name."

"Consuelo, listen to me. Those names are aliases he gave you. No one knows his real name; he is known on the street only by El Fantasma. I presume that those who know his real name are his most trusted men. Whatever Manuel told you is a lie. Maybe he even gave you a false name for himself."

Consuelo sipped water and said, "Maria, do you believe Manuel, or whatever his name is, knows the true identity of El Fantasma? Possibly he is one of his most trusted people, and he also knows his address. Perhaps he is even his right-hand man. Answer me this: why are we still alive? We know what that animal looks like and could identify him."

"Consuelo, we can conclude Manuel knows the man's name. What difference does that make? Do you think he is going to publicize it in the newspapers?" Maria was annoyed with Consuelo, feeling it was her fault they were prisoners. In her heart, however, Maria knew no one was to blame except Mr. Gonzalez.

Consuelo talked only about escaping. Maria said to her, "Oh, hell, it is no use getting upset. We will be lucky to live one more week."

"Do you remember Manuel? He informed us we were the property of the organization. Who are we going to communicate our story to that will be willing to make a difference? Otherwise, Manuel would have killed us."

Consuelo started meditating when she looked up and saw dust swirling in the distance. She kept staring at what seemed like a cloud of dust traveling in their direction. After a few seconds, there was a vehicle.

Consuelo whispered to Maria, "Do not look now, but there appears to be a vehicle approaching us over your left shoulder."

Maria looked discreetly, and it was a Jeep. "I hope it is immigration, and we get deported." Maria did not want others to hear their conversation.

"Maria, we need to be careful that a person seems to be coming too fast in this direction, as if looking for something. That could be why we are waiting here.

"Consuelo, this could be our opportunity to escape. You keep speaking about it, especially after we crossed the border. Well, we are in the United States, and here is our chance, this is what you keep saying. These monsters cannot have much power on this side of the border."

"Maria, we do not know who is driving in this direction; it does not look right. We need to wait." Consuelo was concerned Maria was going to do something stupid. "This is not the appropriate moment. We have to make sure we can escape before making our move."

"Consuelo, there is only one way to find out," Maria commented. She stood up in plain sight so the vehicle could see her from a distance. However, she looked in the opposite direction with her back toward the approaching car.

Maria and Consuelo had been given a stern warning before leaving Mexico on their journey: when they were resting, they were to stay hidden.

If they were walking by areas where they could take cover immediately, they should always be ready to do so if they saw anything suspicious.

One of the men with them quickly rushed over to Maria and pulled her down. He said, "You want to get us all captured or killed? Get down— there's a vehicle coming in our direction."

It was too late, and her objective was successful. The driver was heading their direction. Maria was successful in being spotted, and they could make out that it looked like a government vehicle.

A Border Patrol agent stepped out of the Jeep. The driver stopped about five feet from them.

Maria broke loose from the man and ran toward the agent, her hands up in the air as she screamed, "I give up! Help us, help! Help—we have been kidnapped!" Maria did not notice that a second man was stepping out.

Then she saw Manuel Mendoza. Maria fell to her knees while trying to avoid running into him.

"Maria, good to see you again. I am surprised you miss me that much. It must be the moment we shared in Mexico. I mean, the way you ran over here to greet me! On the other hand, I told you that you would not have the opportunity to embarrass me again." Manuel took out his automatic handgun and shot her three times in the chest.

Consuelo ran over to Maria, who was barely alive. She muttered something to Consuelo and passed away.

Manuel asked Consuelo, "What did the bitch say?"

Consuelo looked at him with hatred in her eyes and responded, "I was not able to make it out. I think she was praying."

Manuel did not believe a word Consuelo said, but it did not matter— not where she was going. Manuel realized he had acted too hastily, and El Fantasma was not going to be happy. The man has already designated Consuelo and Maria for two exclusive men's clubs. Eliminating both of them was out of the question. The monetary loss was going to be too high, and that would make his boss very unhappy.

Manuel retrieved the gold chain with the locket. He made a feeble attempt to clean the blood and then placed it around his neck. Manuel saw the three men standing around in disbelief. "What are you looking at? Bury her."

Armando, aka the Coyote, walked over to the Jeep, pulled out two shovels, and said to one of the three men, "You are going to need this, Pablo." He gave Pablo the shovels and added, "I want her buried deep."

"Yes, sir. I will take care of it."

As the men carried away Maria, Manuel signaled Armando over and said in a low tone, "There are too many witnesses. See what you can do about that."

"I understand that. I will wait until they are finished. That is why I have the shovels in the Jeep. I was going to do that anyway; it was next on my bucket list. Besides, I need to cut expenses. In a growing company, that is essential." Armando had a big smile on his face, and then he checked his weapon and started following them.

Ten minutes later, the men were digging the grave for Maria. Armando watched them from a distance as he yelled, "Make that hole deeper. I do not want the smell to attract attention. Do you?"

It had been a long, exhausting trip. The sun was setting, and daylight was diminishing fast. Pablo, who appeared frail from the trip, was struggling to help. Pablo had become distrustful of Armando; furthermore, he was concerned for the men with him. He talked them into working for Armando.

Pablo noticed the two men who had arrived in the Jeep had already loaded the backpacks into the Jeep, yet their transportation was late. Pablo was concerned now that Manuel had killed Maria. They had been promised free passage across the border once they completed their agreement, and they would receive documents. They had accomplished their five trips carrying the backpacks across the border. Pablo was promised transportation to California, a designated sanctuary state, with false documentation.

"That's deep enough. Drop her in," Armando called out to them.

Consuelo wondered whether she was going to be the only one left alive. *If they are going to kill me, get it over with. I do not want them to rape me again; I prefer to join Maria.* All of a sudden, she heard three shots ring out.

After what seemed like an eternity, one man screamed out, "Please do not kill me! I will do whatever you want. Please!"

As he was pleading for his life, two more shots rang out, and after a few minutes, three more rounds.

Consuelo cried silently, tears streaming down her eyes.

"Consuelo, you have nothing to worry about—as long as you cooperate. One day, you may learn to love your work. I told you that my boss has a knack for placing persons in the proper job, and he has hired you. You are going to be working in an exclusive club." There was a smile on his face that was more of an evil smirk.

However, Manuel stared into her eyes, and the look he got back from her told him he had eliminated the wrong woman. Manuel had an uneasy feeling that sent chills down his spine as she stared back at him. He wanted to terminate Consuelo; this was the first time in five years Manuel had had that feeling. He found himself reaching for his weapon.

Thirty minutes after the last shot, Armando returned and announced in a loud voice, "All done." Armando said it as if he had accomplished a noble task.

"What took you so long?" Manuel had wondered about the long delay.

"Some refused to die, and I dropped them in with Maria. I thought they'd keep each other warm; it is going to be a cold night."

Consuelo observed Armando and could tell something had gone wrong; there was a look of concern. He seemed to be trying to hide something.

Manuel handed him a white envelope and added, "This should cover your expenses, plus what we agreed on. I will see you in Mexico City next month; I will have another run for you. Do you need a ride?"

"No, thanks. I have arranged for my transportation. They should be here in a few minutes. Manuel, are you still picking up these whores at Margaritas Diner?"

"That is just one of the places I find these bitches. I make my rounds to that location every three months like clockwork. I give that voucher time to recruit fresh meat for our clubs." He paused for a few seconds. "Normally, we overbook the trip by about twenty-five and transport them into factories to work off the money they will need. We need bait when making trips like today and notify the Border Patrol where they are crossing. After their deportation, we track them down with the help of the Mexican Police, and afterward we transport them to our factories.

"Armando, do you know we earn more money having them work in factories? And some are skilled, so we insist they stay a few extra years," Manuel explained. "You see, it's unfortunate that they lose their money." He had a wicked smile on his face, and no other words were necessary to know the people behind those assaults.

Consuelo took mental notes about everything she had been observing from her capture. *If by some miracle I survive this tribulation, I will make them all pay, one by one, for what they did to Maria and my uncle.* Consuelo knew of the robberies; the story had circulated in town since her arrival. Maria and I were stripped of our financial value and, more significant, our honor.

Maria noticed the man in the Jeep was not a government official. He started eating an egg sandwich and drinking strawberry fruit juice.

Manuel walked over to him and lost his mind. He screamed, "Are you crazy, bringing eggs and strawberries around me? You ever do that again, and I will bury you out here!"

"Manuel, I have a few potential candidates, however there is one problem: they are my next-door neighbors. If you decide to take these families, I need a solid alibi, like being out of the country. I am not talking about being in Mexico. Or do you think I should move? We should give them a permanent vacation?" Armando said, even though he knew the answer.

"Tell me how many girls they have under fifteen."

"There are two boys, aged five and seven, and three girls, aged eight to twelve; the best part is all are Yankees. All the children have blond hair and blue eyes. Now for the best news: one of the women is pregnant. I have been studying these two families' habits. I think the best time to grab them is when they are all together. The good news is that they always plan their vacations together because the women are sisters."

Manuel listened attentively with excitement as Armando described the children, however when he heard one of the women was pregnant, he said, "El Fantasma will pay you handsomely if we can confiscate the entire package. We are always on the lookout for younger blood. Furthermore, one of the women being pregnant is the grand prize. We will need your assistance and will need to plan this carefully. How friendly are you to these families?"

"Are you crazy? I want to stay away from them."

"We will need to scout these families before taking any further action. I want to see these people before presenting this package to El Fantasma."

"There is no way I am presenting them to you or anyone. You are not grabbing them anywhere near my home. The police officers will paint a bull's-eye on me if those families disappear into the abyss anywhere near me. I had problems in the past with the law. The authorities will automatically start an investigation into me if something happens to them and I am within a hundred miles."

Manuel smiled at Armando. He had a method of approaching a person when he desired to con them into doing his bidding. "How many months is she pregnant? Cousin, I will ensure you have an unshakable alibi."

Armando had heard it before and was annoyed. "You are trying to play me. I am not one of the flunky workers you can bullshit. You are not visiting me or getting any details about these families until I am sure my alibi is unbreakable. But I will tell you the woman is no more than two months."

"Good, that gives us plenty of time to work out a plan. Ideally, we would like to have the infant within days after birth. We will have to talk more about this in Mexico City. Presently, I have a few packages to deliver." Manuel was about to get into the vehicle and then looked at Armando. "In the meantime, you need to befriend these men to get as much information from them as possible."

"Take them out to a bar and buy them a couple of prostitutes—no, better yet, take them out to a couple of our exclusive clubs. Make it look like you are paying for their drinks and a piece of ass. I will clear it with the managers. Armando, you will need to call first, give the manager a heads-up. These men will tell you everything we need to know after a couple of trips. Armando, let's keep this between us for now." After Manuel finished talking, he jumped into the vehicle and drove off.

Back in New York City, after dinner, Richard was having a conversation with Michael while Jayda was in her office attending a called she had received from the hospital. It seemed that one of her patients had taken a turn for the worst. She was unsure whether she would have to rush to the hospital.

Richard said, "Michael, are you sure you want to handle this by yourself? You know that I have your back. However, in my opinion, you should turn this over to the police department." He was concerned for Michael if he continued on this path. Michael would be walking into a hornet's nest, and it was a world he had no knowledge of; he wouldn't know how to deal with them. *I should have never agreed to help Michael with this investigation. I have already taken out an insurance policy, and the paperwork has disappeared.*

"Richard, as far as the police handling this case, they have done a bang-up job. What is it now, twenty-two years? I will not wait for another twenty-two years to see the killer of my father incarcerated; he may die of old age first. What do I own you?" He understood that Richard meant well. He hated the justice system and they had handled the murder of his father.

Michael remembered reading about a case where a man had been beating his girlfriend, and with each beating, it escalated. The last assault sent her to the hospital with a broken left forearm. The judge, upon seeing them for the third time, ordered him to stay away from her.

The woman begged the judge, "Your Honor, you have to do something—he is going to kill me."

The judge responded, "I have told him to stay away from you." After that, the judge never had to worry about seeing them again, because the man killed her.

CHAPTER 4

THE ODD COUPLE

"Michael, this one is in the house. I can never repay you for what you did for my family. On second thought, you can manage my branch here in Manhattan; I need someone with your expertise to manage the office. I have not found the right individual for this position."

Richard was thinking the leads were slim and next to none, and the chance that Michael ran into a dead-end was good. However, Michael had a determination unlike anyone he had ever met. He has an obsession with finding the killer of his father. *Still, I want him to run my office in New York. Hell, I could see him moving into the main office someday in the future.*

Dr. Jayda Manford was in her office reviewing her cases on Wednesday, December 27, 2017. Wanda walked into her office. "You have a visitor in the waiting room who wants to talk to you."

"I thought that I did not have any appointments until this afternoon."

"You're right. The next patient is at 2:00 p.m. This handsome gentleman wants to speak to you in private on a personal matter. Jayda, if you are lucky, he may want to give you a complete physical. Do yourselves a favor; this one looks like a keeper. Give him a chance. Otherwise, if you are going to kick him to the curb like all the others, do you mind if I write down his number?"

Jayda tried to maintain her composure, but there was a slight smile while she thought, *Sometimes this woman comes out with the most outlandish remarks.* "Wanda, you are a married woman. How could you?"

"Jayda, have you seen my husband lately? Leonardo resembles a man who swallowed a medicine ball. Hell, his idea of physical fitness is asking for a beer and reaching for it while watching football. When the season is over, he will play reruns of the game as if the damn scores will change."

"The other day, I was lying on the couch, and Leonardo reached over and touched my breasts. I thought for a minute I was going to see some action. The man had the nerve to say, 'Excuse me. I was reaching for the TV remote.' Jayda, I have worn out my vibrator waiting for Leonardo; without it, I would die of old age before getting any satisfaction."

"Jayda, one day I will throw the TV out the window. On second thought, I will fling his ass out—the TV is worth more than him. If you are sure you do not want to see him, do you mind if I give him an exceptional examination in the back?" They were both laughing.

"Wanda, ask the gentleman for his name and number; I will try to call him back this afternoon. I am jammed up in paperwork right now."

"Well, if that is the case, can I take a five-hour lunch break in one of the examination rooms? I want him to have a thorough examination by me. I want to practice being a doctor."

"Wanda!" That was the clue to get back to work.

"Yes, boss, I am on my way out."

Before she left, Jayda asked, "Wanda, what is the gentlemen's name?"

"Richard Livingstone and he is handsome."

"I will see Richard for five minutes."

"So the name of the man who finally turned your head is Richard. Do you want me clear your schedule for the day? Five minutes is not enough for a rabbit to warm up his engines."

"Wanda, please show him in."

"Yes, boss, I will show Richard in right away. The man is handsome and a keeper, Doctor."

A minute later, Wanda was showing Richard to the office.

Jayda thought, *Maybe I can find out what Michael is planning.*

"Richard, what brings you to this side of town? Please come in and have a seat. How can I help you?" She turned to Wanda and said, "Thank you. That will be all for now," Then she turned back to Richard. "I wanted to take a moment and thank you for the flowers the bottle of wine, which I am going to save for a special occasion."

"That was my pleasure, Jayda. I do have a serious question for you. I am opening up a branch here in NYC. I need the advice of a person who is intelligent and knows this city to show me around the best restaurants and sites. I require the services of a trustworthy person. First impressions are important in my business. I often entertain potential clients."

"Richard, I have never heard that line before. Does it work for you?"

"I do not know. Why not let me know over lunch? I am assuming you have not eaten."

Fifteen minutes after Richard entered the office, they were walking out.

"I will be back in one hour," Jayda said as she looked at Wanda.

"Yes, Miss Manford. Did you want me to cancel your next appointment and make reservations for you?" Wanda said that with a double meaning, and she wanted to stress that Jayda was single.

Before Jayda could finish her thoughts, Richard cut off Wanda. "No, thank you, Wanda, for your kind offer. I have already made reservations at the Olio e Piu; I understand Doctor Jayda Manford prefers to have lunch in that restaurant."

"Yes, sir." Wanda had a big grin on her face. She was happy for Jayda; this was one of the few times the doctor had taken some personal time for herself. Jayda has dedicated her entire life to Michael and her job.

Jayda walked out of the building with Richard, and she had one question on her mind. "Richard, Wanda does not use a name tag. How did you know her name?"

"Jayda, I am not in the habit of listening to other conversations;

however, Wanda left the door to your office ajar. She does have a boisterous voice. I did overhear something about an exceptional exam, a hotel room about Mr. and Mrs. Smith, and a five-hour lunch break. With those types of benefits, can I work for you?"

Jayda turned red and could no longer look him in the face. She desired to disappear as they got into a taxi. Richard had a gentle smile on his face that eased her embarrassment. However, she would have a long talk with Wanda. *She should at least make sure the door to my office is closed.*

In an unknown part of Texas, Consuelo had almost given up the prospect of ever escaping. The grasp of these barbarians seemed overwhelming at times, if not for the memory of Maria. Her last words kept playing back in her mind like a recording. Consuelo would never trust anyone ever again, especially when someone was offering great deals.

Consuelo was meditating on one of her clients. Mr. Andrew Grierson was in his mid-eighties, and he had white hair with a well-trimmed mustache. This man never seemed to have a hair out of place, and he was about five feet ten inches and 205 pounds with deep brown eyes and a sad smile. He was always well dressed and was a retired college professor. Grierson reminded her of the actor Cesar Romero.

Mr. Grierson always had a walking stick, as he called it. She asked him about it because he did not seem to need a cane to walk. Mr. Andrew Grierson said he had a car accident, breaking his right leg, in the first year of his marriage to his wife, Janet. Janet had designed the cane for him. A month after the death of Janet, Mr. Grierson started using his walking stick again; he said it felt like having a closer connection to her.

Like Mr. Grierson, Janet had also been a professor in college as an art teacher. As strange as it sounded, he was not interested in sex at all. This man simply wanted Consuelo's warm body in his bed next to him at night, and at times he cuddled up to her and cried. *I never told Mr. Grierson about the circumstances that bought me to the club. No use; it would cost both our lives. The men in the organization have threatened us: if we talk, they will kill us and whomever we related our story to. There are wiretaps in all our rooms, and some of the women are not to be trusted.*

Consuelo continually looked for vulnerabilities in the club's defenses; so far, it seemed hopeless. In time Consuelo learned the information she required to escape: the schedule and the wiretaps in the room. Consuelo was still looking for a way to escape while causing the maximum damage to the club. She hoped to catch all the men inside.

In time she learned to trust Mr. Grierson; he had been a widower for ten years. Consuelo would never have faith in humanity, but there were some exceptions. Her strength to escape did regenerate with Andrew. Consuelo had been El Fantasma's slave for approximately six months, and absconding from their grasps was not an option here; life depended on it. *They have implanted me with an item that will track me no matter where I go. At first I thought it was a way of scaring us, until I learned the truth.*

These men checked them every week to ensure that the devices were working. They were all given a stern warning about their conduct and what would lead to torment. Consuelo knew that because she was new, they would keep a closer eye on her. They also informed her that Mr. Grierson would be punished in the same manner. Although her number one priority was to escape, she knew he would be another victim. Consuelo thought, *These men will play under my rules one day.*

Consuelo remembered there was a girl nicknamed Italy because she had a birthmark resembling the map of Italy. Italy's attempted escape was futile; she managed to evade them for only a few days. The other girls were gathered together and shown photographs of her body; furthermore, Italy's tattoo was on display, stretched out across a picture frame.

Consuelo knew that once Mr. Grierson left, she would be shipped off to another club; that was their practice. *After all, we are not human-being in their eyes.* When she first arrived, one of the women informed her, "We are all moved to different clubs. There are rumors of one girl who has never moved." Consuelo thought, *They have not moved me because Mr. Grierson will only deal with me.*

Consuelo learned that Mr. Grierson was moving to Arizona within a few months. She knew that once he departed, they would have her transferred to another hellhole. Originally, she had thought the implanted GPS was a joke the girls were playing on her. She did not know that such things existed.

Michael had a tip on a Mr. Pablo Fernandez; he may know the whereabouts of Armando Sebastian De La Rosa Santana, aka the Coyote. Finding Pablo Fernandez has turned into a nightmare; all leads had gone cold. It seemed that tracking down Armando Santana depended on hunting the whereabouts of Pablo Fernandez, and that was like chasing a ghost.

Armando Sebastian De La Rosa Santana, the man who had killed Michael's father, had been on the loose for over twenty-two years without facing justice. Even if the information was correct and Pablo Fernandez was in San Antonio over six months ago, Pablo was the only person who may know his whereabouts in the past year. Pablo had relatives in San Antonio who had been deported various times. Michael hoped Pablo was still in the area.

Today, Michael was following up on information that Pablo worked for Armando, but it was a dismal lead. Still, it was the only lead he had acquired since arriving. Michael thought he had to be careful around this area; it had a reputation of being tumultuous.

He knocked on the door. After a few seconds he heard, "Yes, can I help you?" There was a man at the door who barely cracked the entrance open, looking like he had just stumbled out of bed. He was unshaven, his hair was in a ponytail, and he was about five feet nine inches and 185 pounds. He spoke English with a heavy accent. "You look lost. Do you want directions out of this neighborhood?"

"No, sir, I am not lost. My name is Michael Jayden Manford. I am looking for Mr. Pablo Fernandez. It is my understanding Pablo has lived in this area and has visited your family."

"I have never heard that name; your information is wrong. I cannot help you. You could have an incorrect address. Sorry. Now, get lost, Yankee."

"I am willing to pay for any information you may have of him. I need his help. I do not care if Pablo is in the country illegally; I am not here to hurt him."

Michael soon understood he had underestimated the man. The man's posture alternated dramatically as he became irritated. "Money, money! You Yankees are all alike. Your resolution to solving problems is to buy your way out. Get lost, and stop saying that you are willing to pay for information. You will wind up in a dumpster. We do not need those types of problems in this neighborhood."

"Victor, let him in. I want to hear what he has to say. Come in, sir," a man from inside said in Spanish without showing himself.

Victor was confused. "Cousin, you are making a big mistake. We should not become involved in this man's problems."

However, the person insisted on conversing with Michael.

Michael was fluent in Spanish, but at present he was better off playing dumb, like he does not understand the language.

Victor opened the door just wide enough so that Michael could walk in.

Michael looked around the area. Some houses in the area should have been condemned a long time ago, including this one. He stepped carefully into the living room. Michael noticed it was clean, simple furniture that was well taken care of; he was somewhat apprehensive about walking into the house.

A man sat on the sofa and looked very fragile; a blanket covering his lap. Michael kept a close eye on Victor, who seemed to want to jump him.

"How can we help you, sir?" The man on the sofa asked in Spanish.

Victor, who was unhappy with letting Michael into the home, found himself being their translator.

"I am looking for this man." Michael said as he reached into a thin briefcase and pulled out a picture. "I want you to understand this is an old picture; he is much older now. I also have some composites made of what this man may look like now. His name is Armando Santana."

The man on the couch looked at the picture without showing any emotions. "I thought you were looking for Mr. Pablo Fernandez. Who is Mr. Santana?" The gentleman passed the photograph to Victor. "Do you have the composites with you?"

"I had three different composites made of what this man may look like now." Michael passed them to the man on the sofa while keeping an eye on Victor.

Victor was too busy looking at Michael and translating; he was not analyzing the pictures. Victor finally glanced at the photograph and stopped cold. He then examined the composites. Victor could not contain himself. "Cousin, this is the man who shot you. And this Yankee is working for Armando." Victor started to reach for a knife he had behind his back while holding a composite photo in his left hand.

Michael said, "Victor, please do not pull that knife; you will not have the time to reach it. I am not working for whoever you are referring to, especially that man, I can assure you."

The man on the sofa sensed the tension building up between his cousin and Michael, and he started speaking English. "Victor, you have not offered Michael here anything to drink. That is rude. Besides, I want to talk to him alone."

As Victor went toward the kitchen with his head lowered, he looked like a scolded child.

The man on the couch spoke English with less of an accent than Victor. "Why are you looking for Mr. Armando Santana—if that is his real name?"

"I take it you are Mr. Pablo Fernandez. How badly were you hurt?"

"At your service. I have told my cousin never to play poker. I was shot by him a couple of times, once in the right hip and once in the back. I was lucky I can still walk, according to the doctor who treated me. I will recover according to the physician. That is more than I can say the people who were accompanying me.

Michael, if you are after revenge, I will not help you. I will not have anyone else's death on my conscience. There is enough violence in this world without me seeking it out in the last days of my life. What has he done to you or your family to invoke that type of wrath? And how long have you been trailing him?"

Michael said, "He killed my father. No, I am not after revenge, however I will not lie to you. That has crossed my mind; at one time, I would have placed two bullets in the back of his head without giving it a second thought. My aunt raised me to know better; otherwise, I would not have hesitated to end his miserable life. I have been searching for Armando for years. I will turn him over to the authorities. That is a form of torture and slow death. By the way, you speak English well."

"At first I was not sure I could trust you. However, I am going to take a chance."

Victor listened to their conversation with interest as he returned from the kitchen with a soft drink in his left hand. "What makes you think that you can trust Michael? Pablo, why are you wasting your time listening to this Yankee? If you tell him what you know, he will get captured and be tortured to death.

On second thought, maybe if Michael is lucky, they will kill him right away. Yankee, why not you stand up slowly and leave quietly with your drink?" As Victor gave Michael a soft drink with his left hand, he pulled out a knife with his right hand. "What are you going to do now, Yankee?" He had a big smile on his face.

"Victor, you have to stop calling me Yankee. I honestly do not like it. For your information, I am a Mets fan. However, if you approach any closer with that knife, I will be forced to blow off your family jewels." As Michael said this, he glanced down at his right hand, which was clutching a .45 automatic.

"Will you two boys please stop comparing your manhoods? Do not forget children are playing in the backyard, and I am willing to bet that those boys have bigger manhoods than both of you put together. Michael, I will help you with the information you are searching for, however first I need a favor from you."

"Pablo, there is no way I am going to work with this Yankee. He will get all of us killed!" Victor emphasized the word *Yankee.*

"Good, then it is settled. You guys will work together. Michael, I am not going to ask you to do anything illegal, but what I am requesting of you could be dangerous." Pablo went on to explain that he had started working for Mr. Armando Santana to obtain fraudulent documents to live in the United States. Pablo never told Michael what was the alias name he used. "Furthermore, I am not talking about monetary compensation. You may find yourselves at times walking a thin line between legality."

Pablo described how he had commenced moving drugs or something illegal for Armando. "You and Victor are going to have to work together as a team."

"Pablo, I have no idea what you guys are discussing. However, if I agree to help you in doing whatever it is you want, I do not work with amateurs."

Consequently, Pablo narrated the story to Michael. On his last trip, Manuel, who worked with Armando, had killed three people. Pablo informed Michael of the two women who were kidnapped and forced across the border with them. Maria tried to escape, and Manuel killed her in cold blood. The other woman, named Consuelo, was being forced into prostitution.

Finally, it dawned on Michael that Pablo wanted him to team up with Victor to rescue Consuelo.

"Pablo, I will try to rescue Consuelo from whoever has her. However, finding her is not going to be easy, if not impossible. I cannot take Victor with me—no disrespect to you." He looked at Victor. "I will need the help of professionals."

"Michael, I'll have you know Victor is a marine with combat experience; you should not judge a by its cover. What experience do you have to call him an amateur?"

"I am a Navy SEAL, and I would prefer to work with an apprentice than someone I have taught their ABCs."

"What is a Navy SEAL?" Pablo asked.

Before Michael could answer, Victor replied, "A fish with the intelligence of a rock."

"I sense you two will work great together—if you don't let your egos get in the way."

CHAPTER 5

THE PLAN COMES INTO FOCUS!

Michael made up his mind to help free Consuelo, along with any other women in the club. He was going to help Pablo clear his conscience for taking part in human trafficking and other illegal actives. Michael had his selfish motives and reservations about it, and Victor's competence was questionable; the man did not seem capable of sustaining himself, let alone rescuing someone.

Victor was unshaven and sloppily dressed; he looked like a reject from hell. *I will cross my fingers and hope for the best. I have instructed Victor to follow up on a lead about Consuelo's whereabouts.* The problem was that finding her was not easy. Michael had been reading about human trafficking, and it was a huge business. *These people are ruthless. Given what Pablo went through, we will have to be careful.*

Their chances of finding Consuelo were astronomical at best. Pablo had overheard their conversation as to where they were taking her.

We were lucky that Pablo was close enough to hear them talking where they were transporting Consuelo. I have become more concerned about kidnapping two families. The problem with finding Consuelo is we cannot walk into the club and ask for her.

The chances are Consuelo has already been moved several times. When the women and children are no longer of monetary value, the evil bastards discard them. Human traffickers are worse than wars in society.

Tonight Michael was going to attend a human trafficking seminar. He wanted to learn much more about how these animals operated before taking them on.

Pablo gave him a breakdown of any information he could find out about Consuelo and her possible whereabouts. Pablo was a good artist and had drawn several sketches and portraits of the men and Consuelo. Pablo remembered details of Consuelo; he had never seen a birthmark on a woman on that part of the body. *Pablo's portraits and sketches are essential to our plans. We know what some of them look like, and they have no idea who we are. They do not know us; that is the perfect combination.*

That presents us with a slight advantage over them, but we will still be outnumbered. The importance of this drawing helps us locate Consuelo because we have never seen her before and cannot count on Pablo to point her out. I presume we are wasting our time. If those traffickers stick to their MO, Consuelo definitely would have moved—if they have not disposed of her.

There are two families in mortal danger who don't have a clue. A target is painted on their backs because of their children, and one of these women is pregnant. I want to prevent that animal from destroying these families.

I feel that we are better off trying to find the whereabouts of Armando, aka the Coyote. Pablo may know more about Armando than he lets on, regarding the alias the man is living by nowadays. He was tight-lipped about the information. Pablo is hiding something that became obvious when he would not sketch Armando or what he looks like presently. There was another man whom Armando works with, and Pablo omitted drawing Manuel. I will play along for now, however I will not allow Pablo to hold on to that information much longer.

Pablo is under the impression we are going to torture him. I could convince Armando or anyone else without utilizing violence. Torture is not my style; there are ways of making him talk without resorting to brutality. All I need is time, and I will have him squealing like a pig. I have a proven method that is efficient; I can resort to the other way, however I do not want to do that again.

Pablo was writing letters in the living room when there was a knock on the door. He almost jumped to his feet. Then Pablo slowly started to reach for an automatic weapon, which was in between the cushions on the sofa.

"It is Michael," the oldest son, Victor Jr., said as he opened the door.

Michael walked into the living room and could see that Victor had not returned. However, he could see that Pablo was hiding something in between the cushions, probably a weapon. Pablo was trying to cover it with his blanket. Every time there was a knock on the door, Pablo was ready to shoot the first person to walk in. The problem was his hands were shaking so badly that the only ones in danger were his family. "I see Victor has not returned. Any word from him?" Michael asked.

Pablo looked up from the sofa as he eased his hand away from the weapon. "Victor should be back soon." Pablo started sealing two letters in a white envelope.

"Pablo, I know you are concerned about being found here, because they may go after Victor and his family. I can move you to a comfortable place, and everyone will be secured. I understand you have a concern, but the longer you are here, the more the danger increases. In my opinion, Armando believes you have perished in the desert."

"Armando's way of thinking is that you could not have survived given the condition you were in. Furthermore, they were aware you did not know the area. Honestly, I am surprised you made it out; I do not think they will be trying too hard in their search."

"That is easier said than done. I do not have anywhere to go, or any money. On the street, I would be a dead man. As for Victor, he is not exactly a millionaire, and I am no Usain Bolt. No one can outrun a bullet. On the street, I would be a dead man.

You are right: I do not feel safe here. But my biggest concern is for Victor and his family. If they were to find me here, they would not settle just for my hide." Pablo wanted to change the subject, and he noticed that

Michael had a suitcase in his possession that seemed heavy. "What are you carrying?"

"Some materials may help us with the extraction of Consuelo from the club where she is being held captive. A countersurveillance kit, a spy protector box, a camera detector, a mobile phone spy detector, a frequency-finder, a bug detector cell phone, a GPS bug detector, and a few other things we may need. I was also able to obtain a dual-channel acoustic noise generator, a wireless signal detector, and a few other things. And who is Usain Bolt?" Michael had never heard the name.

"I am sorry I asked. The real question is, Who are you? James Bond? I do have a question for you. Why are you carrying all that equipment around when, deep down in your heart, you do not think we will ever find Consuelo alive? In the past, you made yourself clear by your reaction. Whenever her name is mentioned, you have shown no real interest; in your mind, Consuelo is already dead. To answer your question, Usain Bolt is the fastest man in the world, according to some magazines in 2018."

After they had been talking for a while, Victor walked into the house, closed the front door, and ensured the children were in the backyard. "I have good news: I have located Consuelo."

Pablo could not contain himself. "It is a miracle. My prayers have finally been answered, though I do not believe it Consuelo is alive? Where is she?"

"My source has informed me Consuelo is still being held captive at the gentleman's club outside San Antonio, about fifteen miles from here. Consuelo has a client who will deal only with her. However, we have a problem: she will soon be moved out of the state. Once moved, we will never be able to find her.

"But that is not our biggest problem. The club is bugged with cameras and listening devices in their bedrooms, the entrances, and the parking lot. It appears they use the recording to blackmail some of their customers. The women also have GPS devices implanted."

"Victor, I do not mean to question your intelligence, but how reliable is your source? What information did you tell him to obtain the details you have? I hope you did not ask for Consuelo specifically by her name. Please tell me that you did not show your contact one of the sketches we have. If that is the case, we need to pack up our tents now, because we are no longer the hunters—we are the hunted."

"Michael, you said that you did not mean to question my intelligence, but you are questioning my ability to develop leads without jeopardizing the team. Do not forget I have more to lose than you. I live in this city. I should have my head examine for agreeing to work with a marine reject. Marines know better than that. You have nothing to fear."

Before Victor could get another word in, Michael interrupted. "Please do not remind me. Why do you think I am asking, jarhead?"

"Listen carefully, you ugly, unwanted stepchild of the marines. This guy works in the club. Heraldo is illegally in the country and is an alcoholic. His mind goes blanks when he goes into a drinking binge. The man cannot remember what happened the night before, and he will answer all questions. He will not remember what we have talked about the night before, for all intents and purposes. There could have been a naked woman with him the night before, and he would not recollect.

"When Heraldo is intoxicated, he will talk about his job nonstop and answer all your questions. Long before you came upon the scene, I worked on him, and I have already tested my theory. Once, I told Heraldo about a couple of prostitutes we had bought the night before and informed him mine was great. Then I asked him about his woman. Heraldo never stopped boasting about a woman who never existed."

"That woman had better not exist. If I find out you have been thinking with your small head, I will decapitate it along with your family jewels for letting it do all your thinking," Annabelle said as she walked out of the kitchen. She had snacks, coffee, and tea on a tray, which she placed on the coffee table in the living room. There were two cups of coffee and one of tea, and she took a cup of coffee.

Victor quickly tried to assure Annabelle, "Honey, no woman ever existed." Then he reminded her she was one cup of coffee short.

Annabelle glanced at the trade and then replied, "No, I am not short. That is for our guests. You can have your nonexisting girlfriend make your coffee." She said that while walking toward their bedroom. As she walked past him, she elbowed him in the stomach.

Victor looked at both of them and said, "I do not want to hear a word from either one of you." He was embarrassed by what his wife had done; she was a very jealous woman and was going to be angry at him for weeks. Victor wanted to change the subject. "Michael, that reminds me: you owe me $478.00 for expenses I incurred getting Heraldo drunk."

"There is no way you spent that much money in one afternoon on drinks just for both of you. Victor, you want me to believe that you spent that much money on liquor in one day? Not even a mindless jarhead could drink that much alcohol without going into a coma. Furthermore, can you give me a rational explanation of why I should pay?"

"Hey, fish head, I have been on a recon mission developing this lead for weeks before you came on the scene. In an exploration of the club, I learned of Heraldo's medical condition. I befriended him to obtain information. Now, because you have insisted on being in charge of this operation, that makes you responsible for all my expenditures that transpired while working on this assignment. Pay up, Yankee."

"Okay, jarhead, you're right. As soon as you show me the receipts." Michael had a big grin across his face that said, *I've got you.*

Pablo interrupted. "I am happy to see that the two of you are learning to work together. Michael, when are you planning on rescue Consuelo? I know that you like to plan everything down to the last detail before taking any actions—I can tell from all the equipment you have in that suitcase."

"I have been contemplating for a while. With the new information, we will need to learn more about the tracking mechanisms before considering any actions. I am not making a move until we know how to neutralize the GPS. Are these ladies ever allowed to leave the club, and what are the circumstances? Hey, jarhead, did Heraldo say anything about that?"

"Hey, Yankee! I know you are not talking to me. When you recompense my previous covert operation, we will talk. Now you are asking for me to continue working without payment? I do not work for free. Furthermore, I want you to understand one more thing: I will not accept checks, especially from deadbeats like you."

"Victor!" Pablo shouted.

"Okay, okay! Cousin, this is just for you. I will refer to this for a later occasion. Michael, you still own me for my first covert operations. The women are controlled to the extent that all their items are purchased for them, including clothing and even Tampax. At times women are let out of the club with their dates for the night, in small groups under surveillance. The men pay extra to take them and are allowed to do whatever they want."

"Furthermore, there is a team of two men team periodically checking on them. I did omit one thing: Heraldo is one of the chauffeurs and knows the inner workings of the club. He is a treasure trove of knowledge about the procedures of the club. One more thing that you will find of interest. I have obtained a blueprint of the club showing the electrical cables, water pipes, all exits, and alarm system, just in case you want to try a frontal assault."

"Victor, I am impressed by excellent work for a jarhead. How did you come across those documents?"

Victor thought, *That is the first time Michael has called me by my name and congratulated me.* "I could tell you, but then I would have to kill you." He gave a big grin.

Pablo said, "Victor, a frontal attack is out of the question; some women may get hurt. We know now there are members of the police department protecting the club. We will require a distraction at the club. Do you have any ideas?

Michael said, "These blueprints could provide us with a means of creating chaos in the club. Heraldo seems to be a loose cannon; let us see what other information we can extract. He is your contact, Victor; keep working with him. Let find out if there are other weak links that we can exploit. We should record him."

"Michael, you spoke about attending a course tonight. What type of seminar is it? How does that relate to what we are trying to accomplish here?" Pablo was not only curious; he also felt that time was running out.

"There is a seminar on human trafficking here in San Antonio, sponsored by the Interfaith Group of San Antonio. I was reading on Deacon Alex Bermúdez, who travels across the country lectures on human trafficking. Deacon Bermúdez has been on a mission for over twenty years. Fifteen years ago, they kidnapped his daughter. They wanted to teach him a lesson, but it made him more determined."

Michael turned to Victor. "The seminar will start at 7:30, but I want to be there at 7:00. Pablo, there has been something on my mind for a while." Victor was about to leave the room, so Michael added, "This includes all of us, and I want this decision made together."

At a quarter to seven, Michael and Victor were on their way to the seminar. "Victor, why has Pablo become so engrossed in rescuing Consuelo? Now that we know her whereabouts, I am all in. That was excellent work on your part; I honestly did not think we'd find her alive, but I am sure that is of no surprise to you. I assume Pablo feels it is more than a novel task, however it seems to be personal; he appears to be on a mission to protect her."

"Pablo did not have the strength to outrun them. He stayed close to them. One time, someone almost stepped inches from his hand. Pablo kept moving to areas they had searched. Armando stopped searching for Pablo and lied to Manuel while waiting for him to depart. Armando continued his search for Pablo with two other men, who appeared in a Jeep." Victor wanted to change the subject. "Thank you for moving Pablo. My wife has been nervous ever since he arrived home. Annabelle kept saying men were going to break into our home and kill all of us."

"There is one more thing: Pablo is dying, and it has nothing to do with bullet wounds. Pablo arrived home haunted, and he wakes up at night screaming in a cold sweat. Pablo told me in his nightmares, he sees Maria and Consuelo asking for help while they are covered blood, or they curse him out for not helping them.

"Michael, you speak about catching the killer of your father as an obsession. I am concerned that you believe it was a contract hit. Do you have any evidence to back up your suspicions, or are you on a fishing expedition?"

"Victor, my main concern now is the safety of these two families; I am not after retribution. Is Pablo aware of his medical condition?" Michael thought, *Is there anything we can do for him?* He also wanted to avoid answering the question about a contract hit.

"Right now, all Pablo wants is to atone for what he has done. He feels responsible for the death of his brother and helping guard the women." Victor was choked up, and his eyes started to tear; he was unable to speak further.

"Victor, you said something about Pablo feeling responsible for the death of his brother?"

"His brother Filiberto was with Pablo on the last trip."

"Victor, we need help with what we are planning—someone who can be trusted. Do you have anyone in mind?"

"I have a friend, Jason Morison, who has been watching the house while I am out. Jason and Filiberto were good friends. I felt that my family was safer while he kept an eye on the house. I had to keep working, and for appearances, everything had to seem normal at home. Besides that, we needed the money. The good news is that he is a marine. The bad news is we are still shorthanded."

"Don't tell me I will have to deal with another mindless jarhead. Now I have to babysit two of you? And Victor, we will not be shorthanded. I have a good friend coming in from Dallas, and better than that––a Navy SEAL."

"Great! Just what we need, another brainless, smelly fish. Do not worry; the marines will save the day. Michael, we will need some hardware because it could get ugly fast."

Michael nodded. "Pablo is so adamant about not using weapons; there is no way of explaining it to him. Are you sure that the best you can do is to come up with another jarhead? This job calls for someone who can think before shooting."

During the seminar, Victor received a call from Annabelle asking him to return home. There seemed to be an emergency Michael was ready to cut the evening short, however Victor assured him that it was personal and nothing to do with their mission."

Michael stayed after the conferenced because he desired to speak to Deacon Alex Bermúdez. He walked over to the keynote speaker and introduced himself, and they struck up a conversation. Michael had never had problems introducing himself to strangers.

Michael sized up Deacon Bermúdez from the minute he observed him at the podium. He was about five feet eleven inches and 220 pounds, with dark brown eyes and a hairline starting to recede. He was in his late sixties, was well educated, and was a distinguished speaker.

"Deacon Bermúdez, my name is Michael Jayden Manford. I was very impressed by your seminar; the extraordinary stories you related were profoundly moving. I never thought that someone could be so cruel to another human being. Families in various parts of the Orient really sell their daughters into prostitution?

The deacon said, "The fathers disown their daughters because they were bringing disgrace to their families. In Venezuela, a woman was walking her seven-year-old daughter to school when a van pulled up next to them. One of the men grabbed the child; another man beat and stabbed the mother to death when she tried to rescue her daughter. Eight years later, her father found his daughter on the street begging for money. Both her arms were amputated so that they could collect more money from the tourists, who felt sorry for the girl.

"Mr. Manford, the stories I related tonight were not the most horrifying ones. I had a lady in the audience break down crying hysterically. I thought for one minute she was going to have a heart attack. I felt compelled to check in on her after the seminar. At first she was so inconsolable, and it was difficult to understand her. The woman finally stated she had given birth to a girl in Bogota, Colombia, five years ago. The next day, her daughter disappeared from the hospital.

"Here are some statistics that you may find interesting from Texas alone."

"In AUSTIN, there are more than 300,000 victims, including almost 79,000 minors and youth. The youth victims of sex trafficking and nearly 234,000 adult victims of labor trafficking. According to a groundbreaking study by the Institute on Domestic Violence & Sexual Assault (IDVSA) at The University of Texas." Deacon Bermúdez read from his notes.

"Call me Michael, Deacon Bermúdez. I was astonished at the numbers you were giving out on human trafficking. Those numbers sound unbelievably high. Please do not misunderstand—I am not questioning you. I am simply wondering how they arrive at those statistics. That is my concern."

"These seminars have become my mission in life. What good would it does to embellish those numbers? Besides, the numbers I stated tonight could be cross-checked by anyone on the Internet. To tell you the truth, I believe those numbers should be much higher. Think of all the cases around the world not reported of persons who go missing every year. There is no way of knowing how many of those persons are victims of predators. That is the reason why I believe those numbers are higher."

"What are the statistics of children under the age of ten years old who fall at the hands of human traffickers?"

Deacon Bermúdez was struck by the question and studied Michael. There seemed to be something more than just curiosity on his mind. "I really cannot tell you; there is no way of knowing. However, here are some numbers for you to contemplate."

Deacon Bermúdez checked his notes, "I wish you would have asked these questions during the seminar." While talking to Michael, he checked his documents.

"In 2002, the UNODC, United Nations Office on Drugs and Crime reports the percentage of child victims had risen in three years from 20 to 27 percent. Of every three child victims, two are girls, and one is a boy. There are about 20.9 Million victims of Trafficking Worldwide as of 2012; the United States accounts for about 1.5 Million victims."

"The breakdown of gender globally: over fifty-five percent are women, fourteen percent Men, seventeen percent girls, and 10 percent were boys. 600,000 to 800,000 women, children, and men bought and sold across international borders every year.

"Michael, what is your interest in all this? It seems to be more than just curiosity."

"I am thinking of writing a book about human trafficking." The question did not surprise Michael; he had been expecting it for a while. However, words seemed to flow out of his mouth. After all, what was he going to tell the deacon? *I am heading a group of vigilantes who will storm a house of prostitution, where we know they hold several women hostage to rescue them.* He was sure that would not go over at all.

"Sir, can I have your business card, just in case I need to verify any information that I may come across, and to quote you in my book?"

CHAPTER 6

SOUL SEARCHING

Michael went over the details of their plans. Things were starting to fall into place. Heraldo had been of enormous help and had invaluable information details of personnel's work habits in the club and their schedules. The maintenance of the building was due. However, getting Heraldo drunk was costing a mint.

Michael was bothered. It reminded him about his uncle, an intelligent man who was an alcoholic and had died at an early age due to alcoholism. This made him feel complicit in the demise of Heraldo. He was amazed that Heraldo could have a sharp mind when it came to his duties while he was working, yet his mind was a total blank when it came to what happened the day before when he was on a drinking binge.

Victor was correct: all the years of drinking have affected his Heraldo, and the next day, he cannot remember anything. We usually show Heraldo pictures of a woman we photograph out of magazines. Let his mind run wild with his own story of what happened the night before. He has a vivid imagination. At least we have one more way inside the club. This person has helped us in different areas of our operation. All we can do is pray that his information is correct.

Pablo had passed away a week ago and delayed the team in setting the operation into motion. He left two letters in a large envelope with strict instructions that they were not to be open until the team rescue Consuelo or discovered she was no longer alive. *I feel sorry for his family. In the end, he was trying to repent for his past actions. My main concern has to do with the two families that are in deep pearl.*

I have been doing some soul searching about being more interested in finding Armando instead of rescuing the women in the club, and sometimes I honestly wonder about myself. We have no leads about where to start looking for Armando Santana. It has been almost seven months since these animals targeted these families. There is a woman who has given birth or is about to go into labor. Either way we are running out of time.

On Thursday, two weeks before Mr. Andrew Grierson was to depart for Arizona, Consuelo was meditating. *In a few weeks, I will lose my teacher and the only person who protects me in this place. Maria was correct: they will use us, and afterward they will dispose of us. We are not human beings in their eyes.*

I will not give them the opportunity or the satisfaction of using me until I am no longer of any value to them. I will find a way to hurt them and their income. I cannot take it anymore. Consuelo had stolen a razor blade from one of her clients.

Consuelo was walking toward her room when she noticed a man working on the air condition system. For some reason, he seemed to be staring at her. *What, has this man has never seen a prostitute?* "Hey, pal, take pictures; they will last longer." She said in a low voice. *Is this the first time he has worked in a house of ill repute? I hope that I have the correct word; I want my teacher to be proud of my progress.*

The manager of the club, Mr. Ramon Guzman, insisted that the women address him by his surname. He had taken over for the previous manager, who had taken a permanent leave of absence once it was discovered, or at least suspected, he was skimming money from the club. Guzman walked past Consuelo to question the maintenance man. "What are you doing here, and where is De La Cruz? I have not seen you here before. And why is De la Cruz working on my system?"

"Sir, he called in sick this morning. I have my ID card here, if you want to call my office to verify the information." As the man said this, he turned his body slightly from the top of the ladder to show his ID to Mr. Guzman. "The office was supposed to call you and inform you that I would be taking his place. I will wait here until you can verify my identification, if this is a problem for you."

"Sir, you have a phone call in your office. Should I inform them you will call him back?" a secretary told Mr. Guzman. "It is a long-distance call, and he insisted on speaking with you".

Mr. Guzman was about to say something to the maintenance man but decided that it was more important to take the call. "I will attend to the client in my office."

While Mr. Guzman was walking toward his office, the maintenance man went back to work.

Consuelo noticed the maintenance man seem to point a tool at her; it looked like a laser pointer without light. He then took time pointing it at all the girls. *What a pervert. Is this how some men get their thrills?*

Mr. Guzman went to his office and picked up his phone. "How can I help you, sir?"

"My name is Christen Roberson. May I speak to the manager, Mr. Ramon Guzman? I require his assistance."

"Mr. Guzman speaking. How can I help you, sir?" Mr. Guzman had never heard the name and apprehensive about new people. He always remembered the names and voices of persons in his business.

"I am going to be in San Antonio on a business trip this weekend. I have three clients whom I need to entertain while they are in your city. I understand your club has a strict policy of being very discreet."

"Sir, may I ask you who refer you to us?"

"Mr. Crawford. He also mentioned that I should inquire if you still have on sale Crown Royal XR LaSalle."

Mr. Guzman thought, *He knows the password.* Then he started quickly checking his computer; he wanted to make sure this was not a sting operation by the police. He saw the name Crawford. He read the details in the system but changed them as he spoke to the new client. "Oh, yes, Mr. Tom Crawford from Los Angeles. He was here over a week ago, if I am not mistaken."

"Sorry, sir, I do not know Mr. Tom Crawford from California, the gentlemen I am referring to is from Seattle, Washington—Aladdin Crawford. He was there about three months ago and owns a law firm."

Guzman relaxed because the person had passed his test. "Okay, let us get down to business. Can I have your full name again? How many escorts will you need for this weekend?"

He repeated his full name and added, "I will need four escorts for this weekend, starting Friday afternoon."

"I assume that you want one of our conference rooms?"

"No, sir. I have made a reservation at the Hotel Emma at Pearl, on the river walk. I do not want it to seem that I have hired …" Mr. Roberson hesitated and seemed at a loss for words. "Well, huh, you know what I mean? Meaning no disrespect to you or your club, sir."

"Sir, I understand what you are trying to say. Did Mr. Crawford make any recommendations of hostesses in particular, or would you prefer that I make some endorsements? It seems you will not have the time to evaluate members of our staff yourself." He thought, *I will check his story about reservations later.*

"Mr. Crawford has shown me several pictures with a brief description of how these young ladies are. He recommended Barbie, Misumi, Esmeralda, and Amanda; he felt that these women were the best suited and that they would be perfect for my needs."

Mr. Guzman was upset this man knew what these ladies looked like— now he would not be able to substitute any of them. *I hope they are still in the club.*

"Sir, I must say you have made excellent choices. Let me see if they are available." He checked his computer to see whether any of them were about to be moved and gave a sigh of relief. "I do not see any problems with your request."

Mr. Guzman started writing a note on his computer to remind his staff not to move any of these women until further notice. "You know, that is going to cost you extra for having them the whole weekend. These young ladies are in high demand."

"I understand, Mr. Guzman. I can count on you to have them ready by tomorrow afternoon? I will call you if there any changes in the time of my arrival in San Antonio."

"Sir, I do not see any problems with that. Can I ask you what credit card you will be using?"

"I will be paying for your services in cash. My sister-in-law is the vice president of accounting in my company; you can understand I cannot have these bills pop up on any of my credit cards. Mr. Crawford informed me that you made special arrangements in these types of cases. As you are aware, he has a similar problem, and you have shown sympathy for his dilemma."

"Sir, we have ways of making it look like those bills are legitimately coming from restaurants and other business locations around San Antonio, which you will need for your taxes. We will give you an itinerary justifying all your expenditures, and this will be all tax deductible."

"I understand, however it is not the IRS that concerns me. I prefer to face an audit by the IRS than my sister-in-law. As you may gather, we are not on the best terms. I am going through a divorce, and these expenditures need to stay away from these women. You made an exception for Mr. Crawford, and he told me that it should not be a problem."

Guzman thought it over. *Well, I could charge him extra and leave that out of the record books, as I have done with others in the past. And maybe in the future, Mr. Roberson will make contributions toward my retirement.* "Did

Mr. Crawford say that you will need cash up front and that it will cost you extra? Will that be a problem?"

The next day at 4:25, Heraldo was driving four escorts to the Hotel Emma at Pearl on the river walk, delivering four women to Mr. Roberson. He had to pick up an envelope for Mr. Guzman and noticed that a couple of the women were not taking; they seemed preoccupied. Esmeralda seems to be hiding something in her small purse. These women were not supposed to carry anything in their possession, just lipstick and a comb.

I hope she is not thinking of doing something stupid by trying to escape. That will not end well; I am going to report her.

Heraldo approached the hotel and noticed a stretch limousine parked in the front of the building with the engine running. Heraldo thought he recognized the chauffeur, though it was difficult to see his face; the driver seemed preoccupied with reading something. He kept staring at the driver as another man stepped out of the back of the limousine and approached.

Back at the gentleman's club, it had been an unusually slow afternoon, and the women were preparing themselves for the evening. Friday nights were one of the busiest nights during the weekdays. "Amber, would you move your ass? It is going to be 4:30, and you are not ready to greet our guest. Who do you think you are?"

Amber, almost in tears, ran into one of the rooms in the back.

Mr. Guzman thought, *That stupid bitch ran into the back? Oh, I forgot she has only been here since this morning. I will have to check the paperwork on her.* He turned around and walked back into his office.

Five minutes later, the lights went out in the club. Mr. Guzman came out of his office, yelling at no one in particular, "Will someone please check the fuse box?" He found it strange that none of his men were by the front door; he had not noticed that before. He walked back into his office, and the lights came on. After a few minutes, there seemed to be a loud noise, and it sounded like it came from the computer room.

He ran into the room only to find that water was pouring into the room from the ceiling, and one of his men was trying to cover the computers. It was a lost cause because it seemed that all the water was pouring down directly onto the computer system. There were two laptops on the desk that were ruined. Mr. Guzman stood there in disbelief, not knowing what to do.

Simon, their IT man, had several choice names and was the most polite computer nerd. Finally he stopped, looked at Mr. Guzman, and added, "Okay, sir, we backed up everything on portable hard drives about fifteen minutes ago, on our secondary system, and there are no water pipes in that area. I know that because I checked the blueprints before I had the system installed there."

As they were talking, the fire alarm went off. Simon and Mr. Guzman ran out of the room and onto the corridor. The hallway was full of smoke, and they tried to make their way to the back of the building to where the computer system was located. However, flames were now visible from the back rooms.

A police officer was yelling, "Evacuate the building now!" Mr. Guzman saw a number of the women heading toward the main entrance, following instructions.

Mr. Guzman walked toward the office and informed Simon, "Help me secure the accounting books."

Simon informed Mr. Guzman that the secretary had placed the books in the safe before going home.

Mr. Guzman headed out of the building, and once outside, he did not see any of the women or his men—and the police officer was no longer in sight. He did notice that a vehicle was rapidly departing the area. He quickly called the two teams he had working on the street to alert them on what was happening. He realized that this was not a coincidence—this was a coordinated attack on the organization.

Mr. Guzman needed to recuperate all the women working in the street and return to their safe house until they could transfer to other clubs. He needed to find who had attacked them. "I have to find another location and have it operational as quickly as possible," he said to Simon.

After a few minutes, Mr. Guzman decided all these women needed to be scattered around the United States or to other countries. *We may even have to dispose of them. One of these bitches has to know something. My men have worked for me for several years, and I will have them check.* He was concerned that some of the women may try to escape.

Simon informed him that he could have a new system up and running in a couple of hours, but he needed to buy some equipment and computers, and he asked for a credit card. *We will have all the women back in custody within an hour or so after the system is operational. I hope that none of the women are inside the club, which is engulfed in flames.*

A few minutes earlier, back in front of the Hotel Emma, Heraldo was being approached by a well-dressed man in a three-piece suit. "Heraldo, I have an envelope for Mr. Guzman." As he said that, he reached inside his jacket for the envelope. However, he dropped it and kneeled down to retrieve the envelope.

Then he looked at the women inside the vehicle. "Ladies, will you please step into the limousine? We are running behind schedule."

A few minutes later, Heraldo was about to drive off when he received a call from Mr. Guzman. "Yes, sir, the women are with Mr. Roberson. I have your envelope and am about to return to the club. I do not understand, sir. You want me to escort the women to our safe house now? Do you want me to give the envelope back to the gentleman?"

Sir, that is going to be impossible. Mr. Roberson just left in a limousine." Heraldo was confused. *They must be on to Esmeralda.* "Sir, you want me to open the envelope and tell you how much money is in the envelope? I have been instructed in the past never to look inside any of the envelopes regardless of the circumstances."

Mr. Guzman went ballistic on the other end of the phone.

"Yes, sir." There were a few seconds of silence as Heraldo opened the envelope, which was difficult for him.

A few minutes before Heraldo had received the call, Esmeralda waited for the other women to step into the limousine. There was a suitcase in the back seat, and she thought, *Oh, no. These men may want to play kinky games.* Esmeralda looked around the area and saw that the man in the suit was returning to the vehicle. She thought that she recognized the driver. *Wait—that is the pervert repairman from yesterday.* She clutched her purse for dear life.

The man in the suit called to Esmeralda, "Please step into the vehicle; we have to move."

Esmeralda stepped in the limousine while leaning against the door. The man went in with the driver and took off the surgical gloves he was wearing.

All the women found that action as unusual and became concerned. The men wanted to feel the merchandise while selecting their preference.

As they were ready to drive off, Esmeralda took out the makeshift knife. "I am leaving. Take me to a bus stop, otherwise, I ruin your perverted night." She put the knife to her throat.

The other women rushed to the other side of the vehicle while pleading with her not to hurt herself.

"Esmeralda—or should I call you, Consuelo Rosa Fonseca?—my name is Michael Jayden Manford. I am here to help you escape. First, I need you to put that away; if my man starts driving quickly, I do not want any accidents. You are going to ruin that beautiful dress, and the color matches your eyes." He had a pleasant smile and seemed friendly.

"What did you say my name is? I have not heard my true name since being kidnap. I have no idea what you are thinking of doing. We are prisoners, and escape is impossible for us. They will track us down no matter where we go. We have something implanted that will lead them to us. Why you are doing this? When they track us down like animals, they will kill anyone who is with us."

"We know they will not be able to track anyone for a long time. We need to move now. We will remove your tracking devices, and it could be painful. We will help all of you reestablish your lives, however we need to move. Now, please put that away. Victor, hit it; we have been here too long. Every minute that we are here is dangerous for all of us."

While Michael was making his point to Consuelo, Heraldo said into his cell phone, "Sir, the envelope is filled with cut-up newspapers the size of dollar bills." His voice was cracking, and he was very nervous, hoping that Mr. Guzman did not think he was trying to steal the money. "I will follow them and keep you informed as to their location."

As Heraldo started to drive, there was a loud noise from under the vehicle, as if a tire had blown. Then the engine stopped running. He stepped out of the vehicle, and smoke came from the engine. The tire was also flat. "What the hell? This is a new car." Now he was beyond being nervous as he called Mr. Guzman.

The women looked back as they drove off; "Heraldo is not following us," Barbie said as they all broke down crying, this time with tears of joy. They hugged each other, but there was also fear of the unknown.

"Ladies, we are not out of the woods yet. There is a suitcase in the back seat. Change your clothing, because we have a long road ahead of us. We will raise the partition to give you privacy. There are a few—" Michael did not have an opportunity to finish his thoughts.

"Sir, we are being followed," Consuelo said as she pointed to a black Lincoln Continental three cars behind them. "Those two men work in the club. They are surely going to relay our location to Mr. Guzman."

"Victor, we are going to plan B. Take your next right turn. Once I am out, drive them to our location. Ladies, you have to change your clothing. I will meet you all at our designated location after I eliminate our tail."

As Michael stepped out of the vehicle, he had one question on his mind. *What the hell is plan B?*

A few seconds later, Michael stepped out of the limousine and was surprised Consuelo followed him. "What are you doing? You are placing your life in danger."

"More dangerous than attempting suicide? You will need to bait them, and these guys do not know you. However, they have orders to return us to the club. What do you want me to do? Michael, hurry up—they will be coming around the corner soon."

Consuelo followed his instructions, yet she did not know what he was up to as she started crossing the street to make herself a moving target. Consuelo made sure they spotted her and then turned and walked back onto the sidewalk, past Michael, at a fast pace as if she was going to run away from them.

"Marcos, there is one of the women. You get her—she cannot run fast in that dress. I will pull over to the curve." As he pulled over to the curb, he added, "Do not kill that stupid bitch. Mr. Guzman wants them alive."

Marcos pulled out his big knife as he opened the door. "Relax, Jack. I simply want to stress the point that she needs to come with me." Their eyes were glued to their target, and they were not paying attention to their surroundings.

Michael rushed over to them and slammed the door shut to the vehicle. He pulled out his .38 revolver with a silencer and shot them both in the head. Then he walked away as if nothing had happened.

Consuelo rushed over to him, holding his arm hand while helping him cover the weapon; they walked away from the scene looking like a couple out on the town.

Back at the club, Mr. Guzman needed to recover all the women as quickly as possible before someone paid him a final visit. All the women from the club were still missing.

The club was up in flames, however the safe was fireproof. *There is a little over a million dollars that need to be delivered early tomorrow for El Fantasma, along with all the accounting books. I will have to wait until the fire is under control. The fire chief in charge is a regular customer; I work it out with him. I can enter the building once the fire department gives the all-clear.*

Mr. Guzman was trying to communicate with the only team that had eyes on some of his women. Heraldo gave the information and the direction they were traveling. Simon called him to say that he would be up and running in two hours.

Mr. Guzman had called all his men, and they should be arriving soon. He did not understand what had happened to the five men who were working. His secretary had gone home earlier for the day before any of this happened. A half hour passed, and the only team he had on the road had not reported back.

After forty-five minutes Michael and Consuelo walked into an isolated house he had rented in Live Oak, about sixteen miles from Hotel Emma. He had chosen this location because it was outside of San Antonio in an isolated area, and it was easy to spot vehicles and the men Mr. Guzman had from a distance.

When Consuelo walked into the house, the women from the club mobbed her and were in tears.

"Ladies, may I have your attention for one moment? This is just the beginning of your journey. First, we will need to remove tracking devices. Then we will be moving a few times before this is all over."

"Have you ever done this before?" Consuelo asked.

"No. The way I look at it is if someone threatens to cut her throat with a rusty razor blade and jumps out of the safety of a vehicle, she should volunteer. If you do not make it, we may have a problem." Michael smiled at her. Then he turned to Victor. "Any news on the other team? Have they reported in yet?"

"After they finish playing cops and robbers at the club, they had to speed up. One dropped off the ladies and afterward follow up on our inside man. As you predicated, he seems to have his plans." Victor laughed as he spoke.

"Victor, do you have somewhere to be? Has the limo been returned and the other vehicle picked up?"

"Yes, on both accounts. Just leaving, fish face."

"Ladies, I am going to need a volunteer to assist me."

Back at the club, Mr. Guzman was conversing with one of his personnel on the cell phone. "Simon is not in his apartment? Are you sure? And his neighbor said that he moved out yesterday? The landlord added that he hit the lottery and was moving to California?"

"I want you to find him and bring him back to me alive. Check the airport first. I will send you help." Mr. Guzman no longer had to wonder whether Simon was involved. The question was how many of his men were involved.

One hour fifteen minutes after the fire started at the club, Simon returned to the hotel room he had rented the previous night at the Travelogue Alamo. He had bought some items and was entering the room. The lights went on, and Simon nearly jumped out of his skin. "Oh, hi, guys, I was about to call you."

"Simon, we were supposed to meet at the zoo about forty-five minutes ago. I guess you decided to take a trip without saying goodbye. Can you believe this guy? What do you think we should do with him?"

Simon nearly collapsed on the floor in fear. He could see that Amber was carrying a canon for a weapon with a silencer. "Look, I was going to call you. I could not escape Mr. Guzman—he kept me by his side for almost one hour! I had to invent …" He did not have time to finish his sentence as Amber cut him off.

"Simon, stop lying to me! You are hurting my feelings. Once the building went up in flames, you jumped into your car stop to buy a one-way ticket for Las Vegas via American Airlines, leaving at 7:50 tonight. We told you that traveling through the airport is dangerous. You are diverting from our original plans."

"I was unable to open the safe, and I thought you would be under the impression I was trying to keep all the money for myself." Simon was a bundle of nerves; when he tried to laugh, it sounded like a hyena.

"Simon, concentrate! What about the books, the two laptops, and the credit card?"

"Yes, they are over there," Simon said as pointed to the closet. He figured that he did not need them; he would disappear with all the money.

"Simon, you have to learn to relax. I believe you. Do you believe him, Jason?" Amber asked her partner. The man did not say a word and stared at Simon like a cat would size up a mouse trapped in a corner.

Amber looked at the refrigerator and continued. "Simon, you are not a good entertainer. You have not offered us something cold to drink. Never mind; I will take a cold bottle of water."

Simon seemed to freeze and then turn pale.

"Okay, forget it. We are not thirsty; you should keep your water in the refrigerator and not this backpack. Your share of the money is in the freezer. You had better hurry up—you have a plane to catch." Amber picked up a backpack.

Simon could not say a word. He defecated in his pants when he saw Amber pick up the backpack and Jason put his hand over his weapon. Then she left the room.

Jason looked at Simon, pointed his weapon, and added, "Charging the airplane ticket to the credit card of the club? That is stupid. They will know where you are going I voted to take all the money and put two in your head. I will settle for leaving you with half of your share."

"Before leaving the room, take a shower and change your clothing. You really should wear diapers, Simon—you are not cut out for this line of work."

After they left, Simon walked over to the refrigerator and opened the freezer. To his surprise, there were two stacks of hundred-dollar bills.

A half hour later, Simon was leaving for the airport he spotted two men who worked for Mr. Guzman—and they were not there to wish him farewell.

He quickly jumped into his vehicle and drove out of the parking lot while looking in the rearview mirror at the men to see if they were following him. He then looked forward and had to swerve hard to avoid hitting a couple walking on the sidewalk. Simon drove on, distracted by the men who were now pulling up behind him. He was looking back instead of where he was going; otherwise, he would have seen the gasoline truck crossing the intersection as he ran a red light and drove into the vehicle head-on.

The two men who were starting to follow him watched in disbelief as the vehicles burst into flames.

Back at the club, a fireman walked over to Mr. Guzman. "Sir, I know you are waiting to enter the building to retrieve documents from the safe. However, we will not be able to allow you to enter the building—there are several bodies in the building, and the fire is suspected to be arson. We are waiting for the Fire Marshal to arrive."

The fire chief in charge walked up to them to intervene, and he looked at the name tag. "Fireman Baily, I will escort Mr. Guzman back there. I will ensure that he does not disturb the evidence." He then looked at Mr. Guzman. "Sir, put on these surgical gloves and these shoe covers; you will need to follow me carefully and step where I walk."

Mr. Guzman wondered to himself as he walked. *Simon is a computer geek, he is smart when it comes to computers, but he does not have the smarts to pull off something like this by himself. The answer is simple: someone is pulling his strings.*

Once they were inside, the fire chief was nervous. "Mr. Guzman, I am taking a risk allowing you to enter this area. You will need to grab your documents quickly—and please do not go near the bodies."

"You have nothing to worry about. I am going to take care of your bill; the pictures will disappear. The bodies found—are they women or men? Will you excuse for one minute? I need to be alone." Mr. Guzman was carrying a suitcase one of his men had provided for him earlier. He suspected the bodies were his men.

"We believe they are men; we will not know for sure until the autopsy is complete. There is one more thing: we believe they died before the fire started. Please keep that information to yourself. I will wait for you out here."

Mr. Guzman went inside and opened the safe; he was in complete shock as he quivered with fear. The safe was empty except for one white envelope addressed to him. Someone was blackmailing him. Now they were taunting him. He whispered, "I am a dead man."

CHAPTER 7

CONTROL DECEPTION

Mr. Joshua Estrada was in his library room listening to opera and trying to relax. He was also reading and answering some last-minute emails before going out for the evening.

His wife walked into the library and asked, "Have you read the news from San Antonio?"

Mr. Estrada knew his wife expressed herself casually, yet something dangerous had happened to their operation. *She never makes spontaneous comments without having a deeper meaning, especially when it pertains to business. And she is vague in her questions; she is like the typical hypocritical politician.*

Mr. Estrada waited for his wife to depart from the room without saying another word. Then he started checking the Internet for news related to San Antonio. He was not sure what he was searching for; nevertheless, all he knew was the news related to one of their businesses.

He read about a man driving a stolen vehicle, a 2009 Corvette. The driver drove into a Sterling Condor fuel truck. Bystanders who attempted to save his life were unable to help the driver; the vehicle burst into flames, trapping the man inside. The identification of the individual was pending examination by forensic science. The driver of the truck escaped with minor injuries.

Mr. Estrada commented aloud, "What a fool, a teenager out on a joy ride." He continued reading. *I know she was not referring to this news.* He kept checking until he found what she was suggesting.

A fire at a gentleman's club in San Antonio claimed the lives of five individuals. Their identification was pending notification of their families. Mr. Estrada checked his schedule on his iPad and made a call.

"Sir, how can I help you?" the man answered at the other end of the line.

Mr. Estrada went straight to the point. "Manuel, have you seen the news from San Antonio? I want you there tonight. I need to know what happened to our number one club. Take your colleague and muscle. I want you to secure the payment."

"Sir, I am in Mexico City, inspecting merchandise before we distribute them to the appropriate locations as per your instructions. We need to move them to different factories by this week; furthermore, you have a two-man team that will handle the commodities; they have never had any problems collecting payments in the past."

"Manuel, Mexico City will have to wait until we can determine what happened to the club. I want you to find out if it was incompetence or worst, and I want you to make an example of whoever is responsible. Check the accounting books for discrepancies; I need you to be meticulous. Call me by midday and let me know what you have discovered."

Mr. Estrada continued thinking. "Regarding the merchandise, you are right. We need those laborers in our facilities. Have two men stay behind and instruct them as to what they need to do." He hung up without saying another word.

His wife walked back into the room; obviously she had been listening to his conversation. "What do you think? Is it possible that someone is trying to move in on my business, or is this just coincidence?" she asked.

"Unknown at this stage. Nevertheless, I never believed in coincidence. We will know more by midday tomorrow; I have arranged for our best man to investigate. Once he contacts our personnel in the police department, we will know more. We have to prepared for all scenarios; another organization could be probing us for signs of weakness."

Mrs. Estrada became enraged and slapped him across the face. "When I want a flunky to handle my business, I will hire one. I want you to fly down there and find out what happened. Do I make myself clear? You make sure nothing happens to my money. Make yourself useful for once in your life. Furthermore, you had better stop your special inspections of your prostitutes."

"Consider this your first and final warning. Who do you think you are? A doctor? If you keep this up, you will regret it for the rest of your life. Now, do something about your lip before it stains my carpet. Hurry up and get ready. I do not want to be late for the opera; I have been looking forward to this show."

Mr. Estrada was not surprised, and this was nothing new. The slap across the face was not the first time, nor would it be the last. *After all, I am nothing more than a figurehead for her organization. Hell, sometimes I wonder why she accepted my proposal of marriage. There is no way I could make a move against her—or should I say El Fantasma.*

Well, El Fantasma, the mistake is that only a few people within the organization know she is the boss. She has spies watching my every move; once they are out of the way, I will personally cut off her right hand while she is still alive. I have already discovered some of her informants, and they have had their severance payment; I made it look like accidents or killed in the line of duty.

In Mexico City, Manuel Mendoza wondered what had happened in San Antonio, because his boss sounded nervous. "Armando, I am leaving my team here to handle the merchandise. Have your men meet us in San Antonio tomorrow morning. Mobilize as many men as you can." Mendoza then checked the news on his iPad.

"What about the primary assignment here? We have not finished with him. I just started to enjoy myself. What are you going to do about Pancho? He has not given us the information; I need at least two more hours."

Armando pointed to Pancho, who was bloody and barely alive, tied up to a chair and waiting for his faith.

Manuel pulled out a switchblade and responded, "Give me one minute, Armando. Let me see what I can do about that." He then cut off the right ear of Pancho.

Pancho had been tied to a chair for over an hour, and he was resigned to his destiny, preying they would leave his family alone and finally kill him quickly.

Manuel took the tip of his switchblade, drove it into the right eye of Pancho, and popped the eyeball out of the socket. "Spare yourselves all this pain. Talk." The eyeball hung by the side of his cheek. Manuel added, "Are you ready to affirm what we already know?"

Armando laughed while looking at Manuel. "You may want to remove the gag from his mouth; the man sounds like he is ready to tell us everything we need to know. He is making so much noise, and the way Pancho is crying, I say you will have to shoot to him to shut him up."

"I wanted to make sure Pancho knew that I was serious. Oh, hell, we do not have time for this shit. We probably will not be able to understand this ignorant asshole anyway. We already have all the information; there is no way of recovering the money." Manuel took out his weapon and shot Pancho twice in the face.

Afterward, he turned his attention to a police sergeant in the room and said, "Secure the rest of the women. My men will be handling the merchandise tomorrow, and they will transport them. Hang his body in a public place as a reminder this is what happens when you steal from El Fantasma. Send the head back to his wife, and call me when you have new personnel."

In San Antonio, Mr. Guzman was in his home and very nervous. He read the note addressed for him.

> Mr. Guzman, you seem to be missing something. You
> have the information we need. Do you want to recover
> your merchandise? We will be calling you soon.

Mr. Guzman contemplated who would be stupid enough to take on this organization. Presently no one in the area had the connection, the men, or the money to take them on. When are they going to call? What information did these people want? Whoever it was, they had astutely pinned him in the middle.

Mr. Guzman wondered whether he had hidden enough money in his house. He needed at least $1.3 million. Maybe he needed to disappear, but even with that money, he was considering making like the invisible man.

A while back, Mr. Guzman had devised a plan to leave in case of an emergency; maybe it was time to place it into action. The problem with that is replacing the money would not leave enough money to escape. On the other hand, making a run with the funds meant he would be dead in a week. Mr. Guzman had been working hard to make it look like he had recovered the money and maintained order. *If I can pull off the first part of my plan, this should work. That is my only hope for survival.*

Mr. Guzman started to implement his plan. First, he visited Mrs. Annabelle Alvarez, the secretary of the club. She was very nervous, and it was difficult at first to calm her down. He informed her Simon had several portable computer drives, and he wanted to know if she allowed him to save them in the safe before going on vacation for a long weekend to visit family and friends in New York. He had several portable computer drives that were full of sensitive information.

He never informed Mrs. Alvarez that Simon had stolen the money or the books, or that he had perished in a fiery explosion. On the contrary, he thanked her for allowing him to secure those portable hard drives; that was his main concern. He did inform Mrs. Alvarez that she had been an enormous help, and he would be paying her for the month. Once he was able to retrieve the money from the safe, he would called her when he had a new location for the club's operations.

Afterward, he departed to the police station to give his statement on the events of today. He also wanted to build up an alibi; while police officers were taking my affidavit, a couple of my most trusted men waited outside the home of Mrs. Alvarez for her husband and children to return home.

Mrs. Alvarez and her family took a permanent vacation. She and her husband were entombed alive, but not before Mrs. Alvarez was informed her children were going to become movie stars, all thanks to her subjection of having young children who were twins in the same porn movies. *I will make sure those boys donate to my retirement to make up for the cash I have lost today. I will have the children disposed of if my clients grow bored with them.*

Mrs. Alvarez placed my life in danger. Having her disappear will buy me much-needed time with all their items removed from the house. It will look like she conspired with Simon to steal the money. They set the club on fire to create a diversion while covering their tracks. The authorities suspect arson; the police want to question all personnel employed at the club or fired in the last six months.

Mr. Guzman was contemplating how to influence Captain Robinson of the police department to corporate with his version of what had transpired at the club. It should not be a problem because Robinson was interested in money. Fire Chief Duggar would go along with whatever story he contrived; all he wanted was the homemade movies of him with underage boys.

However, convincing El Fantasma or the man he sent to investigate was going to be difficult. Guzman was not taking any chances. He set up the alarm system in case he had an uninvited guest. Mr. Guzman checked his weapons to ensure they were clean and loaded. His men roamed the street to see if they could spot any of the women.

Back at Live Oak, Texas, it was 9:00 p.m. Michael was reviewing their commando raid on the club with Amber Fisher, Victor Fernandez, and Jason Morrison. They informed him of the details of the operation and discussed what their next moves should be. The women were in the bedrooms, sleeping.

"Michael, there is no reason to move within three days; we should stay here. These women need to rest more than anything else. We are safe here, and it is time to start considering returning them to their homes. You have already removed the tracking devices from the women and destroyed them, right?"

"Our information is that it will take them at least one day before they can have a new system up and running, which will be worthless anyway." Jason seemed to be interrogating Michael more than making a statement. "Why did you leave Mr. Guzman a letter?"

Michael smiled. "On the contrary, Jason, their tracking system is worthless to them, but not to us. We need their system operational by tomorrow. Remember, we need to know their location so we can control their movements. You want to know why I left our enemies a note? Well, we need them fighting among themselves, chasing ghosts and not looking for us. I have some ideas on how to make that happen. How does that sound to you?"

"As for staying here, Jason, let me ask you how long you think it will take before some nosy neighbor calls the police, imagining this is a brothel. We do not need that attention." Michael seemed annoyed that Jason did not see the logic of his strategy.

"Michael, you are right. We will start standing out in no time if we stay here too long; someone will call the police believing this is a cathouse. I do not know what you are planning, however you can count on me. Besides, there is something I need to do first," Consuelo said as she came out of the hallway and sat in the living room.

Michael counted the money confiscated from the safe of Mr. Guzman. "Victor, you have been of enormous help to us. Without your expertise, we would not have been able to help these women escape. Your wife has been a gem, helping us with details and scouting for us."

He gave Victor the money. "I will understand if you want to walk. I know Annabelle is nervous, and her concerns are well founded—we are dealing with animals. Anyone else wants to walk away, I will understand no hard feeling. I am grateful for all your help." Michael turned his attention to Amber and Jason and gave them each one hundred thousand dollars.

Victor saw something wrong. "Wait one minute. Why am I getting more money than these guys? And for your information, I am not going anywhere. I will see this mission to the end—do not insult the Marine Corps."

"Partner, the marines have nothing on Navy SEALS. Besides that, I have to make sure that these empty heads do not screw up a simple mission," Amber said with a smile.

Jason seemed to want to walk away, but there was something else on his mind as he looked across the room in deep thought. He turned to Victor. "You are going to need my help. There is no way I am leaving you alone with these two mindless fish heads."

Michael looked at Victor and added, "Amber and Jason wanted you to have half of Simon's share; they felt he forfeited it. I almost forgot." He tossed Jason a white envelope. "This should cover your expenses you occurred while conducting your covert mission on Heraldo. That was an outstanding job. By the way, you have nothing to worry about—no personal checks in the envelope."

Michael took the money he had spent in the operation and on any further expenditures he was expecting to incur in the future. "I want to thank you guys; the four of us should be able to pull this off without any problems."

"I do not know what marines or Navy SEALs are. However, you guys cannot count worth a shit. I come up with the number five." As Consuelo said that, she stood up, walked over to the kitchen table, and sat down in a chair. "Okay, Michael, what is your plan?"

"Victor, that reminds me. Pablo, may he rest in peace, left two letters. Those letters were supposed to be opened when we rescued a certain young lady." Michael looked at Consuelo as he spoke. "Since she refuses to stay out of danger, I say we have completed our mission." When Michael opened the envelope, there were two letters, one addressed to Consuelo, and the other to Michael.

Mr. Guzman was having a telephone conversation with Darrell McCoy. "Sir, I will be in San Antonio tomorrow afternoon. I should have the system operational in two hours after setting up the equipment. Sir, I want you to remember the radius of the signal in these trackers is only fifty miles."

"Darrell, why are you waiting until tomorrow? I need you here tonight. Like told you, I believe Simon perished in the fire. I lost all the merchandise and need to recover it as quickly as possible. Darrell, as you alluded to before, I am running out of time."

"Sir, I understand what you are saying, however when you called earlier to inform me, Simon did not back up the program to the GPS. I will have to start from the beginning. I cannot believe that idiot did not save a copy of the program, especially after I instructed him to do so."

"Mr. Guzman, when you informed me of what happened to the club and the loss of your commodities, I made it clear to trace those items. We need to purchase the same equipment implanted in the merchandise."

"Regrettably, this is a tracking device not sold in San Antonio. I will have to buy it tomorrow. When you first called, I did check. Otherwise, Sir, I would have been on a plane. I will not be able to obtain the tracking device until nine tomorrow morning."

At 6:00 a.m., Mr. Guzman's cell phone rang. "Hello?"

"This is Manuel Mendoza. I am going to skip through the pleasantries.

We are here to collect the money and examine the books. I will also need to talk to the secretary; we need to meet somewhere we can speak in private, without any interruptions. Do you have any questions for me?"

Mr. Guzman swallowed hard. He needed to control his nerves. "Not at all, Manuel." *It does not take long for the vultures to start circling. I am sure he is accompanied by the Coyote, his faithful henchman, who does the killing for Manuel. If they are not out entertaining themselves; they are enjoying torturing their victims.*

"I have the money in the house; we can meet here. This is a quiet neighborhood, and we will be alone. You can pick up the money at the same time. As far as books, we have a problem. Although I cannot prove this, the fire may have destroyed the accounting books."

"Mr. Guzman, I was under the impression the books are supposed to be locked up in the safe. How is it that you have the money and not the accounting books?" Manuel was on speakerphone so Armando could hear their conversation; he wanted to evaluate Mr. Guzman's tone of voice, in case he tried to avoid answering the questions or seemed to be lying.

Manuel thought, *Never liked Guzman.* He considered the man a buffoon and inadequate to run the club. He first needed to secure the money before determining whether Mr. Guzman was responsible for the fire or incompetent. The most important thing to him was how Mr. Guzman reacted when Manuel subjected him to a private meeting. *There is no organization in this area strong enough to attack us; we have the police officers and local government officials in our books.*

Mr. Guzman said, "I had a conversation at 3:40 p.m. with our, secretary Mrs. Annabelle Alvarez. Yesterday, she stated she wanted to leave the club an hour earlier to take care of her children, and she would return after taking care of the twins." He had to weigh his words carefully around Mendoza. "Mrs. Alvarez's children have behavior problems in school. Afterward, she said she'd return in the evening to complete her work.

"However, Simon, our IT man, was found in the backroom. He

claimed he needed to secure equipment in the safe for the weekend. The fire started at the same time and spread fast. We had to evacuate the building. Davila Soto, the head of security, informed that Simon dropped his rucksack as he ran out of the building; Davila at first thought it was because of the fire.

"Later that evening, to my surprise, the rucksack was filled with blank papers to make it look like his backpack was full. In my opinion, he meant to take the money and leave blank papers.

"Mrs. Alvarez knew when there would be the most money in the club, at shift change, and she knew the busiest schedule. Simon would be knowledgeable about manipulating the wires to manufacture a fire that spread so rapidly. The fire department suspects it was an electrical fire given the way it spread and started. I believe it was a diversion. Mrs. Alvarez and Simon plotted to steal the money. They were observed having lunch together several times in the past."

"Mr. Guzman, if you believe Mrs. Alvarez is involved, why not have your men pick her up before the police question her?"

"I chose not to bring her in for questioning. Simon is still out there, and she is my bait on the street. I want her thinking we are unaware of her involvement. Simon has to be close, and we need her to lead us to him. We need him alive, and he needs to answer questions in case there are others involved. The chief of the fire department escorted me into the building to retrieve the money."

After hanging up the phone, Mr. Guzman started sweating profusely. His hands trembled, and his blood went through the roof.

At Live Oak, Consuelo walked into the kitchen and asked Michael, who was having a cup of tea, "Why were you so interested in rescuing us? You gave your team and us the money from the club. You did not take a share of the money for yourself. Are you only interested in finding the men who killed your father, and nothing else matters?"

"I started off interested only in finding Armando Santana. However, after I read about human tracking and heard some of the horror stories you ladies have gone through, I would not feel right taking that money. I have taken enough funds to finish our mission. I will see the people responsible for the death of my father in jail or dead. Consuelo, from what you are saying, Armando is simply a pawn in their organization.

"My vengeance will have to wait; my only concern now is these two families who are in mortal danger. They are not solitary victims, and I hope we are not late. All we have is an old address, which does not give us much of a lead. The best part is we are going to be using the traffickers' money against them. It is poetic justice, don't you think?"

"Michael, you need to hear this," Amber said as she rushed into the kitchen from the garage. They had a van in the garage set up with the equipment set to spy on Mr. Guzman. "Am I interrupting something?" she asked, somewhat confused—or maybe disappointed.

Manuel was preparing to meet with Mr. Guzman when he received a call from Mr. Joshua Estrada. "Good morning, sir. We are on our way to question Mr. Guzman now. I called Mr. Guzman earlier this morning. There could be a few characters involved in trying to steal the money. Mr. Guzman claimed the accounting books were destroyed during the fire."

"I have some connections in the police and fire department, so I will have more information this afternoon. The good news is I will secure the money. Nevertheless, the person responsible for the fire has escaped for now." Manuel thought he had his reservations about how truthful Mr. Guzman was. However, first, he wanted to solve this case before eliminating all involved.

"Yes, sir, I will secure the money first as soon as I meet with Mr. Guzman. Unfortunately, all the women are unaccounted for, and we do not have a way of tracking them until this afternoon. Mr. Guzman has an IT man coming in from Dallas with the equipment required to track the woman. Sir, you want all the women eliminated? Do you want me to question them first to see if they know anything? Yes, sir, I will use my discretion and then take the appropriate action."

An hour after Manuel had a conversation with El Fantasma, Amber, Jason, and Consuelo were driving down Hays Hill in San Antonio.

"Amber, do you see the for-sale sign sale on that house? It's perfect. I want you to stop here. I will take a closer look over there; pick me up after I take a couple of pictures and a pamphlet." Jason stepped out of the vehicle and reached back for Consuelo. "Honey, you want to take a closer look around the area? I want to take pictures and information about this location."

Jason gave a charming smile while looking at Consuelo, and then he turned and walked toward the house. "Okay, we will compare the information later."

Consuelo turned toward Amber and asked, "Is that man crazy? Amber, if may I ask, you how long have you been in love with Michael? You have nothing to worry about regarding this old prostitute; I am not in your league."

"Consuelo, look at me. Never talk or think of yourself in that manner. What happened to you was out of your control; you had to survive. Remember, you are a young, beautiful woman. Once you are away from all this, put it behind you." Amber wanted to change the topic. "Jason has eyes for you, and he is a good guy. Consuelo, do my feelings for Michael show? I do not want Michael to know. It does matter anyway—he does not even know I am alive."

"That is what you think. I have been around men more than I care to admit."

Three men were standing by a couple of parked cars, talking, smoking, and carrying a conversation as Jason walked in their general direction. He walked past one of the men and noticed that his left shoelace was untied, so he kneeled down behind a couple of the vehicles to tie his shoe. Afterward, he took pictures with a wide-angle lens of the house and the street, and he took a pamphlet of the house for sale.

Amber drove past the men and picked up Jason.

"Jason, are you crazy? I told you one of those men works for Mr. Guzman in the club."

"Well, I was not going to ask the mindless fish here. Heaven forbid anyone looks at her crossed-eye; Amber is liable to beat the crab out of them. I am surprised she did not run them over. Besides, these men are looking for single women. They are not looking for married couple who is house hunting."

"Hey leatherneck, did you plant the bugs in those vehicles and take pictures of those men? Or were you spaced out like all marines?"

After Mr. Guzman met with Manuel, he turned to Davila Soto, his new right-hand man, and asked him, "What do you think?"

Davila thought to himself, *You are a dead man.* "Sir, we have a problem: I think they did not believe our version of the story. We may be in trouble." *I am not settling for a new boss. I will be in charge of a new club. After all, I went through enough trouble to frame the previous boss.*

This time I do not have to plant evidence like the last time. Mr. Guzman, I know Simon is dead, and I buried alive Mrs. Alvarez; her children were used in X-rated movies. Mrs. Alvarez, having an affair with Simon? That is the joke of the year. Finally, where did Mr. Guzman get the money if it all went up in flames?

"Is there any word on the street on the women? I want our men to find the women before Manuel does. We need to question them before terminating all of them; one of the women may have the answers I need to solve this mystery."

"Mr. Guzman, it is a mystery. The women have disappeared, and no one has seen any of them." Davila was at a loss. How could these women vanish without knowing this city? "Sir, it is as if the earth opened up and swallowed them. Do you think someone is trying to move in on the organization?"

Two hours after his meeting with Manuel, Mr. Guzman drove down the streets of San Antonio, checking for the women on the streets. He received a phone call on his unregistered cell phone, which made him suspicious. "Who is this?"

A voice said, "How much do you trust Davila Soto? Because your man is on his way to meet Manuel. If you do not believe me, take a drive to the corner of Wyoming St. and South Cherry St. I figure that is how much time you have before Armando visits you. Who knows what your man will say to Manuel?"

"Why should I believe you?" Mr. Guzman was in the area, and he wanted to confirm the information, just in case. If it was the truth, his life depended on it. He thought, *I need to be on the scene before Manuel,* and he set the address on his GPS.

"My only interest is saving your bacon. Are you inspired to make a deal in a future venture?" Michael wanted to hear him squirm over the phone before hanging up.

Five minutes later, Mr. Guzman approached the corner of Wyoming St. and South Cherry St. Davila was sitting inside his precious car. Guzman stopped his vehicle alone side of Davila and asked him, "I thought that you were going to drive around the Alamo, checking the area."

Davila needed to compose himself quickly, or else Mr. Guzman was going to suspect there a problem. Davila did not anticipate seeing him around this area, and he grasped his weapon slowly. There was some hesitation in his response "Huh, yes, Angel called with information that a few women may have been observed in this area. I am waiting for Angel, and a couple of men are scouting. I will notify you, sir, if something reliable turns up."

"Finally there may be good news. Okay, I will wait for your call. Meanwhile, have the angels open the pearly gates for you."

Davila thought, *Idiot. Just like taking candy from a baby.* He bought the story, hook line, and sinker. He slowly removed his hand from his weapon on his lap. Davila started relaxing, but then something hit him. "Wait one minute—what did you say?" He turned his head toward Mr. Guzman and found himself staring down the barrel of a 9mm.

The last word he heard was, "Traitor."

Mr. Guzman fired two times into the chest and one into the head. Once he finished shooting, his phone rang again. It was the same number that had called him before. "What?"

"Good. Now, control yourself, wipe the weapon down, and drop it; we will take it from here. Drive off slowly without attracting attention; the speed limit is thirty-five. Take the second or third right and keep on driving; we are watching you. Manuel is coming in the same direction. You have about ten minutes to disappear from this area." Michael was watching him with binoculars and hung up the cell phone.

Twelve minutes later, Manuel Gonzalez was driving on South Cherry Street, approaching Wyoming Street. According to his GPS, he was about two blocks from his destination.

Manuel was carefully driving as he looked for Davila and checking parked cars in the area to ensure he was not walking into a trap. Manuel saw a red Toyota in the distance, and he rolled down his window while placing his weapon on his lap. He did not trust Davila.

Suddenly and without warning, a woman ran out in front of the vehicle. Manuel had to brake hard to keep from hitting her. A man rushed up behind the woman and pushed her on top of the hood of the car. The man appeared to be on the verge of striking her. Manuel unable to drive off without creating a scene or having someone reporting a hit and run, furthermore, he did not want to get involved.

The woman suddenly broke loose and ran toward the passenger side of the door. Manuel was caught off guard, but he quickly locked the door and tried to roll up the windows. He was too late.

The woman forced half of her torso inside the vehicle while begging Manuel for his help.

Manuel was angry and yelled, "Get out of my car!" while covering his weapon.

With tears in her eyes, she stopped struggling and got out of the vehicle.

The man forced the woman toward the sidewalk in a harsh manner. When they reached the curve, he threw his arms around her neck, kissing her passionately. She responded in kind.

Manuel lost his temper and screamed, "Get a room!" Then he said to himself, "Some people are just too much. Unbelievable."

Manuel started driving toward Davila, thinking, *If he is out to double-cross his boss, I will eliminate him—after I take care of Mr. Guzman. I could never trust anyone who will backstabs his boss.* Manuel had received a call from Davila, who had stated that he had details about the fire and the money.

Manuel stopped alongside Davila. "Mr. Soto, what is so crucial you could not inform me over the phone?" After waiting a few seconds for a response, Manuel glanced over at Davila, and what he saw caught him off guard. Manuel broke his one carnal rule: never call attention to yourself when there are bodies in the area. He started driving in a reckless manner for a split second without checking his surroundings. Unfortunately for Manuel, there was a patrol car, and it sped up behind him without his lights or siren.

Police officers stopped Manuel Mendoza for speeding two blocks down the street. Another police officer confirmed a dead man was in a car and identified the corpse as Mr. Davila Soto.

A search of Manuel's vehicle revealed a 9mm fired recently—the suspected murder weapon of Mr. Davila Soto, along with leader gloves in the back seat of the car Manuel was driving.

"Armando, you and Manuel have worked together for as long as I can remember. Can you think of any reason why Manuel would kill Davila? There is no reasonable explanation; I think he may have received information about Mr. Guzman and had to act. What could have Manuel learned to move against Davila?"

CHAPTER 8

LET CONFUSION RAIN

Mr. Estrada said, "Babel has confirmed that the police read Manuel his Miranda Rights. He requested a lawyer without answering any questions. The problem is we cannot have our names associated with Manuel; the implications could be devastating. We need to avoid any direct communication with him, however it is essential to find out what transpired. The only question is why Manuel was there in the first place."

Lawyer Babel had worked for the organization for a long time.

Armando had never dealt with Mr. Estrada, known as El Fantasma, who may have more bosses than he knew. "I agree with you, sir. Presently, he is being held at the 515 S. Frio Street police station. We will have to wait for the lawyer to inform us what happened with Davila."

"I know that Davila Soto works for Mr. Guzman and was his right-hand man. Could Davila have tried to lure Manuel for a hit? Maybe Manuel acted in self-defense; that would make sense."

"Mr. Estrada, I would say that is a possibility, but I seriously doubt it. I would go as far as saying Manuel did not even know that Davila personally, only by name; he has seen him around the club the same as I have. Sir, I was meeting with one of my contacts in the police department on the other side of the city."

"I have no idea what Manuel was doing there or why he shot Davila Soto. I think he did not shoot Davila in self-defense. I have been able to contact our man in the police department, although the police officer is not involved in the arrest or the case of Manuel. The information on Manuel is he's being held on suspicion of murder."

"According to the charges filed against him, they are building up a stronger case. He was speeding away from the crime scene by the arresting officer, however I know he is innocent. Someone else killed Davila."

"Armando, you describe a dream case for a prosecutor to present to a jury. Nonetheless, you are so adamant about Manuel being innocent. I am confused. What do you know to draw that conclusion?" Mr. Estrada wanted to understand Armando's point of view.

"Sir, Manuel does not use gloves when eliminating a person; he believes not using gloves gives him a connection with the armaments he is working with."

"There is a final nail in his coffin: the police found gunpowder residue in his hands. The gloves had gunpowder, and the suspect murder weapon also was recently discharged."

"How can you be so inflexible to say Manuel did not kill Davila Soto? Everything points to him except for the gloves, which were in the car."

"Mr. Estrada, two weapons found, one in his possession, a .45 automatic with an ivory handle, and a 9mm with pearl handles in the back seat. We know the suspected murder weapon is the 9mm. Manuel has always said that he would never use a gun with pearl handles; those weapons are for pips. Manuel considers General Patton his hero, and he has read about the general using weapons fitted with ivory handles.

"Sir, that reminds me: Mr. Guzman has three weapons with pearl handles. Mr. Guzman could be our killer. I know about his acquisition because he was so excited to show us. One of them is a 9mm. Afterward, Manuel commented that pearl handles are for pimps. That's all the proof I need."

"Sir, the gunpowder on the hand of Manuel came from late last night in Mexico City; he shot Pancho Santos, who was stealing money from this organization, and Manuel was not wearing gloves. Manuel wants to feel the weapon in his hand while pulling the trigger."

"However, I cannot testify on behalf of Manuel with that glowing testimony. Presently, Manuel does not have a leg to stand on, and this state has the death penalty. When can I speak with attorney Babel? There is something I need to verify."

Mr. Estrada considered this. "Is there any chance Manuel may turn state's evidence against us, to have his sentence reduce? I am not a criminal lawyer, but He is looking at life imprisonment or the death penalty—not the best choices."

Mr. Guzman thought, *Whoever is moving against El Fantasma placed me in the middle for whatever their end game is; regardless, it will not work. I cannot say a word or move against them until I recover all the books. I will have a play along with them for now, but afterward is a different story. I cannot afford to have this man on the loose. I will eliminate him and his crew.*

Mr. Guzman walked into the spare room. "Darrell, I need that computer up and running now." As Guzman said that, his cell phone started ringing, and he looked at the incoming number. He did not recognize this number, but it was not his mysterious caller. "Who in the hell is this?"

"What, no 'Thank you for saving my bacon,' Mr. Guzman? You are just plain rude."

"Darrell, let me know when the system up and running," Mr. Guzman said as he stepped out of the room and walked into his home office. Mr. Guzman did not want anyone to overhear the conversation.

Darrell replied, "I should finish in about thirty minutes or so."

After a few seconds passed, the person on the other end of the line said, "I am assuming that we are along? I have been looking over the accounting books, and you have been a bad boy, stealing from El Fantasma. What do you think he would say if he were to find out?"

"What kinds of a sick game are you playing here?" Mr. Guzman responded out of anger. He started thinking. The last thing he wanted was to have this man upset at him.

"Sir, how can I recover my books and be of service to you? I do owe you a big favor, as you have reminded me several times. What do you want for my books? I am sure we can work out something beneficial for both of us?"

Michael could tell Mr. Guzman was desperate to recover his accounting books. *It is time to apply pressure on the dirtbag.* Michael had to let him know who was in command. "I will not tolerate insubordination from someone like you. Mr. Guzman, are you aware there was a shooting at the corner of Wyoming and South Cherry?"

"There are rumors of a film on the killing. Do you want to know all the details of the man? I could continue with a full description: the killer, his vehicle, and the license plate. No, wait—I can see his face. Do we now understand each other?"

"Sir, I understand." Mr. Guzman was subdued in his tone of voice because he knew the man was holding all the cards. Although Mr. Guzman was simmering on the inside, it was all he could do to swallow hard, hold back his temper, and play along for now.

"I want the name and address of El Fantasma and Armando—that is not negotiable. Do you have that information at your disposal?" Michael knew the answer to some of the questions he asked; this was his way of testing Mr. Guzman.

"No, sir. These two men are very secretive about any personal information. I do have some ideas. Not too many people would dare do anything like what you are attempting to accomplish. I know El Fantasma is married and lives in Texas. I saw a wedding ring on his finger when he walked into my office, and he removed it when he thought I had not noticed.

"Armando Sebastian De La Rosa Santana is known as the Coyote; his specialty is smuggling things across the border. He uses his first name because in the past, he has tried using different names but has forgotten the alias. That is why Armando has to keep it simple and wants to be known as the Coyote. You may surmise he is not the brightest bulb in the room. The fact is you took out the smart one between both of them—a good job."

"You have until tomorrow to fill in the missing information." Michael was tightening the screws one way or another without giving Guzman a chance to breathe.

"What do I get in return? I mean, you hinted if I wanted to recuperate my personal property."

"I will give you one book for every piece of information I establish is correct on a person. How does that sound to you? Give me what I ask, and I will reciprocate."

Mr. Guzman thought, *How can I let him know I want to cooperate?* "I will give you the cell phone numbers they are carrying, however those phones are throwaways. Once they leave San Antonio, those numbers are history. Similar to what you have been doing now." He gave Michael the numbers.

"That still leaves one of the books and the video identifying the killer of Davila Soto. I am interested in finding out who killed my man. After all, I have to protect my personnel." Mr. Guzman was not going to admit he had killed Davila Soto over the phone; this person could be bluffing about a recording. "How do I retrieve those items?"

"You mean the book that has the information showing you have been stealing from your boss and blackmailing your clients without giving El Fantasma his share? Now, your concern about your man Davila Soto touches my heart. Excuse me; I need to shed a tear. You are only interested in one book because in the wrong hands, this could be detrimental to your health.

You work on retrieving the first two books. Start by taking baby steps before trying to run. In the meanwhile, you need to start looking for a location to open up a new club."

After forty minutes of an unpleasant conversation with this mysterious caller, Darrell rushed into the room excited. "Sir, I am tracking five of the thirteen women, and they are still within range. Their movement is minimal; they seem to be practically stationary. They must be in a confined area."

"Darrel give me their location. What about the others? Do you have anything on them?"

"Mr. Guzman, I may be able to amplify the frequency—something that I discussed a while back with Simon. The five women are at Potter Creek Park Road in Canyon Lake; it should take your men about an hour to get there. If any of the women move, we will be able to relay that information to the team you send to recover them."

Michael called Jason. "You will have company coming in about one hour. Do not get cute and remember what we have discussed: wait until they are all on the scene. We want them to do all the work, remember, just one close two both teams, and then move out of the area. Make sure both groups are together before you shoot; do not hit anyone."

"Look, I understand Navy SEALs are mentally defective, and that is why you have to repeat yourselves. However, I am a marine, remember? You do not have to repeat yourself on my account; we are not mindless fish heads like you."

"No, we have to reserve our baby talk for jarheads like you. Otherwise, it will never sink into that thick skull you have." Michael had a smile on his face as he hung up the cell phone.

"Consuelo, we are going to be having guests for dinner. You need to stop visiting our friends. Do not worry about them; they will be all right. Trust me. You have nothing to worry about. I will not let anything happen to your friends—they are brave to corporate with us. I will give you my word they will be all right."

Armando was wondering what else could go wrong today. His partner was in jail. Manuel had tons of information about him and El Fantasma, and he could turn that over to the police for a plea deal. His cell phone started ringing. "Who is this?"

Angel Castillo had been driving for almost forty minutes; he was in charge of a team of three men to recover five women from the club. He had never been in this part of Texas, so he was unsure of the area. Angel was trying to understand why Manuel had killed Davila Soto. They had been close friends since childhood. Nothing seemed to make sense in this business; life seemed to be cheap.

Angle did notice that a vehicle had been on the same road for the last twenty-five minutes, and he asked the group, "Have you guys seen any of those men in the black Lincoln Continental?"

Figueroa instantly recognized the driver, Richardo. "He works for Manuel and was around earlier yesterday. He also works for Armando. Are those guys following us?"

All men started checking their weapons.

Angel quickly reacted. "Everyone, stay calm. I am going to verify if they are following us." he started to slow down the vehicle without making it look obvious. He turned to the man sitting next to him and said, "Move to the back. Everyone on the floor. I want them to think I am alone." Angel held his 9mm automatic on his lap the way a toddler would cling to a security blanket.

The van had back windows with contact paper they could see out, but no one could look in; it looked like a commercial vehicle. Mr. Guzman transported his women from one location to another in this manner.

Ricardo was driving the Lincoln Continental, and he was concerned about the van that was in front of them. He did notice that the driver was now slowing down. He passed the van and observed the driver was alone. Ricardo thought, *It is just a coincidence that we are traveling in the same direction.*

"We should be arriving in fifteen minutes."

A few minutes later, the driver of the van passed them at a high rate of speed. Richardo wondered aloud, "Where are the police when they are needed? It must be time for their donut break."

The men laughed and then broke out jokes about police officers.

Angel Castillo figured out that they were both traveling to the same location. Angel had his orders: the women had to be picked up at all costs. However, he knew he had to eliminate them before they fell into the wrong hands.

Manuel Mendoza sat in a cell at the police station, knowing he had been set up by Guzman. *I miscalculated the man. I did not think he was intelligent enough to pull off something like this.* Mr. Guzman had sacrificed Davila Soto. Mr. Guzman was playing chess and had sacrificed his queen. Now Mendoza did not know whom he could trust, especially his lawyer.

Attorney Babel is not representing me but El Fantasma, the man whose only interest is for me to keep my mouth shut. DA Fitzgerald has never prosecuted a case; she has only been working for one month after passing the bar. Oh, hell, who I am kidding? I could get a conviction in a case like this without finishing high school. Manuel recounted the events of today.

Then one of the guards called out, "Manuel Mendoza, your lawyer wants to speak to you."

Manuel found it strange because Babel had informed him that he would wait for the DA to arrive. The guard was now escorting Manuel to the telephone, for Manuel to speak in private with his attorney.

Mr. Manuel Mendoza picked up and said, "Is there a problem, Babel? Something we should discuss before meeting with the DA?" He speculated what else could go wrong.

A voice unfamiliar to Manuel said, "Do not disrespect me by comparing me to that dirtbag. Now, shut up and listen carefully to me—your life depends on it. DA Lara Fitzgerald will be arriving in twenty minutes. For your self-preservation, inform her you want to converse with her alone. Attorney Babel will not be representing your interests, and you know that.

El Fantasma has a contract out on your head, so now you have a dilemma: turn on him or sit in your cell and wait for your termination letter."

Manuel Mendoza broke out in a cold sweat as he responded. "You are dead. I am going to kill you, you son of a bitch. You set me up!"

"At your service. No need to thank me; it was my pleasure. You want to kill me? Those are empty threats. Whom are you going to tell before finding yourselves facing the wrong end of a gun? There is no one you can trust from this moment on; El Fantasma has ordered your demise."

Michael was exaggerating at this moment, but he knew Manuel would come to the conclusion that El Fantasma would order termination. "Manuel, you cannot trust anyone, not even your friend Armando—you know him as the Coyote. How long before he starts considering your termination? The way I see it, you can continue to make empty threats, or you can try to save your pathetic existence." Michael hung up the phone while thinking, *That will give Manuel an added incentive to turn on his friend and the organization.*

DA Lara Fitzgerald was enthusiastic about having her first murder case. She was there to charge Manuel Mendoza with first-degree murder, and the evidence against him was mounting faster than Mount Saint Helen blowing up.

Mr. Mendoza had a long, questionable history for the last ten years. Cases were dismissed, evidence disappeared from the evidence room, and victims recanted their statements or vanished. This time the witness was the morgue, the evidence looked overwhelming, and she would keep a close eye on the evidence.

Just in case Mr. Mendoza has connections in the police department, I cannot believe this man is that lucky. The weapon used, a Ruger 9mm, was recently fired. I am waiting for the ballistic report of the evidence founded: the vehicle he was driving away from the scene, the bullet extracted from Mr. Davila Soto, and the bullet shells on the street.

Attorney Asher Babel had been preparing himself to represent Manuel Mendoza. In the past, most of his cases dealt with bailing out prostitutes or bouncers from one of their clubs. El Fantasma had given him instructions to ensure Manuel kept quiet. His boss has invariably stayed anonymous.

Attorney Babel had defended Manuel and his partner in the past when the evidence looked overwhelming. However, as time went by, the evidence seemed to vanish in the same way as James Hoffa. Except for this time. He did not see this happening for this case; everyone seemed to have been caught off guard.

Attorney Babel was waiting for the DA to arrive, and he just finished updating his employer, who did not sound pleased. He believed Manuel would be better taking a plea deal; contrarily, he could be facing the death penalty.

The way Babel saw this young DA, her first murder case being a quick conviction would be perfect for her record. Attorney Babel was going to take advantage of her inexperience to get his client off with a lighter sentence rather than life imprisonment without the chance of parole, or the death penalty.

Fifteen minutes after Manuel received an unexpected call, DA Lara Fitzgerald arrived at the police station where the defendant and attorney Babel waited. She walking from the parking lot toward the police station, and a woman came marching out of the police station straight toward her. DA Fitzgerald tried to avoid the woman and walking toward the main entrance, but she noticed the woman kept walking at her.

The woman had large sunglasses, and a red wig practically covered her face. She had long, wine-colored gloves. She gave the DA Fitzgerald an envelope. DA Fitzgerald read the note on the envelope: "Read this before meeting Manuel Mendoza and his lawyer." DA Fitzgerald tried to question the woman. The woman ignored Fitzgerald and quickly stepped into a vehicle with tinted windows, which drove off. DA Fitzgerald walked back to her car, where she could have privacy to read the note.

I am willing to turn over state's evidence by giving you full details of human trafficking operations in San Antonio and across the United States.

Attorney Babel works for El Fantasma and the organization, not for me. I did not kill Mr. Soto. My life is in danger. I will deny everything if you bring up this subject in front of Attorney Babel. Furthermore, you will have signed both our death warrants within days.

After reading the note, DA Lara Fitzgerald placed it in a large brown envelope and then headed and back to the police station. She walked directly to the police captain on duty's office, and attorney Babel approached her. She put her hand up politely as if saying, We will talk later.

Babel had a way with words and expressions. She always knew he was as crooked as a politician and worth as much as a three-dollar bill. There was something that gave her a creepy feeling about Babel. She never trusted him. Her first impression of the man was correct.

DA Lara Fitzgerald conversed with the captain and wanted to see if he had ever heard the name El Fantasma. DA Fitzgerald would not ask direct questions about El Fantasma regarding the case she was working on, and she kept the letter a secret. However, she wanted to know whether such a person did exist.

Five minutes after DA Lara Fitzgerald had a conversation with the police captain at the station, the rumors started to circulate that Manuel may be contemplating turning over state's evidence for a lighter sentence.

Within minutes, Armando was having a telephone conversation with a police officer who seemed to have firsthand knowledge of the details. Armando walked up to Mr. Estrada. "Sir, we may have a problem. My source in the police department informed me that Manuel may be contemplating turning over state's evidence for a more moderate sentence." Armando relayed the information to Mr. Estrada. His only concern was

Manuel would turn information on him because they knew too much about each other.

"Mr. Estrada, DA Fitzgerald was asking questions about a person name El Fantasma and human trafficking, which means she has to know something. The only way she could have received that information is through Manuel. Sir, this DA is too new in her job to know about your code name and the human trafficking in this area." Armando was concerned El Fantasma would start firing personnel—and in this business, retirement was a coffin. He wanted to cover up for the fact that Manuel was his friend.

"Oh, just what we need. The news has gone from bad to worse. I received information that Mr. Guzman gave the order to Davila to have Manuel killed. They must have set a trap for Manuel; he must have caught on and acted in self-defense. The man just called me to give us a lead on five of the women from the club. Whoever is giving us this information has inside information into the operation. What does he want?"

"The man could want to show you his loyalty to you before he makes himself known. Sir, call in an insurance policy, so you will not eliminate him once Mr. Guzman is out of the way.

"Armando, we need to cut ties with Manuel Mendoza. Do you know anyone who could serve him a notice of termination?"

According to the GPS, they would be arriving in minutes. Angel hoped to take the persons holding the women by surprise. He was able to lose the El Fantasma men, however that was temporary, and they needed to act fast.

He turned on to Creek Park Road in Canyon Lake. The GPS said, "You are arriving at your destination in three hundred feet." There seemed to be a shack or abandoned home on the left side of the road. Angle called Mr. Guzman. "Sir, we have arrived on the scene. I will call back when we have secured the women."

Angel stopped the vehicle, and all the men headed toward the rundown cabin. The men drew their weapons as they ran into the shack.

Angle entered the structure, and to his surprise there were only five dogs tied on long leashes. They checked the area, turned around, and headed back toward the van as the black Continental pulled up alongside their vehicle, blocking their way.

Angel started to approach Ricardo while lowering his weapon; he needed to defuse the situation. The tension was too high, and they all seem ready to start shooting. Angel holstered his gun and wanted to show Richardo he was not lying. "There is no one there; check for yourself."

Both groups aimed weapons at each other. Richard and his men did not believe a word Angel said. The men were within ten feet of each other. Angel wanted to calm down the situation. The strain on the men was so much that any wrong move could set them all off. He was trying to talk to Richard, who seemed to be in charge of the group.

Angel was starting to relax because his plan seemed to be working: all the men lowered their weapons.

Then without warning, a single shot ranged out. The bullet struck Ricardo in the right eye, and the projectile came out of the back of his head. Everyone started shooting before the body hit the ground.

The groups were now firing at one another, and Angel was trying to stop them from killing each other. He was shot multiple times.

CHAPTER 9

THE SPLINTERING OF THE TEAM

Eight days after Michael conducted a daring daylight raid against El Fantasma's establishment, nerves were starting to become frayed. Michael had worked on reuniting all women with their families or wherever they would like to settle down. Some women wanted to start their lives over again in different locations, which was understandable. Five women had been kidnapped from different regions of the United States, and they were already repatriated to states of their choice. Two women wanted to return to their country of birth, Mexico. Five other women wanted to return to their families.

Some of the women figured the money was a fortune in their country, and they would be able to elevate themselves and live quiet lives. Those same women were showing signs of anxiety about returning to their families and how their families would accept them; they were from different parts of South America or Mexico.

Michael felt the tension among the women building up as they got closer to their departure date approaches. There was no way of calculating the physiological damage these men had inflicted on them.

The biggest problem Michael had was finding the parents of Amanda. He believed she was underage when taken. Amanda remembered asking her mother for permission to play outside of the house before her birthday party started, and someone offered her a candy bar. Once Amanda consumed the candy, she did not remember anything afterward. All Michael knew was she was from the United States.

Amanda had been a victim of underground pornographic movies since she was at least five years old. The stories Amanda recounted to Barbara were horrific. Amanda communicated only with Barbara about what these people did to her as a child. She had all types of nightmares and often woke up screaming.

Michael thought, *I cannot believe what these animals have done to Amanda during the years of her captivity. How can a human being be so cruel?*

The only time Amanda had a peaceful night was when she slept with Barbara. *Whenever she was alone, Amanda started sucking her right thumb. I have become concerned about her psychological well-being. Amanda changes dramatically when a man walks into an area when she is alone. I have instructed Jason and Victor to be aware of her fears whenever she is around, and to avoid being alone with her.*

Ironically, Barbara was named Barbie by the barbarians—the same nickname her parents had called when she was a child. Barbara never protested. She learned that Nicky Muller was used in pornographic movies, and when they no longer had any use for her, they gave an overdose and left her to die on the sidewalk.

Barbara never heard any rumors about Terrie and was unaware of what happened to her. When she learned what had occurred to her girlfriends, Barbara showed no emotion. Like Consuelo, Barbara was always looking for a weakness in their defenses; they even spent some time comparing notes.

Michael recalled the conversation with Deacon Alex Bermúdez, who said *children are exploited early as eight years old. Adolescence between the ages of 15–17 years; have been exposed to hard-core porn. The largest population of Internet porn users between 12–17 years old. The solicitation of youth in chat rooms is sexual. Children between the ages of 7–17 years old would voluntarily give their home addresses online.*

"Mendoza, you have your lawyer on the phone," the guard said as he opened his cell. "It will be easier to cover all the details of your defense when they are here to converse with you."

Mendoza was not sure who was at the other end of the line, and if the police were to become aware that he had received calls from someone who was not one of his lawyers, it would create more problems for him.

The voice told him, "Mr. Mendoza, I am sure you recognize my voice. You have a problem. Mr. Guzman is trying to strike a deal with El Fantasma, and their first task is your head as a trophy."

"What do you want, and what is in it for me?"

"I will stop your next assassination attempt. I could get you out on a technicality. Or there is proof you are an innocent man: or a film could magically appear at the DAs office proving your innocence. Which one would you prefer? You have always claimed to work for the organization, however you have not admitted to killing Mr. Soto, so you could be out on the street. That would give you a better chance of survival."

"You son a bitch. You know I am innocent, and you frame me. Now you are telling me you were recording when Soto was killed."

"As your lawyer, I am asking you a theoretical question regarding whether there could have been someone recording or taking pictures around the area that could prove that you are innocent or cast some doubt to your guilt. Now, let us get down to business. What is your friend the Cayote's complete name? Has he already kidnapped the two families living next to him? Where does he live? If you lie to me, I will let them take you out."

"When you get me out, then we will talk."

"That's the wrong answer. Get one thing straight: you have nothing to bargain with. You may not even survive the next attack. I have already stopped two without asking you for any favors. I will call you tomorrow if you are still breathing." Michael did not say another word, acting as if he was about to hang up.

"Wait!" Mendoza yelled.

"I thought you would have a change of heart."

Michael received more information than he was hoping. He had the Coyote's name, and other information checked out. He had no reason to believe that Manuel had lied about the address and additional information. Michael was disappointed that Manuel did not know the details of El Fantasma. Now more than ever, he wanted to foil their kidnapping plans. He wrote down the information and made notes, but his thoughts were interrupted.

"Consuelo heard the conversation he had with our jailbird, and they got into an overheated argument. She became infuriated when I suggested to Manuel there could be a film establishing his innocence." Michael needed his cooperation while letting him think there was a chance of escaping. She would not listen to reason.

"Consuelo, I have no idea what those animals did to you and Maria. I am sorry for everything you and all these women have endured. There is no way anyone could ever make this up to you. Manuel is giving us and the DA information that will put others out of business and save other women from going through the horrors you ladies have endured."

"Sure you are." The eyes of Consuelo were burning red, but no tears or any signs of breaking down crying from all the hurt in the past. "I will tell you what. Clear that table and let me pay you the only way I know how. Maybe this will change your mind." She started to raise her dress and lower her panties.

Michael jumped to his feet and angrily said, "Get dressed now. Let us understand each other. Let this be the first and last time you ever try something this stupid. The men who are here, including me, have treated you and all the ladies with respect. Never forget that. You are not the only one in danger here, and this animal has valuable information we can extract from him. Am I making myself clear to you?" Michael was now furious.

He waited for Amber to return with groceries and necessities for the team. When she pulled up, Michael and Barbara went to help her.

"Michael, I want to contact my parents in Canada. I see Consuelo is on the warpath again, and you are her target," Barbara commented as she went inside with bags of groceries.

"I was wondering when the two of you were going to lock horns. Consuelo has been pushing your buttons, and I am getting fed up with her." Amber commented.

Later on that evening, Barbara had a conversation with Michael about her communicating with her parents. Unfortunately, Amanda was scrutinizing their conference. She was always hiding in different locations, and today it was a closet.

Amanda had become anxious about learning Barbara would be moving back to Canada. She waited for Barbara and Michael to finish and afterward left the room without being observed. Amanda felt no one wanted or cared about her. Amanda never heard the dialogue in its totality, and she headed back to her room in tears.

Two hours later, Amber was making her rounds and checking the area. She saw Amanda, who seemed to be walking toward the main road. Amber noticed that her eyes were red; she seemed to have been crying, "Are you all right, Amanda?"

"I have nowhere to go, no one who cares about me. I just want to die."

"Amanda, how can you say something like that? We all love you. Speaking for myself, I will always be there for you whenever you need me. Michael and I have been working hard trying to find your parents." Amber noticed there was a strange look on Amanda; she seemed to become more upset. Amber wondered what she had said wrong.

"Amber, you and the others here are saying that, but none of you mean it." Amanda then turned around without waiting for a response. While Amanda was returning to the house, she mumbled, "I am going to sleep."

Amber went back to check the area.

The next morning, Barbara walked out of the bedroom and headed toward the dining room. "Has anyone seen Amanda? I have not seen her since last night, and she did not sleep in the bed."

Amber became concerned and related to them the brief conversation she had had with Amanda.

They all became concerned about Amanda and quickly mounted a search. After a quick search through the house and grounds, they realized Amanda was not in the area. They threw caution to the wind while walking about the neighborhood. Amber and Michael headed toward downtown San Antonio in hopes of spotting Amanda.

After twenty minutes of desperately searching for Amanda, Barbara started calling them back to the house. Barbara sounded distraught over the phone and was crying.

Barbara was hysterical, and no one could calm her down. Barbara was crying nonstop, and finally, she pointed to a tape recorder. They gathered in the dining room.

Amanda was illiterate and could not read or write. She was learning to read and write from Barbara. Amanda had recorded the inhuman treatment she was enduring since the kidnapping. Amanda was too ashamed to tell anyone face-to-face what she had experienced.

They were all listening to the recording, and their nerves were to the point of shattering as Barbara turned the recorder on:

> "Barbara, I lied to you. I do know my mother and father: Warren and Silvia Bridgemore. My real name is Amanda Bridgemore. I tried to be a good girl and never cried, no matter what my parents or brother did to me.
>
> Barbara, I want to apologize to you; for not being truthful. After tonight, I will no longer be a burden to you or anyone else. I was just a child when my parents sold me to Mr. Guzman.

Let me see how I can explain this to you; maybe it will make sense to you, though I will never understand it. Mr. Ramon Guzman was visiting my parents. He looked at me then said, "I needed a girl for movies who's under ten."

My mother quickly volunteered me. "In three months, Amanda will be eight." My mother always looked at me a certain way. When she walked into the room with a candy bar, I ran to my father.

My father picked me up, and I have never been able to forget these words. "Amanda here is smart and pretty, with big blue eyes and curly blonde hair. And look at this body."

There was a prolonged pause. Amanda was sobbing on the recording and seemed troubled to assemble her thoughts.

Barbara could not endure hearing the recording again. She departed the dining room in tears.

Amanda continued.

My father started undressing me while I begged him to stop. I closed my eyes because I feared what was next. It was the same way I used to do whenever my father walked into my bedroom with my mother at night with a chocolate bar.

Barbara, all the stories I related to you are true, except most of them happened while living with my parents, who had their way with me. After my father removed my clothing, I closed my eyes. He said, "Fifty thousand."

Mr. Guzman responded by saying, "Make it twenty, and we have a deal." I do not remember anything else afterward.

They were all shaking with fear, imagining what Amanda was planning on doing. It was not as if the women had never heard similar stories, however it was difficult for them to understand parents could be so horrible to their children.

No one in the room said a word, and their silence was deafening. Finally, Michael broke the ice. "We have to find Amanda."

Consuelo was going to protest because she was anxious to leave.

Jason answered before Consuelo could say a word. "I will help with the search. Victor has the documents, and he will not be back for at least a few hours. We will not be able to do anything without her identification papers."

Michael turned to Jason. "I know that you and Consuelo have something pending, but this takes precedence."

While Jason was speaking, Consuelo gave him a dirty look.

"Jason, thank you, we do need your help. Amber, please talk to Barbara and explain we need her help." Michael had noticed Consuelo, and judging from his expressions, she was ready to attack the first person to look at her. However, the foremost concern now was finding Amanda.

At that moment, Victor walked into the house upset. There was something on his mind. "Michael, Jason, Amber: conference room, now. We need to discuss something."

The women wondered why Amanda never been transferred from the club. The mystery was solved. They gathered around Consuelo, questioning her about the remark Michael made.

"Victor, we have a problem with Amanda. She has disappeared. Whatever it is may have wait for another time."

"Michael, I saw it in the news. Amanda has committed suicide, and we need to break the news to the girls."

CHAPTER 10

A RUNNING DISPLAY OF
BOOKS AND TAPES

After learning that Amanda had committed suicide, Barbara seemed unable to console herself; all her fears were confirmed. She was crying, yet they were tears of hatred. The other women tried to calm her down. They misread her tears as ones of resentment. Everyone felt deeply affected by the demise of Amanda. It seemed that when new women arrived at the club, they felt compelled to protect Amanda, and now they all seemed to blame themselves.

Consuelo and Jason asked for a ride to San Antonio International Airport, where they rented a car. Consuelo seemed to be interested only in obtaining her documentation. They planned to drive to Mexico. Nevertheless, Consuelo objected to giving two women who were going to travel in their direction a ride.

Victor tried to talk Jason into waiting a few days, however he managed to turn a friend against him. Jason had his marching orders from Consuelo, who seemed to be in charge; Jason followed her every command. To say Consuelo and Jason became furious with members of the team was an understatement.

The number of women with them had dwindled to five. Michael hoped Jason would have taken two women across the border. They were having a conference in the library about several subjects. The tapes Amanda left behind were foremost on their minds.

"Amanda requested that Barbara take part in the decision on how to utilize the recording. We will table that until Barbara can join us."

Suddenly Barbara burst into the library, where Michael was holding his meeting on their present problems. "Michael, what the hell have you done?"

Michael was stunned and had no idea what was going on. Their problem was Jason and Consuelo had been very careless and placed them all in danger of being exposed by El Fantasma or Mr. Guzman. They were leaving a trail of bread crumbs more extensive than a four-lane highway, which could inadvertently place everyone in danger. Barbara could not be talking about Jason and Consuelo being in danger.

"Barbara, I have no idea what you are speaking about. Calm down and explain to me what is going on."

"Michael, you understand damn well what I am talking about. It's leading the news today. Michael, to think I defended you to Consuelo, who told me not to trust you. I feel like such a fool! Consuelo said you were going to release the video we have of Mr. Ramon Guzman killing Davila Soto."

Michael realized what Barbara was talking about, and he did not say a word but shot out of the seat. He walked over to where the videotapes were. Michael felt betrayed. They may have their differences about how to tackle this organization, however he never thought Jason would resort to such a treacherous act. Jason knew where Michael was hiding all their evidence.

"There was no way I would allow Manuel back on the street, innocent or not. I was leading him on to extract information, which was working. I needed the film to obtain evidence against Mr. Guzman. I have lost my number one aces I had against him.

"Barbara, we are no longer safe here. You need to trust me: we have to move now. Have all the ladies pack. Barbara, regardless of what you think, we need to work together."

Barbara realized that Consuelo had lied to her and made Michael the fall guy, but what was she after? "I am sorry for doubting you, Michael." She turned around and headed out of the library.

"We need to clean up the area; I do not want to leave any evidence that we were ever here. I will also cancel our reservation and make new ones. Amber, you're driving point. I will bring up the rear. Victor, you are responsible for communications. We will stay in a hotel tonight." Michael contemplated changing vehicles before the move. After three hours, Michael moved everyone for their safety.

DA Fitzgerald was receiving calls from reporters for an interview. The reporters wanted to question her about the rumor that she had received a package establishing the innocence of Manuel Mendoza in the murder of Davila Soto.

DA Fitzgerald was waiting to have a meeting with DA Thomas Bolton, nicknamed the Tasmanian Devil. No one knew why, but there were all kinds of gossip around the office. It seemed to be due to the way he ripped his attorneys when they lost a case. Some presumed it was because he had over a dozen action figures of the cartoon Tasmanian Devil.

Fitzgerald thought it was the way he handled himself in court when questioning a defendant in court. DA Bolton was known as a staunch defender of women and children in court, and he was rumored to be running for mayor of San Antonio. He always encouraged the personnel in the office to contribute to those foundations.

At the district attorney's office, Detective Carl Fillmore had worked with the attorneys for six years, though he tended to stay away from the personnel. He wanted to keep it on a professional level—except with DA Fitzgerald. He felt she needed guidance and protection. He knocked on her door and walked in without waiting for an answer.

"Carl, if it is about a case, it will have to wait. I have a meeting with DA Bolton." Lara Fitzgerald was concern about the conference; Bolton was on the warpath, according to some colleagues.

"This is about your meeting with DA Bolton. Listen carefully to what he has to say. It is very important you do not interrupt him; otherwise, he will be yelling for an hour after that. Inform him you are contemplating contributing to a couple of charities from this list and ask for his opinion."

Detective Fillmore passed her the list of charities. "Finally, do not ask him about the Tasmanian Devil collection he has in his office; ignore those items. Also, don't read the passages he has around his desk. Look him in the eyes, but do not stare or interrupt him. After he finishes with the lecture, file it in your memory cabinet under 'Consign to Oblivion.'"

Ten minutes later, DA Fitzgerald entered DA Bolton's office. DA Bolton told her to have a seat. The man looked like he was setting her up to jump down her throat.

DA Fitzgerald was about to have a sit when he started speaking. "Did you bring the infamous video?"

"No, sir. I have my suspicions, and that is why I sent the evidence with the original letter to the forensic laboratory. I have a copy." DA Fitzgerald was confused by the statement to "Consign to Oblivion," and she wondered what Detective Fillmore meant. She would follow through on the rest of his advice.

"DA Fitzgerald, let me see what you have." DA Bolton was upset she had sent the video to the forensic lab without consulting him. DA Bolton read the document and looked at her in a suspicious manner. He then raised his right eyebrow above the round rim of his glasses.

"According to this note, Mr. Manuel Mendoza is innocent, and the video proves it. Did you at least look at the video to try to determine the validity of the film?"

"No, sir. I became suspicious of the items in the box. I believe the man could be working with someone outside and may have rigged the package to make it look like we damaged the evidence."

"DA Fitzgerald, would it have been better to consult me first? We could have reviewed the film and evaluated it together. Jointly, we could have determined the guilt or innocence, instead of running to the first reporters on the street and creating this debacle."

DA Fitzgerald was insulted at the implication that she had leaked information to reporters. *Does DA Bolton assume I am a cheap politician for sale?* "Sir, I can assure you I had nothing to do with leaking the information to the reporters. I am sure Mr. Manuel Mendoza is behind this. The last thing I wanted was anyone tampering with evidence or being foolish enough to leak erudition to the press."

"A police officer was transporting the evidence to the forensic laboratory earlier today." Detective Fillmore insisted on transporting the film to forensic laboratory and not to present it to DA Bolton.

"What evidence do you have to base your assumption on? The film has been reconstructed?" DA Bolton thought, *This is not the publicity my office needs before announcing my run for mayor of San Antonio.*

"The anonymous tipper stated there is a film that establishes Mr. Mendoza is innocent."

DA Bolton felt the pressure from all directions. *The mayor has an interest, and attorneys for Mr. Mendoza and others have continued to call, all demanding to know why he is still in jail.* "DA Fitzgerald, did you have any reason to believe the film has been tampered with or is fraudulent? I hope you are correct, because the city and our office will be looking at a lawsuit. Finally, you will also be out of a job."

"Sir, I reviewed the criminal history of Mr. Mendoza. A long, extensive criminal record: suspicion of murder, assault with a dangerous weapon, armed robbery. His criminal past reads like a dictionary from A to Z; you name the crime, and he has been involved. Victims or witnesses have all recanted their statements or died mysteriously, and evidence has disappeared from the evidence room. Finally, a film magically appears clearing his name? I would say there are plenty of reasons to doubt this evidence."

"DA Fitzgerald, you discovered four corrupt police officers in this department. We are all grateful to you for cutting a cancer out of the city. However, before taking any action, you should come to me first. Do you think you have a strong case on those police officers? You have not obtained a conviction—you will have to prove their guilt in court. Do not let the arrest and their confession go to your head. I am still your boss, so when you receive any evidence, you come to me.

"Finally, Mr. Mendoza approached you with evidence about human trafficking, and their leader named is El Fantasma. That means the Phantom in English. You should have contacted my office. Mr. Mendoza may have a long, extensive criminal record, but regardless of how compelling the evidence, you will not stand a chance against a film casting doubt on his guilt, as described in this letter."

Mr. Guzman was in his home wondering how he had men looking for these women all over the city, yet out of nowhere Amanda chose to end her life at the main entrance of his club. *That bitch could not find a tree somewhere else?* DA Fitzgerald requested Guzman's presence at her office about the fire and the five men who perished.

Mr. Guzman recognized damn well if he failed to appear, the DA would probably send police officers to his home with a search warrant. He commenced dealing with his attorneys and received a tip from her office that this was all a maneuver to question him about Amanda.

Once Mr. Guzman finished consulting with his attorney, one of his men walked into the living room. "Sir, I am sorry for the interruption, but one of the men recognized a woman. Unfortunately, they were unable to follow her as instructed. Even so, they could pick up her trail. The woman identified as Esmeralda, aka Consuelo. "Our man said she was placing a white rose where Amanda had hung herself."

"Javier, let the men know I want her taken alive or followed. If there is anyone accompanying her who is not female, eliminate them. We need her breathing; she may be able to lead us to the other women."

Around the same time Mr. Guzman was consulting his lawyers, Mr. Manuel Mendoza was conversing with his lawyers. "Does anyone have any idea when I will be able to leave this place? I have always maintained my innocence, and DA Fitzgerald has the evidence establishing that I am not guilty."

Manuel thought, *This man works fast. This will complicate my escape. I am wondering how his organization plans to move against El Fantasma. Well, that is no longer my problem. I will have to vanish until I can find a new continent on which to operate. I may have given this man too much information about where to obtain additional intelligence on the organization.*

Amber rushed up to Michael. "You have to hear this. Mr. Guzman has discovered Consuelo and Jason. Mr. Guzman men are closing in on them."

Michael had tried to prepare for all possible circumstances except for being double-crossed by one of their own He was still furious with Consuelo and Jason, yet he wanted no harm to befall them. Simon had wiretapped the residence of Mr. Guzman to keep track of their every movement before they raided the club.

Simon had been preparing to steal the money for himself; it was not difficult to convince him to work with Michael. Simon helped place Amber in the computer system, making it look as if she had been their captive for several years and transferred there.

Simon knew the schedule of Mr. Guzman and had been useful as a team member. Michael did want Simon to escape; unfortunately, Simon got too greedy and did not use his comment sense.

Two hours after DA Fitzgerald was in court, pleading her case that defendant Manuel Mendoza be denied bail because he was a flight risk, she declared that they were waiting for forensic laboratory on the legitimacy of the recording.

Before taking any further actions, presently, the defendant was being held on murder charges. DA Fitzgerald enumerated the evidence against the defendant validating his guilt. She further claimed that the safety of Mr. Mendoza was a concern; he could be in danger on the street because he had turned state's evidence against a criminal organization.

The attorneys for Mr. Mendoza claimed the DA was withholding evidence from the court establishing the defendant was innocent. Furthermore, Mr. Mendoza volunteered to cooperate with DA Fitzgerald, and he was anxiously looking forward to cooperating with the DA's office to clear his name.

After the judge questioned both sides and heard their case, he ordered the defendant to be released on two million dollars bail bond and had the defendant turn over his passport. Judge Falcon found this decision difficult. He did not want this person on the street, however he felt granting the defendant bail set at two million was correct. The judge thought, *This man will not be able to post such a high bond.*

Mr. Manuel Mendoza immediately posted the money. He was anxious to walk out and wanted to disappear. The attorneys were escorting Manuel out of the courthouse, feeling confident in winning their case in court. Manuel thought there as a large crowd in front of the court, and he needed to disappear before El Fantasma hired someone to kill him.

Manuel saw the reporters rushing toward him. His attorney had warned him not to make any comments because they had already prepared a speech. Then from nowhere, Manuel saw Consuelo and remembered the same look on her face at the border. Manuel had a cold shiver run down his spine as fear overcame him.

Consuelo rushed Manuel as she threw her arms around his neck as if she was going to kiss him. She ripped it off his neck gold chain with the locket that belonged to Maria and then drove a hypodermic needle into his neck. She whispered, "Maria was thanking God that her suffering in life had come to an end, and she asked him to help me escape. Now, I am here to send you to hell. I will take this—it does not belong to you."

The lawyers at first were surprised and then started to pull Consuelo away from him.

Manuel realized that he had killed the wrong woman. He felt his knees going weak, and he had trouble breathing. Manuel felt his throat swelling up, and he lost his balance, falling backward. He did not know what was happening as he lost his vision. Everything went dark.

DA Lara Fitzgerald had been reluctantly watching from a distance because she felt Mendoza would skip bail. Mendoza and his attorneys were having microphones shoved at them. Then out of nowhere, a woman jumped on Mendoza and threw her arms around his neck. The lawyers tried to pulling her away from him.

DA Fitzgerald thought, *Groupies. There is no accounting for their taste.* Then people started screaming and running in all directions. DA Fitzgerald saw police officers draw their weapons and run toward Manuel Mendoza, who was now on the sidewalk. His lawyers stood around in disbelief.

A minute later, Detective Carl Fillmore rushed up to DA Fitzgerald. "Mr. Mendoza has been killed, and I am going to escort you out of this area." Detective Fillmore was concerned for the safety of the DA. Once she started receiving evidence against the organization working human trafficking in San Antonio, someone would try to have her killed.

Manuel Mendoza had expired for over an hour. DA Lara Fitzgerald walked toward her vehicle with Detective Fillmore and noticed her car had been open. She said, "Great, just what I need. Carl, could this day get any worse? First I lose my number one witness on four cases. My tires require replacement, and the only thing that works is the radio. Now that is gone."

DA Fitzgerald worked full time to attend college and law school. All she could afford was a 1991 Ford Escort pickup, and the air conditioner did not run.

Detective Fillmore smiled at DA Fitzgerald as he inspected her vehicle. Nothing was tampered with or taken. "We must have chased them away. It seems they had a lookout, and when they saw us walking in this direction, they took off. They must have been after the package you left in your pickup. In the future, never leave anything in plain sight—you are asking for trouble. Well, you hit the trifecta today."

DA Fitzgerald was confused, "What?"

"It's the trifecta because you still have your radio, Mr. Manuel Mendoza will not sue you, and his guilt or innocence is irrelevant." He liked this new DA. *She is intelligent, dedicated, and honest. However, she needs to learn the ropes.*

DA Fitzgerald looked inside to see for herself. She observed a white envelope. "No, I know what the trifecta is. What I do not understand is this package. Who is arranging this? Carl, I am confused. I have no idea what to think anymore. Can you follow me back to the office? I have a feeling this is going to lead to another unpleasant meeting with DA Bolton."

Michael was unable to stop Consuelo and Jason before they killed Manuel. *Their actions could have killed an innocent bystander. Jason has placed us in danger, and he's being controlled by Consuelo.*

Michael's number one rule was they were not getting involved in shootouts unless it was necessary. Jason had informed him he had been detected and had to shoot. Michael never believed the story Jason said about being spotted when he killed the first man. *Furthermore, he is an expert at concealment in the Marine Corps, credited with over forty kills while serving in Afghanistan.*

Consuelo has wrapped Jason around her pinkie and was using him for revenge. Jason was either in love or infatuated, and he would do anything for her. Michael had been watching DA Fitzgerald as she drove off with a man who appeared to be a police officer in civilian clothing.

Michael learned the DA had sent the film to the laboratory, and the results would not be back for at least two weeks. Michael needed to act before Mr. Guzman was identified as the killer of Mr. Soto. Michael thought, *I will have to act fast.*

Mr. Guzman answered the phone. The voice said, "Sir; your information was correct. I am going to allow you to redeem yourself and win the other book back."

Mr. Guzman, who had made arrangements to disappear, was listening skeptically. "What good is that going to do me now? It is all over the news that you released the video to the DA."

"Your safely has been secure; that recording did not show your face or the car. The proof is the police have not visited you. Am I correct? Manuel needed to be on the street; his usefulness has expired. You are aware Manuel Mendoza was a liability; neither one of us could afford to have him speak to the DA or be questioned by El Fantasma."

"When can I expect the first book?"

"Do you want all your books back, Mr. Guzman? Let us stop playing games with each other. Allow me to enlighten you. I require films of children entertaining adults. Mr. Guzman, do you know where I could obtain such movies?"

"Why are you asking me? I would not know where to find those types of movies. Those types of films are disgusting." Mr. Guzman acted indignant and was not sure what this man wanted.

"Mr. Guzman, we were doing so well; I was hoping we could become friends. You see, I was under the impression we could learn to work together in this film industry. Shall we say a new private club will be advantageous to all? Your present procedures for those movies are unsuitable, according to my information.

"I suppose I could strike a deal with your previous partner. Mr. Guzman, I think you have a decision to make. I will call you back— unless I decide we have no use for a new partner." Michael waited to see if Guzman's selfishness would overwhelm his common sense.

"In all seriousness, how could we work together while you continually blackmail me with a video and the books? In a partnership, there has to be mutual trust between partners. What can I expect from you outside all my books and the video? And are we talking about a fifty-fifty partnership? You can see I have been cooperating with you. What is in it for me? Where is the sign of good faith on your part?"

"Your cut is 20 percent; this is not negotiable." Michael was not giving him time to reflect; he wanted to dangle a golden hook out there. "The reason I asked for the entertainment recording is that we need to see if your equipment is up to par or if it needs upgrading. You are not making anywhere near this amount; no one will give you 50 percent in a partnership where you are not putting up any money, and you know that."

"Mr. Guzman, we have customers who demanded high-quality work and are willing to pay through the nose. At least six different moves should tell our experts all we need to know, however the more movies available, the better. When we meet, I will lay out my plans for the future."

"Where do you want to meet?" Mr. Guzman had been waiting for this opportunity; he had anticipated this moment since the nightmare had started. He needed to see his enemy in person—and plot his demise.

"I will call you in an hour with instructions on where we are going to meet. I also want to know how many videos you have in storage for us to inspect. You will recover all your books. I want from you the following in exchange for the books..." Michael hung up the phone without waiting for an answer.

"Michael, do you believe he will go for it?" Amber was concerned Michael could be walking into a trap.

"Presently, we need to destroy them or rekindle the war between them, which seems to have come to a halt. Once that video returns from the laboratory, we do not have anything to hold over the head of Mr. Guzman. Has Victor had any luck in contacting Jason or spotting Consuelo?"

"Michael, I guess you have not seen the news today. Consuelo was the one who tackled Manuel; she threw her arms around him before Jason killed him. A reporter called it the final embrace of tenderness." She smiled.

Joshua Estrada was in his hotel room when Armando Sebastian De La Rosa Santana arrived. "You took a hell of a chance in killing Mendoza. That was stupid and one hell of a shot. I thought my orders were to question him before his demise."

"Sir, I cannot take credit for that hit. We were going to follow Manuel. I was going to wait until he was alone, or at least in a different location. We needed him alive, and I had no intention of making it a public execution. Mr. Guzman has to be responsible; we spotted a number of his men in the crowd. That was a professional hit. Mr. Guzman must have hired a professional to move against us."

Mr. Estrada received a call around the same time, and he looked at the number and excused himself as he went into another room. "Who is this?"

"Mr. Guzman has an accounting book in his possession that shows the money he was skimming from the club before he had it burned to the ground. You heard me correctly: he orchestrated the destruction of the club. He informed you there was a conspiracy between his secretary and the IT man. Mr. Estrada, have you not found it odd they both disappeared without a trace?"

"I would say they are no longer in the land of the living. Before I forget, Mr. Guzman has hired a hitman—one target down, and two remain. Do you want to guess who the other two targets are? I will give you one guess. He also has a child pornography enterprise. Are you getting your cut considering he was using the club?"

"Wait, I have some questions for you." Mr. Estrada tried to elicit answers, but the line went dead. He wondered how this man knew so much about Mr. Guzman.

"Mr. Guzman, we have spotted one of the women by the name of Esmeralda. My men are tracking her now."

Mr. Guzman was in his home to consider the pros and cons of the information he had received and the deal offered. However, this was an opportunity he needed to explore. Mr. Guzman called Javier into the office. "Javier, I need to review six movies of the videos we have. Do we have movies with our two new actors?"

Mr. Guzman was thinking of the phrase "children entertainment movies." *I have never heard it phrased that way. I like it. I have not been able to decompress since the fire at the club. I need something to ease my anxiety.* He stressed to the men not to lose Esmeralda; when she settled down, he wanted her alive.

DA Lara Fitzgerald held the letter while listening to a recording of Amanda before she had supposedly committed suicide. She requested Detective Carl Fillmore for his opinion. "What do you think?"

DA Lara Fitzgerald always insisted that Detective Fillmore address her by her first name. "Lara, if this letter is correct, the body lying in the morgue is Amanda Bridgemore. Her mother and father are Warren and Silvia Bridgemore, who sold her into sexual slavery. According to Amanda, she was sold to Mr. Guzman when she was seven. First, we will need to establish she is the daughter of Mr. and Mrs. Bridgemore.

"Lara, I believe it is Amanda is in the morgue as Jane Doe. I have been researching the last name Bridgemore and found one family fitting the description on those recordings. While living in Newark, New Jersey, Silvia Bridgemore gave birth to a baby girl named Amanda. Eight years after the birth of Amanda, they moved to Oklahoma City without the girl."

"Silvia posted on Facebooks that her baby girl, Amanda, died in Newark, New Jersey, due to a car accident. They even asked for money to help bury their daughter. Research shows there is no death certificate on record in Newark or in Oklahoma."

Detective Fillmore was becoming concerned for DA Fitzgerald. *She has already created enemies in the police department, and she is not popular in her department. These traffickers control powerful government officials, and they will come after her.* "Do you want to place this case in your backlog? I will understand."

"Detective Carl Fillmore, I am surprised at you. How could you think of asking me to drop this case? The day I start thinking like that, I will quit." She was surprised to hear him say that.

The next day, DA Lara Fitzgerald was in her office waiting for the documents she had requested. As she was about to say something to Carl, she received a call on her cell phone. "Hello? Who is this?"

"I am going to assume you have heard Amanda's testimony. The information in the letter is on the level. She has suffered all her life; it is only right that the judicial system work on her behalf. Mr. Guzman is involved in human tracking, children pornography, and who knows what else. Are you going to allow him to continue?

"There is an accounting book Mr. Guzman possesses pointing to the guilt and to Mr. and Mrs. Bridgemore. I will call you when Mr. Guzman has children pornography films in his possession. I do warn you that the list of the persons involved in this business is long; be careful whom you trust." The line went dead.

"Whoever is sending you this information knows you would not be aware that he had your cell phone; that was original. He is determined to maintain anonymity." Detective Fillmore was not sure whether this man was a friend or foe.

"Why give me information about Manuel Mendoza and send me the video freeing him, only to him kill?"

"No, that was not our anonymous caller. The death on the street of Mendoza was his organization. They wanted Manuel dead to send a message: stool pigeons will not be tolerated."

Mr. Guzman had waited a long time for this moment, and today he would stop living under this blackmailer's nightmare. He followed instructions to drive to the San Antonio river walk. Mr. Guzman had been warned by his anonymous caller that any deviation on his part would end all communications. He would have to deal with the consequences. The instructions were simple: Mr. Guzman had placed the porno videos in the box on the front seat. His men were not to be in the vehicle or follow him.

CHAPTER 11

HOW THE MIGHTY HAVE FALLEN

At the corner of East Commerce Street and Bowie Street, a woman in dungarees with a bright red blouse would meet him. Once she verified some movies, his new partner would meet him at the river walk. He would receive all three accounting books and the video of him shooting Soto.

Mr. Guzman felt proud of himself. He had talked his mysterious blackmailer into giving him all the books and the video at this meeting. He was very familiar with the river walk and instructed his men to position themselves in different locations.

Today, I will end my blackmailer, and I will retrieve my accounting books and the video. I will depart from the area, and my men will track them all down. I will have to be careful—these people place themselves in an area where they could escape within the crowd.

Traffic was almost at a standstill during this time of the day. Then someone knocked on the passenger side of the window of his vehicle. It surprised him there was a woman with large sunglasses, a red wig, and large gloves. He noticed it was his contact and let her in.

Amber carried a briefcase as she slipped into the back seat of his 2017 BMW. "Do you know how to drive to Biga on the Banks Restaurant from here, or will you need instructions? Are these the movies that I am supposed to examine?" She did not wait for an answer. She leaned over the front seat and picked up the box of movies. Then she arranged them in the back and brought out a computer from her briefcase. Amber started examining the videos.

"We are supposed to meet in the river walk. If your boss wanted to eat, there are several exceptional restaurants in that area; I eat there all the time. Explain to me why I should not call off this meeting? He should have notified me first of his change in plans. This unexpected, last-minute switch in our schedule is suspicious."

Amber could sense the tension in Mr. Guzman; he was ready to walk away. "Sir, my boss had a busy schedule this morning and wanted to treat you to lunch. He desired to seal the new partnership at his favorite restaurant. Now, drive. I need to examine these movies." Amber was becoming sick to her stomach. She wanted to authenticate a few more videos to verify there were porn movies with children. After a couple of minutes, she could not take anymore and placed the computer back in the briefcase. "I will take these movies for further evaluation. Drop me off at the corner of East Commerce and South Alamo."

Mr. Guzman thought, *When I recover my books and the film, I will depart from the area. Then my men will follow isolated and eliminate him. I would like to terminate her too.* She looked familiar to him. *Today, I will cut off the head of the snake; then the body will die.* "Under what name are the reservations, in case I arrive before him? And please join us? You never told me your name."

"Sir, I have to evaluate all these films, and that will take hours." Amber thought, *After what I have seen, you do not want me anywhere near a steak knife.*

Michael had anticipated the arrival of Amber; he had been against her going on the mission because Mr. Gonzalez had seen her before and may recognize her. However, she insisted. "Mr. Guzman will be more relaxed with me instead of a man in the back seat."

Michael saw Amber on the street and gave a sigh of relief as she gave him the signal.

After the distasteful encounter with DA Bolton, Lara Fitzgerald studied the autopsy report while looking at the pictures of Amanda Bridgemore and consulting Detective Fillmore. "Carl, do you think I have enough evidence for probable cause to start an investigation against Mr. Guzman?"

"You would have probable cause against Mr. Warren and Mrs. Silvia Bridgemore if they were living here, but not against that animal. The best you could hope for is that your admirer digs up the evidence he promised you. Have you rigged up your cell phone, just in case he keeps his word and calls you?"

As they were conversing, Carl received a phone call.

"If this is your boyfriend, should I ask him if he knows the whereabouts of Jimmy Hoffa?" They both laughed.

"Very funny, Carl. Do not give up your day job."

Carl responded without looking at the phone number; his wife commonly called him around this time.

Mr. Guzman had been waiting for his mysterious blackmailer for over twenty minutes, and he now suspected he may have been set up for a hit. Two police officers walked into the restaurant, one man in a cheap suit, to have lunch. Mr. Guzman felt relief to have the police officers there; he felt that no one would dare move against him while the police were present. Since Mr. Guzman had walked into the restaurant, he could not take any chances of contacting his men.

"Excuse me, sir, is your name Ramon Guzman?" Detective Fillmore asked the question loudly because he purposely wanted to create a scene while approaching Mr. Guzman.

The people in the restaurant stopped to look at whom the man was directing his question to.

"Yes, officer. May I ask what is this all about?" Mr. Guzman said in a low voice as if to signal the detective to lower his voice.

"I'm Detective Carl Fillmore. We have a search warrant authorizing us to search your 2017 BMW 7 Series. Would you please come with us and open your car?" The detective gave Mr. Guzman a copy of the search warrant.

Mr. Guzman thought, *I am glad that the woman took the porno movies with her, and that her boss is late. Otherwise, I would also have the accounting books and the video in my possession.* "Officer, I am not sure what you are looking for, however I believe in cooperating with the law," he said.

Mr. Guzman walked out of the restaurant toward his vehicle and saw DA Lara Fitzgerald arriving on the scene. *Well, she is too late, and once I make a call, she will be history.* Mr. Guzman walked over to his vehicle and opened the door wide.

He asked, "Does this search warrant cover the trunk?" He was overconfident and being sarcastic. Mr. Guzman wondered why no one had called to warn him from her office or from the court. "Officer, I am a law-abiding citizen, and this is embarrassing. I would like to call my lawyer." He noticed three additional uniformed officers had joined in on the search. One officer was watching him and was not involved in searching because he was filming the proceeding.

DA Lara Fitzgerald answered Mr. Guzman, "Yes, sir, call your lawyer. You will also need to observe the officers searching your vehicle. Furthermore, the search warrant has all the information regarding what these officers are searching for. You may want to take a minute to read it to inform your attorney."

Officer Sanders found the accounting books noted in the search warrant. However, she found no porno movies. She notified DA Fitzgerald. "The only other things I see are DVDs of cartoons underneath the seats."

"Officers, keep recording. I want all those films checked one by one, bagged and tagged along with the books. Mr. Guzman is not married and has no children. Do you think it is odd a man his age would have all these cartoon movies? Detective Fillmore, will you check these DVDs? I am curious to see those cartoons."

Detective Carl Fillmore had hoped the DA would not ask him to check those movies. He had a horrible idea of what those movies contained. The first DVD was titled *Let Daddy Teach You*, with the name of an eleven-year-old boy on it. The second was *Ride Them, Cowgirl*, with the name of a thirteen-year-old girl. This went on for three more films. Fillmore was trying to control himself from beating the hell out of Mr. Guzman.

"Detective Fillmore, what do you have?" She noticed Carl was holding a DVD title: *A Virgin's Way to Heaven*, with the tagline "Amanda, seven years old." Another one was titled *Double Your Pleasure* and had the names of two boys who were ten years old.

Officer Sanders felt bad for neglecting the fact Mr. Guzman was a single man without children. She walked over to examine the next film.

DA Lara Fitzgerald had a smile that said, *I got you*, and turned her attention to Mr. Guzman. "Detective Fillmore, read Mr. Guzman his rights. There is enough to hang him three times over. Sir, have you called your lawyer? He may want to alter his route and meet you at the police station."

A couple of hours after the arrest of Mr. Guzman, Joshua Estrada had received the information from his informants. He contemplated how this man could be so stupid to carry incriminating evidence in his vehicle, particularly exploitation movies of children and the accounting books he claimed were consumed in the fire. *However, he managed to keep that enterprise away from me. I wonder what other businesses he may have that we are unaware of? I never had any idea he was cutting into our enterprise.* "Armando, do you have the connection that wanted to help us?"

"Sir, that is going to be more expensive now that Mr. Guzman is under arrest. I understand he has not talked and claimed the police framed him. They have him in protective custody as if he's the most valuable treasure in the world. I have a few connections. Once it is out that he is a child molester, more inmates will volunteer to take on the job. Maybe one of them will be willing to risk it all for the right price. I will make some calls."

DA Thomas Bolton was in his office, fuming. DA Fitzgerald had failed to follow his instructions. She had never contacted him about obtaining the search warrants for Mr. Guzman without consulting him. Then she obtained incriminating evidence against two or more defendants without notifying him. He had tolerated her disobedience for long enough.

"Sir, I understand you wanted to see me," she said, nervous because of what she had learned in the last twenty-four hours.

"Have a seat so that we can speak in a civilized manner." DA Bolton waited for her to sit down before he started tearing into her.

"No, sir, I will stand. What I have to say will not take long."

"Have a seat! I called you into my office to have a conversation about your work performance. To say it is wretched would be a generous statement. I am a patient man with my subordinates. I tried to mentor you the same way I have with all the new attorneys in the office. However, your work is dismal at best, and you are disobedient and refuse to follow instructions."

"I hired you because of your grades in law school and your score on the bar exam. I was hoping you would one day sit in this chair, with my mentoring. However, you have been nothing but trouble. Following orders is nonexistent on your part. I have informed you in the past that if you received possible criminal activities, you should bring it to me first."

There was a knock on the door, and DA Bolton barked at whoever was at his door. "I am busy—go away!" He wondered why his secretary had not stopped them.

DA Fitzgerald responded, "Come in," as if she was in her own office. Detective Fillmore walked into his office.

DA Bolton growled, "This had better be earth-shattering news. Otherwise, Detective, get out now!"

DA Fitzgerald ignored Bolton and asked, "Detective Fillmore, have the arrest warrants been executed?"

Detective Fillmore had never liked DA Bolton and ignored him while directing his answer to DA Fitzgerald. "Mrs. Sandra Carlson was arrested." That was Bolton's secretary.

DA Bolton was ready to explode. "You dare to arrest my secretary without coming me first? What are you charging her with? Conspiracy to kill President Lincoln? I guess your second arrest warrant is for me!"

Detective Fillmore looked at DA Bolton and answered, "The secretary of the mayor is in custody for embezzlement. There could be more charges pending. The federal government may also charge her."

"The both of you have gone mad! Detective Fillmore, you just flushed your career down the toilet! I hope it was worth it." DA Bolton stopped himself from saying another word and started considering what had happened.

"DA Fitzgerald, you did not bring this information to me because of the rumors of leaks in this office and what you discovered about these secretaries? Did you know I am hated for prosecuting child molesters and men who assault women? I realize why you failed to follow orders, but you still should have come directly to me. We can disregard this."

DA Bolton did not have a chance to finish his thoughts as two men in three-piece suits walked into his office. "You have nerve to barge into my office. Get out!"

One of the men identified himself as an FBI agent and said, "Is your name Thomas Bolton."

DA Bolton responded unprofessionally without considering his remark. "No, I am the janitor. Do you see the name on the door?" He quickly realized that he was acting unprofessional—something in which he took pride. "I apologize. What can I help you with, gentlemen?"

DA Bolton observed several men in plainclothes going through the work area of his secretary. One officer removed the computer assigned to her. "You may want to remind your men there is sensitive information on the computer!"

"DA Thomas Bolton, you are under arrest on suspicion of murder and five counts of sodomy of a minor," the FBI agent said, and he asked Bolton to stand up and turn around. One agent moved in to handcuff him while the other read him his rights.

"Sir, I am not involved or aware of her criminal activities. Please do not walk me out of this office like a common criminal. This will be devastating to my family!" DA Bolton looked at DA Fitzgerald and noticed she had an evidence bag showing a DVD titled *The Tasmanian Devil.* DA Bolton blurted out, "It was an accident!"

DA Bolton looked like a wild animal trapped and desperate to escape. He managed to break loose before the FBI agents could completely handcuff him, and he headed headfirst into the window, trying to jump through it.

Detective Fillmore tackled him. DA Bolton did hit his head against the window, cracking it. As he slid down, he hit the side of his face on the windowsill. He was not seriously hurt, but he would have one hell of a headache.

"Bolton, you are not going to get off that easy after all the disgusting things you did to that boy. I will make sure everyone knows why your nickname name is the Tasmanian Devil." Detective Fillmore was furious with Bolton and wanted to see him convicted in a court of law.

"So you are concerned about your family? We still have not reviewed over one hundred DVDs confiscated from the home of Mr. Guzman. I wonder how many more videos you are starring in?" DA Fitzgerald said, and she walked. Other police officers and FBI agents entered the office.

The detective followed her, and DA Fitzgerald said, "Fillmore, that was a perfect tackle. Were you a football player in college, or was that a reaction?"

"Lara, in the future, do not walk around with evidence in your purse. You could contaminate the chain of custody, particularly that movie."

"Oh, are you referring to this evidence bag containing a cartoon of the Tasmanian Devil? This is my nephew. I borrowed this cartoon from him because it's his favorite charter. However, after what we witnessed, I will never be able to sit with him and watch this cartoon again. I wanted to see the reaction once he knew we had the video. I'd say mission accomplished."

"I was angry; I did not want that idiot to jump out of a second-floor building; he would fail in his feeble attempt at suicide and wind up disabled. Then the state would have to maintain that human excrement for the rest of his life."

Detective Fillmore received a call on his cell phone. After a few seconds on the phone, he responded, "How did that happen? He was supposed to be kept in isolation. I left instructions to have Mr. Guzman placed in quarantine!" He looked at DA Fitzgerald. "I hope you do not have a hot date tonight. Mr. Guzman is dead."

Jason and Consuelo were in a motel room. They had turned in early for the night, wanting to get a head start the next day traveling to Mexico. While showering, Consuelo wondered why Jason had rented a room with two beds when all they needed was one.

She stepped out of the shower, wrapped a towel around her abdomen, combed her hair, used makeup and perfume, and took a second towel to drape it around her neck, just barely covering parts of her breasts. She realized Jason was backing out; after all, what would his family think if he walked into the house with a prostitute?

She walked into the bedroom, and Jason was checking the hallway through the peephole. He had barracked the room, and one mattress was against the window, with a chair wedged against the door.

Consuelo did remember that the night before, Jason had done the same thing. He also slept with a gun under his pillow. "Jason, what are you doing? They will be looking for us in San Antonio."

"Honey, this is just in case someone tries to break in while we are sleeping. Besides, I am a light sleeper. Consuelo, get some sleep; we have a long day ahead of us tomorrow. We should reach your hometown tomorrow to obtain your birth certificate and return to the United States. We will be married in the home of my parents in Washington. I have already called them, and they are anxious to meet you. I have not told my parents how we met or the circumstances. If you want to inform them of the facts. You can count on me being by your side."

While Jason and Consuelo were having their first serious conversation about what the future held for them, men were closing in on them for an execution. Their boss, Mr. Guzman, was in jail, and he wanted all his enemies or possible witnesses neutralized. First, he wanted several persons terminated.

His men discovered Esmeralda, aka Consuelo and a man were staying at Cotulla Executive Inn off I-35 in Artesia Wells. Javier would not have been able to locate these persons, however he received a tip that Esmeralda was traveling with a man to Mexico. Javier had five men and two missions with at least four executions to complete, starting with Esmeralda and all the people persons in the room with her; they knew that she was traveling with at least one man.

Javier knew that in most hotels and motels, it was easy to sneak up on a person if he knew the location. Mr. Guzman had become paranoid since the club had gone up in flames—not that he was ever a normal man. Javier had his men steal two vehicles and buy surgical gloves and four masks. He just wished they would have purchased different disguises.

Javier needed to obtain the pass key to the room his targets were staying in, bust in, and take out all persons. Once we take out our primary targets, we burn the vehicles and all equipment used. The second target was Angel Castillo and his sister. Javier hoped Mr. Guzman would give him a pass; Angel had almost lost his life while trying to recover the merchandise. *Mr. Guzman wants all witnesses or enemies terminated.*

Angel and I grew up in the same neighborhood. At one time, I dated his sister, and now I will have to eliminate them. I do not want to do this job, however I know damn well what the price will be if I do not complete the assignment. In the end, Angel and his sister are to be terminated. I will not have to worry about supporting my family.

Victor drove over the speed limit because he wanted to save Jason and Consuelo. Regardless of the harsh words they had exchanged, Jason was a brother in arms; they had struggled together in war and had been friends for years.

"Victor, you need to slow down. We will not help Jason if we wrap this car around a truck. We cannot afford to be stopped by the police, not with the arsenal we have in our possession. Victor, we will arrive on time; you will see. I wish Jason would answer his phone." Michael observed the speedometer slowing down; he wanted to believe his own words, yet they sounded empty.

"I have been texting Jason ever since we left the house. He has not answered, and I know that Amber has been calling; she also was trying to communicate with the hotel. I fear he has turned off his cell phone."

Joshua Estrada paid top dollar and wanted to see results for a change since he had started on this trip. He listened to the news and finally heard of a man murdered while in protective custody in San Antonio. The police had no further comments and were withholding the name of the victim until his immediate family was notified.

Mr. Guzman was killed, along with pictures that were confirmed. "Armando, there one more thing the news has to leak: that it was Mr. Guzman. You acted fast; now we can start planning on picking up your next-door neighbors. You have already confirmed she gave birth a few days ago?"

"Sir, the name of Mr. Guzman was leaked to reporters; it should be over the news soon. Furthermore, we informed the reporters Mr. Guzman was arrested and charged with child molestation. Mr. Estrada, I am not trying to tell you how to run this organization, but you should consider eliminating Darrell McCoy, the IT man. It will leave the rest of his men in complete disarray."

"These men have cheated us out of a lot of money since he has been running the club. Our connections in this city with the local government and the police department run deep. The police can help us with Darrell McCoy; my men will handle it from there."

"Armando, how many men do you think we will need to leave behind? I prefer to secure the children first and then deal with this problem. We have a buyer for the baby; this couple made an outstanding offer for the infant. The pictures you shot of the girls and boys have perked the interest of many potential buyers. Once the children are in our possession, they will go up for an audition. I do not want to lose these prizes."

Mr. Estrada thought, *Armando is taking too many liberties. I will keep a close eye on him.* "Presently, the most important thing is to secure the children first; this will be your biggest paycheck in one operation."

Meanwhile, Javier was approaching the motel. He had called the driver on the second car and instructed him to enter through the back to look for the blue Ford Mustang Consuelo was seen traveling in. He hoped they had stationed the vehicle in front of the room they were renting. Javier reminded his second team when they located the automobile, they should notify him and stay there in case Consuelo tried to escape.

Javier drove up and parked in front of the lobby, but they did not see the mustang. He was now waiting for his men to inform him they had found the vehicle. There appeared to be two attendants in the lobby; Javier assumed only one was working the midnight shift, and the other one would be leaving soon.

After a few minutes, Javier noticed that his second team drove past him, and he shook his head in disproval. One of the attendants in the lobby walked out, crossed the parking lot, and drove off in a red Ram Charger.

Javier waited a few minutes and wondered why his men had not reported back. *It should not have taken this long for two-man team to spot a vehicle. I should see what is holding them up. I am sure that the little lady will cooperate with us once we explain our problem.* As Javier thought that, he put on his mask, and the other men followed suit.

Miss Marlin Madison has been working at the Cotulla Executive Inn for almost three years while attending college. She saw many things while working at the inn. Nothing shocked her any more after seeing so many people cheating on their spouses, not to mention other unspeakable things.

Marlin was watching as these four men drove up to the main entrance and parked without a woman. However, the mask of Wonder Woman gave her the chills and spooked her. Marlin wondered, *Do these idiots realize they have been videotaped on cameras without their masks?* She had called the police before three of the men walked toward her.

The first man walked past Javier and through the doors of the lobby. He pulled out his weapon without saying a word. However, the woman was quicker and shot him in the throat. He stumbled backward and fell onto the lobby floor, clutching his windpipe.

Javier was startled to see her reaction and reached for his weapon. Javier and his man fired at the woman, however they were terrible shooters under pressure—the only safe place was in front of them. They started backing away from the lobby.

Jason entered into the fray as he shot a man who came out of the entryway in the left shoulder; the man stumbled backward into the lobby.

Javier was trapped by a crazy woman shooting at them while a man outside was cut off their getaway. He was receiving fire from two different locations.

Javier thought that in Riverdale, Chicago, nothing similar to this would have happened. The lady would have felt overwhelmed without a problem, and no one would have dared come to her rescue. Chicago was a difficult place to obtain a weapon legally, and on the street they were available for a dime a dozen. The problem in Texas was people could buy weapons legally. *After a criminal check, I am moving back.* Javier wondered where his men were; they had to have heard all hell had broken loose here.

He found himself down one man and so ordered the other to attack whoever was outside. They ignored the crazy woman while charging Jason, who was standing between them and their escape route.

Jason saw the two men coming out of the lobby. He took cover behind a large flower pot, and his position was precarious. Jason realized that his other man was shooting at him.

Javier reached the door and then felt something strike him in the back. He started losing his balance and hit the glass door hard. His other man stumbled past him. He made his way to the lobby entrance while considering it was everyone for himself. The man by the vehicle was yelling, "Mr. Guzman is dead! We have to go!"

Javier needed to move fast because his time running out. Mustering up all his strength to reach the door, he turned around to shoot that crazy woman. Javier was too late. Marlin walk toward him and shot him twice in the chest.

Marlin Madison had been trained on the range by her father, and it had paid off because all the bullets found their target. Marlin went outside to help the man who had possibly saved her life.

The second man was unaware Javier was dead, and he was concentrating on Jason while trying to reload his weapon. Marlin shot him in the back of the head. Once the man shooting by the car found himself alone, he jumped into the vehicle and drove off. He drove off hastily without checking his surroundings. He drove the car head-on into a patrol car that was responding to the emergency call. He jumped out of the vehicle and started to shoot wildly at the police officer.

The police officer took cover and returned fire at the man, who went down immediately. The officer ran over to Jason, who was behind the flower containers, seriously wounded. Officer Madison yelled at Jason, "Drop your weapon."

Marlin Madison came running up to Officer Madison, "No, Dad! He saved my life. I will not have survived if he had not come to my rescue. I do not know him."

Officer Madison quickly called for an ambulance as other police officers arrived on the scene. Officer Madison and his daughter started administering first aid to Jason, who was barely alive, while waiting for the paramedics.

Consuelo had been watching from a distance. Jason had been wounded, and Consuelo realized that Jason loved her. She had never expected that until tonight. There was only one thing left for Consuelo to do now. This organization was responsible for all the deaths. A truck driver offered her a ride across the border.

The next day, reporters wrote that four heavily armed men attempted to hold up the Cotulla Executive Inn off I-35 in Artesia. Mr. Jason Morrison, a former marine who served in Afghanistan, came to the rescue of the night attendant. Marlin Madison described Jason as her knight in shining armor.

In a telephone interview, Jack Morrison claimed his son always helped persons in distress. He had a strong sense of duty to his country and fellow man, according to his father. Jason Morrison passed away as doctors worked to save his life.

Consuelo made her way back to her place of birth; she planned to visit several persons. In her mind, these people need to learn how to treat their fellow humans. There was one thing on her mind: *It is time to pay for their past despicable actions.*

A message for Mr. Gonzalez had arrived earlier in the day informing him all future businesses transactions would be handle by Armando. Mr. Gonzalez already knew of the change and had read the news. Mr. Gonzalez was not happy or sad about the death of Manuel in San Antonio. The rumors were Manuel was talking to the police.

CHAPTER 12

THE MANY FACES OF EVIL

> There is nothing uglier than a very beautiful face with
> an ugly heart.
>
> —Edmond Mbiaka

The good news was that he did not have to deal with Manuel Mendoza. *Manuel always thought he was better than anyone else, looking down his nose at the rest of us.* Carlos Gonzalez did not know anything about Armando except his reputation. Today, Mr. Gonzalez was hiring women and funneling them to the organization. Mr. Gonzalez has already interviewed over a dozen women.

El Fantasma himself called, asking for ten women; one of his clubs was out of commission. Another woman was waiting for an interview; he selected all the ones needed for the club. Still, there was no harm in talking to her because she had the looks. El Fantasma was replacing its entire staff with brand-new blood for the club. According to the call, this was an emergency.

Mr. Gonzalez was handling business over the phone when his son, Carlos Jr., walked into his office. "Dad, if you do not want or need the one outside, I will interview her personally. Better yet, why not call her in here? We will work her over. The woman looks like she has a firm body. She looks like a wildcat."

"Her name is Altagracia, and she arrived a few minutes ago. I wanted to turn her away because she looks older than the others, however she is attractive."

Mr. Gonzalez said, "You are not going to double-team this woman. The last time your friends did that to one of the women, we lost money. Altagracia seems nervous, and somehow this one looks familiar to me; I am considering letting her go." Mr. Gonzalez took another look at Altagracia while wondering, *Where have I seen her before? There is something uneasy about her.* He took another peek.

Carlos Jr. wondered why his father was concerned about this woman. *Dad has sold women like her for years. What is important about this one?*

Mr. Gonzalez kept looking at Altagracia. He could not remember where he may have seen her before. He checked his weapon and placed it back on the desk. "I want you to leave me alone with her for two hours. Afterward, if I am wrong, she is all yours. I want you to make sure everyone is out, and lock up. If I do not call you back and pick up your prize, I do not want to see Altagracia ever again."

"I understand. But Dad, if you want Altagracia all to yourself, just say so." Carlos Jr. received a look from his father that meant, *I am serious,* so he turned and walked out of the office.

After Carlos Jr. locked up, Mr. Guzman interviewed Altagracia. "Do you mind if I call you Altagracia? Relax. I do not bite—much. Have you ever worked in a restaurant before?"

"No, sir."

"Can you read, write or cook?"

"No, sir, but I am a fast learner. I noticed that the menu has numbers next to each order." She noticed he was not impressed, so she moved her body in the chair while crossing her left leg over her right. There was a split in her dress moving up her thigh, exposing more of her shapely legs.

Mr. Gonzalez was distracted as his eyes wandered up her thighs. He found it difficult to concentrate on his thoughts and so looked at the desk.

"Well, I require my workers to read a little, or at least know how to cook, even if it is bad."

He wanted to give her a chance to lie to him. All the other women hired today had lied; that would be the excuse for firing them, should the police ask about any of the missing women. "We do not have time to train anyone. However, I will hire you on a temporarily basis. It is late, the restaurant is closed, and everyone has gone home. Can I give you a ride, or is there someone waiting for you?"

"Thank you, sir, for giving me this chance. You will not regret it. I just arrived in town and do not know anyone here or anywhere to stay. Can you help?"

Mr. Gonzalez relaxed; he had nothing to be wrong about this woman. He took a second look at the name. "You said your last name is Montezuma? You are from Mexico City. Do you have a sister named Maria? Have we met before? You remind me of someone who used to work here for two years."

"I remind you of Maria, who used to work for you? What kind of pick-up line is that?"

The remark took Mr. Gonzalez by surprise; he had not expected a comment from a woman who had been so shy the previous hour. "No, you remind me of someone else. She worked here about eight months ago for a few days. She quit for no apparent reason and left, taking Maria with her—my best worker. Her last name is Montezuma."

"I remind you of Consuelo Rosa Fonseca. I am surprised you remembered. Mr. Gonzalez, your senses have always been dulled by the end of the day. The bottle of tequila you bought this morning must be empty, and the lights back here are horrible," she commented while moved nearer to the light so he could take a closer look.

Mr. Gonzalez was beyond astonished. How could she have escaped? Then he took a closer looked at her. He was caught off guard and started to slip his right hand away from the desk. That was not even a year ago, and now she looked like she was in her late twenties. He started to open the desk drawer, where he had placed his revolver. "Is that you? But how?"

"Place your hands flat on the desk, where I can see them. You're too late." Consuelo aimed a 9mm at Mr. Gonzalez. He was unable to reach his weapon. Consuelo placed a hood over his head, took cable ties from her purse, and tied him to his chair while retrieving his weapon.

Consuelo removed the hood from Mr. Gonzalez's head. "I will ask you a few questions. You do not want to lie."

In the past, Mr. Gonzalez had always ensured he had the upper hand. His eyes were bloodshot red and about to tear up now that he found himself in a precarious position. Fear settled in fast. "Consuelo, listen to me, please. This was not personal. It was a business transaction. How can I make it up to you?"

"As I was saying before you rudely interrupted me, I may do something unpleasant to you. Like this." Consuelo took out a knife and stabbed him twice, in the left thigh and in the right shoulder.

Mr. Gonzalez screamed out in pain. "Consuelo, you did not ask me any questions!"

"I just wanted to make sure we understood each other. Now, where do I start? What is the combination to the safe? I know that your son, Carlos Jr., locked up the building. When does he return? Before I forget, is the owner involved? Does the owner know that you are selling women into sex slavery? Finally, how many people have the combination to the safe? Mr. Gonzalez, you have nothing to worry about. If I wanted to kill you or your son, the both of you would be dead already. I want to make sure I am out of here before Carlos Jr. returns."

Mr. Gonzalez was in excruciating pain and also feared for his life. Once she was out of here, he would have Carlos Jr. tracked her down with his friends. Afterward, they would deal with Consuelo. He wanted her to take whatever she wanted and leave as rapidly as possible. He was going to answer all her questions quickly and truthfully.

Consuelo opened the safe after Mr. Gonzalez answered all her questions. "Mr. Gonzalez, how much money did you get for Maria and me?"

Once Mr. Gonzalez told her, she separated the exacted amount and placed it on his desk. She took out of her purse several super glue tubes as she applied them to the open wounds to stop the bleeding. "I told you I was not going to kill you; it may hold you together until proper medical treatment is applied."

Consuelo stared intensely at Mr. Gonzalez. "They cheated you. I made more money for them in one night than what you received for the both of us. That reminds me—you have not asked me about Maria. I know you were interested in her. Do not tell me you have forgotten about her. Are you not the least curious? You had better ask me about her."

"I figure Maria escaped with you and returned to Mexico City, where her family lives. How is she?"

"Well, Maria has breathing problems. Manuel shot her in the chests, and she is dead." Consuelo practically screamed it into his ear as she started cutting Mr. Gonzalez. "You are responsible for everything that happened to us. I am here to pay you back for what you have done to women in general." Consuelo cut his body in earnest while using the super glue to keep him from bleeding out.

Two hours later, Consuelo finished her handiwork on Mr. Gonzalez and changed clothing. She stood outside Margaritas Diner, waiting for Carlos Jr.

Carlos Gonzalez Jr. pulled up in front of the diner and asked her, "Has my father already left?"

"Carlos Jr., your father informed me you could have a job for me. He wanted me to wait for you to interview. Did he call you?"

"Is my father inside, or has he already left?" Carlos Jr. looked around and did not see his father's vehicle.

"Mr. Gonzalez departed roughly ten minutes ago, however he said I could trust you. I am not acquainted with this area; is it dangerous?"

Carlos Jr. thought, *I see my father has worked her over, and she had to change clothes. I want this babe for myself. We will compare notes in the bar.* "Where are my manners? He called me a while back. Please get in."

"Your father notified me about a home where I could rent a room for the night. I have just arrived in this town, so I am basically at your mercy." Consuelo hastily jumped into the seat, and her dress came up well above her knees.

Carlos Gonzalez Jr. drove down a desolated dirt road, and after making infrequent turns, he stopped and said, "There seems to be something wrong with my vehicle. I think it is a flat tire."

"Oh, my. What are we going to do in the middle of nowhere? That is terrible, and we are all alone." Consuelo was acting dumb.

"Can you help me fix the tire? It will not take long." Carlos Jr. jumped out of his vehicle and ran around to her side of the car, thinking, *Before I dispose of her, I am going to have fun.* He opened the door.

Consuelo shot him in the right shoulder when he opened her door.

Carlos Jr. fell backward to the ground and started begging for his life. "Please do not kill me! I will give you all my money, anything you want!" He kept crawling on his back, away from Consuelo.

Consuelo came out of the vehicle and shot Carlos Gonzalez Jr. once again, in the left knee. She yelled, "Carlos, stop moving. If you do not, I will shot you again." She stood over him while he whimpered. "I made a promise to your father: I would not kill you with these hands. If you are wondering whether your father is alive, he is going to need medical care for some time—like you."

She thought, *Perhaps a magician can assemble Humpty Dumpty back together again.* "Carlos Jr, let me explain something about women. They do not want to be dragged into isolated places to be raped. It was up to your father to teach you how to be a gentleman. I do not blame you—this is your father's fault, so he is responsible. Unfortunately, children have to pay for their sins."

"I was not going—"

Consuelo cut him off. "You are a liar, and not a good one. I have good and bad news for you. The good news: I will not kill you. The bad news: your father will." Consuelo took the right hand of Mr. Gonzalez out of her bag, placed the index finger on the trigger, and shot Carlos Jr. several times in the chest.

She dropped the weapon and hand on his chest. Consuelo then jumped in the vehicle and drove off. Jason had given her some driving lessons, which were coming in handy. Consuelo learned a lot from Jason and Michael. Now, she was to put those lessons to use.

Mrs. Montes was sleeping when she was awakened by a phone call. A worker informed her no one had opened the facility, and workers were waiting outside of the diner.

"I am on my way." Mrs. Montes got dressed while wondering what had happened to Mr. Gonzalez and Carlos Jr.

On the way to the restaurant, Mrs. Montes had no time to select the proper clothing and jewelry. For a woman of her class who took pride in her looks, this was infuriating. She was agitated with Mr. Gonzalez while driving toward her establishment. It was his responsibility to ensure the restaurant was operational every morning. When Mrs. Montes arrived, she was fuming.

Then she wondered whether Mr. Guzman had to help transport the women for El Fantasma. *Still, he should have informed me.* Mrs. Montes decided to check the books and pick up her payment for the women. She opened the door to the office, screamed, and passed out.

Minutes later, a paramedic was tending to Mrs. Montes. She had a cut over her right eye, apparently from when she had hit the floor. The medic informed her she should have it examined by a doctor.

Mrs. Montes had a headache, and her head was spinning. It was difficult for her to believe what she had seen. Nothing made sense. She could see police officers in the office as she tried to get her bearing.

A police officer spoke to her. "Do you suspect anyone who could have been responsible for this? We rushed him to the hospital. Mr. Gonzalez is barely alive; it seems they super-glued his wounds closed. We also need to ensure they did not steal the money and afterward close the safe for our report."

Mrs. Montes was trying to collect her thoughts. She wondered whether El Fantasma was behind this attack. "His son is the only other person with the combination. I have been calling and texting him without a response. Did they attack him too?"

Outside, a crowd had gathered. Persons wondered what had happened, and there were all types of rumors. The workers were milling around with a group, waiting for her orders.

A man in his midsixties asked a lady standing next to him, "Do you know what is happening?"

Back inside the establishment, a police officer informed Mrs. Montes, "I sent a police officer to their home, and he was not home. He is not answering his cellphone. Can you open the safe? We need to know if they stole the money."

Mrs. Montes stood up, walked over to the safe, and looked at the officers suspiciously as if saying, Stand back. The officers took the obvious hint and stepped to the other side of the room.

Mrs. Montes opened the safe, and it blew up in her face. The force was so strong that it knocked three officers off their feet. Mrs. Montes received the safe door between the eyes, killing her instantly. The strength of the blast shook the building, and the three officers had scrapes but nothing serious.

Outside of the establishment, loud noise and smoke came from inside the building. Consuelo turned to the man who had asked the question. "I would say the owner of this stinking hellhole is dead."

Rumors circulating among the workers about Mr. Guzman: his tongue and eyes were removed, and the equivalent of four hundred US dollars was glued to his forehead. Finally, a slight cut to the spinal cord rendered him paralyzed from the neck down—if he survived. Furthermore, the sexually assailed women by Mr. Gonzalez admitted he had it coming. The police officer wondered how he was still alive.

Three days after Mrs. Montes had received a permanent face-lift. Mr. Cortez was interviewing a woman to be the nanny of their nine-year-old son. His wife was eight months pregnant, and the last nanny had suddenly disappeared without explanation. "Miss Altagracia Montezuma, you claim to have worked in Tacoma, Washington, for Mr. and Mrs. Zimmerman for over two years. Why did you resign?"

"I was in the country illegally and was caught driving without a license. The police officer turned me over to immigration officers and subsequently deported me under the name of Carmen Soto." Consuelo memorized the account Jason had recounted to her, in case Mr. Cortez had means of verifying the story. *On the other hand, he is scoping my body. He is only interested in my other credentials. Presently, I need a place to hide from the police. They have a couple of sketches according to witnesses who saw me riding with Carlos Jr.*

"You seem to be a hardworking person. I am going to take a chance and hire you. I noticed that you did not say anything about your immediate family." Mr. Cortez thought, *I can check her story through my contacts.*

Joshua Estrada was recounting the details of their next business venture to his boss. "We have acquired all the equipment and should be able to purchase all the merchandise for a minimal cost. I will secure all the artifacts, and the auction will take place three days after that. What do you think?"

"I am not interested in details, just results. You failed me in San Antonio, and that was unacceptable. It was a costly blunder, and I will not tolerate another incident like that. I have many highly valued customers coming in from the Mideast and Eastern Europe. Furthermore, do not play doctor with my merchandise." Once his wife finished speaking, she hung up the phone without saying another word or waiting for his response.

Joshua Estrada rented a house for the job, and he walked into the living room. Armando moved from Texas to California and was on vacation in Spain with all the documentation and pictures; at least on paper, he had a strong alibi.

As Mr. Altermatt and Mr. Jónsson planned their vacation, Mr. Estrada and the men were in place. He had known for a while the route they were taking. Each year Altermatt and Jónsson selected one state where they took their vacation. Today, they were on their way to the Estes Park Aerial Tramway Prospect Mountain. They planned to spend two weeks on vacation, but first Altermatt would visit a family friend, and Jónsson would travel to Colorado from Sorrow, Texas.

"Armando, you will be monitoring the progress of these families; the custom-made van will make it effortless to follow these people. Our three-man team will follow these two families to ensure there are no last-minute diversions to their plans and will help with the transportation of the children.

"Armando, you are responsible for ensuring the parents and vans disappear without a trace. I do not want anyone collecting souvenirs. The boys are to be swiftly transported to California, where they will be auctioned off three days after their arrival. The auction for the girls will take place in New York City. We will have customers participating in the Middle East and Eastern Europe."

Mr. Estrada is a licensed lawyer, and his specialty was foreign adoptions. He prepared the documentation to give the appearance that the child had been illegally adopted. Mr. Estrada was contemplated the situation.

The demand for adoption of children has created a fertile breeding ground for all sorts of illegal activity. The tens of thousands of United States dollars per child, which influential people from all around the world are willing to pay. Nations amid war or in the aftermath, extreme poverty, political unrest, or natural disasters. Combine that with very loose regulations and an almost complete lack of oversight, and you have a powder keg for deception, child stealing, and every transgression imaginable to obtain children to meet the demand.

Joshua Estrada had one request for Armando before shipping the girls to New York, and he instructed him how to prepare them.

Armando had learned something regarding those extraordinary examinations from Manuel, however never with such detail. Armando learned what the exam consisted of, and he could not believe his ears at what this man was saying.

"Sir, are you sure that is what you want me to do? Those children are too young and valuable to be taking chances with their health. What you are subjecting them to sounds dangerous."

"Armando, I did not stutter. You had better learn to follow my orders. Manuel never questioned me before. Do I make myself clear? Or would you prefer I place someone else in command, and you can be his assistant? I need personnel at my side to follow my commands without question. Can I trust you to follow my orders without hesitation? I have plans for expanding this business. You will prosper by my side—or do you want to continue playing second fiddle?"

Armando briefly contemplated the order of El Fantasma. Now was not the time to execute those orders.

The team Debra was heading had been trailing these families since they had left their homes in Socorro, Texas. *These people left their homes in just two hours ago. This has to be another stop for the children. At this rate, we will not get to the point of extraction until sometime next week!* Debra was concerned about the parents discovering they were being followed, which would compromise the element of surprise.

"We are going to be spotted. Bill, call Armando and ask if he wants us to go ahead with these two families. Their girls are letting the whole world know what route they are taking on Facebook. I can keep communicating with them because they are informing us of their every move. This trip was supposed to take fifteen hours calculating for gas and eating. We know the name of the hotel where they are supposed to stay for the night."

Armando received a call from Bill, who apprised him of the situation. Armando realized the schedule was useless; they had not accounted for the five children utilizing the bathroom so often.

Armando agreed with Debra and informed her to continue ahead to the point of extraction and take charge of both teams. "Furthermore, they will not reach our extraction point at this speed, so we will not be able to meet our schedule. We had planned to take possession of the children in six hours or so."

Armando had other concerns on his mind than his new, unexpected orders. However, in his opinion, Joshua Estrada was making a blunder. *That will be costly if it backfires.*

In the trailing team, Bill, the driver, was contemplating how to get out of this job. He had acted very sick since they had left. He felt someone had been following them since starting this assignment. *Something is wrong with this whole assignment. I have worked for Armando for years. He is not a forgiving man, and failure will result in all of us killed.*

Debra instructed Bill to drive ahead. They would meet up with the second team. She changed the plans while asking Carton his opinion, ignoring Bill. "We have nothing to be concerned about. I will continue corresponding with the girls for weeks. Each move their parents make, we will know about it."

Bill had known and worked for Armando for over two years, driving him around the first time he had to transport children cross-country. Bill needed to pull out of this job. He considered his options, but what could he do without Debra shooting him?

They left behind the families. Bill kept looking in the rearview mirror because something was wrong. He was so busy looking in the mirror that Bill almost had an accident. Bill drew the criticism of Debra and Carton.

Armando had followed the families. His concern was with the children. Their traveling plans were useless. He cleared Debra to join forces with the other team and assist in securing the children. Debra was supposed to report back once in position while keeping in touch with the girls until they were secured.

Armando was thankful for the Internet. *Our business is booming. The majority of the children we obtain are through the Internet, and Debra is my specialist. She gains their confidence. Children are so trustful.*

Armando had not heard from his teams for over three hours; it should not have taken them this long. Debra was not answering her cell phone, so he believed there something wrong.

Debra was an hour late, and Frank thought, *Debra should have been here by now.* He then saw a vehicle approaching them from a distance in the rearview mirror. "Ed, Debra finally arrived. Debra and Armando have researched these men, who are good samaritans; they will unfailingly stop to help a woman in distress. She will be standing next to her car with a flat tire. Ed, I think something is wrong—that does not look like her. I was under the impression she traveling with two men and driving in a van. That is a pickup."

"Frank, you are getting too jumpy for this line of work. Besides, I can barely see Debra from this distance. What makes you think that is not Debra? Nevertheless, if it is not our people, they will continue driving."

A minute later, a black Ford 250 drove up next to Frank and Ed with tinted windows. Then the windows on the driver and passenger side rolled down. Barbara had a smile on her face yet had a deadly stare.

Frank and Ed found themselves staring at weapons. They both raised their hands in the air.

"Gentlemen, you have been found guilty of attempted kidnapping and are sentenced to death." Barbara then tossed two hand grenades into the van.

An hour after Frank and Ed were sentenced to death, Armando became concerned. Armando could not understand why Debra had not reported back. "The teams are not reporting their progress. I cannot believe it is a coincidence. I recommend we send two more teams to transport the children. We need to discover what has occurred out there."

Joshua Estrada appeared to be captivated while listening to the radio, so he did not hear a word Armando said. Estrada looked up to him. "Armando, have you not been listening to the news on the radio? Debra and her team were ambushed and killed. It's reported as an automobile accident with no survivors, and there were no other vehicles involved. A reporter just described her vehicle. Now, the news is that a van was blowing up on the same road some thirty miles from the first accident. Ring any bells?"

"Armando, I have suspected for a while that we were being betrayed by one of our own, ever since arriving in San Antonio. This confirms my suspicions. Before we continue conducting business, we need to find the traitors. Is there another organization trying to take over this territory and then attack them? This is not the behavior of the police. We will have to cancel all operations and deal with the immediate problem."

"Sir, are you sure this is the right move? In my judgment, we need to be reconsidering a strategy to obtain those children; we made too many commitments with influential individuals."

"Armando, we have no choice in this matter, recall all our men. We need to know who is betraying us before taking any further actions. I am aware of your loss and will make it up to you in the future; you have my word."

Armando considered following up on his next assignment; this operation was a failure, the loss of his revenue was beyond repair, and El Fantasma would never make it up to him. He moved in behind Estrada, grabbed him by the neck, and lifted him in the air. He plunged his knife deep into the ribs of Estrada and twisted the knife three times. He had to make sure Estrada was suffering did not die immediately—those were his orders.

"Mr. Estrada, you are correct: this is not personnel. Your wife said consider this your notice of divorce. Sir, you were careless with the information on the computer, and the password is a joke."

Michael and Amber busted into the house as Armando was completing his assignment. Armando quickly dropped Estrada and drew his weapon, firing once at Michael and missing his head by inches.

Amber did not miss with one shot, hitting Armando in the forehead. She had to take out Armando, however Michael would never know who had given the orders to kill his father. She tried to save Estrada, who was mumbling something about his wife as he passed away.

Forty minutes after the demise of Mr. Estrada, Michael and Amber were on their way to the hotel. Victor and Barbara had called to claim they had completed their mission without any complications.

Amber was unusually quiet during the ride to the hotel. Michael knew she had to be upset about killing Armando. Richard had warned him once he started down this road, innocent people could get hurt. He felt it was his fault for placing Amber in that situation. Richard further felt whoever was involved could wind up with legal problems. Michael was on a slippery slope.

Michael pulled the vehicle off to the side of the road and looked at Amber. "I never meant to place you in this situation. I should have known better. This mission is going to hell ..."

Amber cut him off. "Michael, I am a big girl; it is a shame you have not noticed. I have been trying to call it to your attention for the last five years. I had no choice with Armando—it was a matter of your life or his. I am upset because you will never know who hire Armando to kill your father. Michael, who do you think took care of those men at the club? And stop mumbling already. Are you finally going to give me that damned ring you've been carrying for months?"

Michael was in utter disbelief. "How did you know about the ring?"

Suddenly behind them, an officer ordered Michael to turn off the vehicle over the speaker. Two officers came up behind them on motorcycles and turned their lights on.

The officers came up alongside Michael and Amber in the vehicle. Officer Morison ordered Michael to roll down both windows. Michael complied with the instructions. An officer walked up to Amber and ordered her out of the vehicle. Officer Morrison asked Michael for his license and registration; he seemed ready to draw his weapon.

Michael wondered whether there was any evidence that could tie them to the killing of Armando and Estrada. Were there any witnesses who may have written down the license plates of the vehicle?

Officer Morison informed Michael he was parked in a no-parking zone, next to a bank. It was making the bank manager nervous.

Officer Bumster, questioning Amber, then commented aloud "I want to hear this for myself."

Michael stepped out of the vehicle.

Officer Morison had been questioning Michael and wondered what his partner had discovered. He slid his hand by his weapon.

"Michael, did you propose marriage to this young lady here?" Bumster had a look of disbelief.

Michael have a sigh of relief. He thought, *We have to stop this mission. We have pushed our luck far enough.*

"Michael, have you taken months to ask this young lady to marry you, and you could not select a better location? I find it difficult to believe you are a former Navy SEAL with combat experience."

Michael replied, "I have simply never been able to find the right moment."

"Do you consider this an appropriate location? You have been carrying around her ring for months. Take out that ring—but do not show it to me. I will arrest you for attempting to bribe a police officer."

Officer Morrison looked at his partner. "I am hungry. Time to go." The officers turned and headed toward their motorcycles.

Officer Bumster looked at Michael. "Do not be here when we get back."

"Michael, are you ever going to give me that ring?" Amber rushed toward Michael to kiss and hug him.

An hour after Michael had proposed to Amber, he was back in the hotel with his fiancée, calling Jayda. "I will be coming home; we are driving to Dallas and taking a flight to New York from DFW. There is a position in Manhattan, and if it is still open, I am going to accept it."

"Michael, that's great. Are you planning to visit your aunt in Houston before driving to Dallas? I suggest you do. Mrs. Veronica Bishop called me yesterday and asked me if I had talked you out of visiting her. In case it does not affect your job prospects, you should at least visit for a day. It seems her husband is abandoning her. Let us keep this conversation between us. I felt sorry for Mrs. Bishop. She suspected her husband is having an affair and using a business trip as an excuse."

Michael had never been interested in visiting Mrs. Bishop. He realized that he could not even call her aunt or use her first name. Michael had used the visit as an alibi for being in that part of Texas. Now there was no reason for being anywhere near her. Nevertheless, it was his auntie asking him.

"I want to check on the job before deciding on visiting Mrs. Bishop. Only if it does not affect my job, Auntie, but I will call. First, there is someone special I would like you to meet." He passed the cell phone to Amber.

In Mexico, Altagracia, aka Consuelo, was walking around the Cortez estate grounds, as he referred his kingdom. She wondered whether it was safe to move. The news of Mr. Guzman was no longer in the headlines. *Besides, the sketches look nothing like me.* She looked around the area; the land was beautiful and deceivingly peaceful.

Consuelo was walking in the direction of a burned-out structure some two hundred feet on a downslope from her location. Then she was called by Mrs. Cortez.

"Can I ask you what are you doing walking around here while you still have work to do? My husband's number one rule: no one walks around this area of his land. Now, Alejandro has a mess in his room."

"Mrs. Cortez, I am sorry, I was unaware that I was not allowed to wander around this area. I was admiring this beautiful sight. I have already cleaned the room, and I meant no harm. I hope you do not hold this against me; it will not happen again. I need this job." She had accomplished her goals, so it was time to move on. *However, first, Mrs. Cortez is a vain bitch who needs to learn a lesson in humility.*

Mrs. Cortez changed the subject. "Do not let it happen again. Men think they run this world, but with the right words in their ears in bed, after flashing your body, they will do whatever you want. Remember that when you have the right man in your sights. You have a good eye for land. Was your father a farmer? I talked my husband into buying those thirty acres down there."

"No, my father used to help my uncle, who was the farmer. I used to know every inch of that land. Unfortunately, my uncle died over four years ago. Was that their home?" Consuelo pointed to the area where there seemed to be a burned-out structure.

"No, that was a barn, I believe, although with these peasants, who knows? It could have been where their daughters slept, and their animals lived in the house. I ordered my husband to burn that monstrosity down because it was blocking my view." The truth was she could not see the structure, not from where they were standing. However, there was no way she was going to admit to a peasant. Mrs. Cortez started laughing.

Consuelo controlled her temper and forced a smile along with Mrs. Cortez. She remembered questioning Michael, whom she had tried to subdue. However, his focus was on Amber, and nothing worked on him.

I had to change my strategy and go after Jason, which I will regret for the rest of my life. Michael was always smiling and acted friendly towards everyone, even his enemies.

He had told me, *"Disarms your enemy long enough to take advantage. Furthermore, always give your enemy hope. Remember, if they believe there is a way out, they will cooperate. Once they lose all hope, you have lost control of the situation."*

Consuelo was still smiling while taking a switchblade out and placed it on the stomach of Mrs. Cortez.

Mrs. Cortez had no time to react and was confused. *Does this woman realize how powerful my husband is?* "What do you think you are doing? My husband will have you killed!"

Consuelo felt there was no use in hiding her identity anymore; it was time to tell her the truth and move on. "I am not going to hurt you unless you try something stupid. You could survive, however your infant will not."

"Mrs. Cortez, you are correct. Some men are easy to control, and you are doing an outstanding job leading your husband by the nose. Giving him one kid with another monster on the way is a smart move, and because they are boys, you hit the jackpot. How do you think he will feel about you if you choose your life over his unborn son? Now, act like you are showing me this area and walk."

"You crazy bitch! When my husband finds out what you have done, you will wish he had just killed you!" Mrs. Cortez realized she had to change her tactics. *I will buy her off. Let my husband deal with this demented woman.* "Altagracia, please let me go. I will give you a suitcase full of money and my jewelry, and I will accompany you off the property. You will be rich."

"Start walking. Your husband is always insisting you exercise; he wants a healthy infant. Mrs. Cortez, this is your chance to comply with his wishes. And one more thing: call me by my real name, Consuelo Rosa

Fonseca. Do you remember your neighbors, Mr. and Mrs. Fonseca, with their three daughters?"

A couple of hours after Consuelo escorted Mrs. Cortez to the farm of her uncle, Mr. Cortez was arriving home with his son and four of his armed bodyguards. He walked into the living room as he called out to his wife. After a few minutes, he walked into Consuelo's room without knocking.

Consuelo was walking out of the shower, and she grabbed a towel to cover her wet body—but not too fast so that Mr. Cortez wouldn't be distracted. She wanted him distracted as much as possible. "Sir, can I help you?" She acted innocent as she reached for her clothing.

"Have you seen my wife? Her car is in the driveway. Do you know where she is?"

"Her mother stopped by a couple of minutes after you left. They left together. She informed me that she would be back in a few hours."

"Well, that means she will not return until tomorrow. Alejandro needs to sleep," Cortez said as he watched Consuelo dress. "When he is asleep, I want to speak to you in the library. I want to go over your duties while working here."

Consuelo observed Mr. Cortez, and she knew his every move like a book. *Working in a cathouse has its benefits.* "Yes, sir. I am looking forward to our meeting. Do you want to have something to drink after your Alejandro is asleep? You have to relax."

Thirty-five minutes later, Alejandro was asleep. Consuelo walked into the library with a bottle of whiskey and two glasses in her hands.

"You are incredible with Alejandro; he is asleep in minutes, whereas it takes my wife hours to have him in bed."

"Mr. Cortez, it looks like you had a difficult today. I believe this is your favorite drink," Consuelo said as she poured him a shot of whiskey. "Your son is intelligent and a good boy. I listen to what he has to say, give him a warm glass of milk, and read a bedtime story." Consuelo chose her words carefully with what she said about Alejandro. Mr. Cortez did not want anyone to correct Alejandro—even his mother could not punish him. Mrs. Cortez never disciplined Alejandro; she was only interested in the material things her husband gave her. Consuelo poured herself a drink. "May I, sir?

Mr. Cortez started to wake up with a headache, and he founded himself in bed. He did not remember a thing about what had happened or how he had made it to his bed.

The last thing he remembered was having a conversation with Altagracia in the library. His wife must have come home early. He was disappointed because he wanted to get to know Altagracia personally. Mr. Cortez thought he heard his wife moving around in the bathroom, but Altagracia came out wearing her birthday suit. He had never taken another woman to his bed, which caught him off guard.

Mr. Cortez tried to sit up to protest her being in his bedroom naked, but he realized she had handcuffed him to the bed. He said, "I am not into kinky sex. Untie me now, or I will make you regret the day you were born."

"Mr. Cortez, shut the hell up and listen. We have your son and wife. The quicker you cooperate with us, the faster they will return to the safety of your home. If you call your men in here before I drive out of your estate alone in your convertible with the top down, you will never see them again. That has to be verified by our spotters. Mr. Cortez, do I have to spell it out for you?"

"Do you know who I am? How much money do you—" He did not have a chance to finish his sentence.

"Your child and wife are safe as long as you are cooperating. We are not drug dealers. I have never hurt anyone with these hands."

Mr. Cortez thought, *After I recover my wife and son, I will deal with them one by one, including their families.* "How much money do you want for the return of my family?"

"First, I need information from you. You are going to tell me what did you do with the bodies you had your son burn alive in the barn. You also encourage your son to kill them."

"I have no idea what you are talking about!" he did not have an opportunity to say more before a sharp pain ran across his chest.

Consuelo placed her knife underneath the left armpit of Mr. Cortez and ran it across his chest. She did not want to kill him—not yet, anyway. "Sir, let me introduce myself. Consuelo Rosa Fonseca. Remember your neighbor, Mr. Fonseca? He was my uncle. He managed to escape and lived long enough to recount how your men raped his wife and girls. You did not have the decency to bury them. Today, I found the remains of their bodies in the barn. Do not insult my intelligence. Furthermore, I know it was your wife who wanted to have a clear view of the valley, and my uncle had built a barn that was obstructing her view."

"There are over five million dollars in the safe. You can have it all. Please do not kill us!"

"Your wife has already given us all the money and jewelry in the safe for her life. What are you going to do to keep your son alive? You will need to come up with more money. What do you think would be a fair price for your life and his?"

Mr. Cortez passed out from the wound while he was listening to her. When he came to, he noticed a stench of gasoline; it seemed to be all around him. "Are you planning to burn down this place?"

As he tried to scream for help, she quickly gagged him. He realized she had already dressed. She walked over to the corner of the room by the door and picked up his Alejandro, who was moving around but seemed to have been heavily drugged.

"Mr. Cortez, I have accepted the money in the save and the jewelry of your wife for their safety. Unfortunately for you, it is not enough for your life. However, if you can escape the fire like my uncle did, so be it." Consuelo threw the key to the handcuffs at the foot of the bed.

Consuelo took a lighter and towel soaked in gasoline, and she set it on fire. Consuelo was surprised when Alejandro took the towel from her hand and made a perfect throw, landing on top of the keys.

The flames were came from both closets of the master bathroom. Consuelo made sure flames did not reach him right away. The bed caught fire.

"Good luck, sir." Consuelo then locked the door behind her and down the stairs. "Fire!" she yelled while carrying Alejandro, who was heavily drugged with the narcotics his father kept for personal use.

"Help! Help! Someone, please help Mr. Cortez!"

The security team of Mr. Cortez rushed into the lobby with their weapons drawn. His head of security tried to grab the boy. She told him, "No—drive me to the hospital. Alejandro needs medical care. He got into the medicine cabinet and has taken medication. He was playing with matches again."

All the men placed their M16s down at the foot of the stairs. A man volunteered to drive Alejandro and Consuelo to the hospital and called the gate. "Leave the gate open for the fire trucks and to rush to the main house. They need help here."

Consuelo was next to the weapons as the men rushed up the stairs. She gave Alejandro to the man who volunteered to take them to the hospital, and he headed toward the door. She quickly picked up an M16 and shot the man carrying Alejandro. Then she turned toward the men who were halfway up the stairs, looking astonished with incredulity. She and opened fire on them.

Afterward, Consuelo walked over to Alejandro, who was trying to crawl his way toward the main entrance. She lifted him by his pants and threw him inside the house. All the years of pent-up anger was finally unleashed. "Help your father," she told the boy as she locked the door.

Consuelo went to the car and started driving. She headed toward the main gate and looked in the rearview mirror. The estate was up in flames. She stopped the car and realized there was something wrong. The men from the gate were running directly at her.

Consuelo hit the gas pedal and hit the horn, throwing caution to the wind. The men moved out of her way. Consuelo reached the main gate and drove towards the home of her uncle, going on the dirt road.

Consuelo stopped in front of the dilapidated house of her uncle. She carried a can of gasoline while keeping hidden from Mrs. Cortez. Consuelo smiled as she walked up to Mrs. Cortez.

Mrs. Cortes was tied up and gagged, in tears. She surrounded by barrels stuffed with money.

"Good news: your husband has agreed to pay the ransom. You will be free soon. You have no worries. Mrs. Cortez, there is no reason to cry; as you can see, I have not taken all the money. It looks like tonight will be cold."

Consuelo had hidden a gas can with a rag attached to it. "My father helped build this house. It was a warm house. Your husband has abandoned this place. I have something to keep you warm until they come to free you. She took out the can, set it on fire, and threw it at Mrs. Cortes."

The next day, the police reported that a rival gang had attacked the Cortez family and killed everyone. However, the police department and fire department omitted the drums of money found that were salvaged from the fire in a burned-out shack along with the body of Mrs. Cortez.

CHAPTER 13

THE DECEPTION OF
HAPPINESS AND PEACE

Mrs. Estrada was acting grief-stricken while receiving the news of the demise of her husband. The detective was going over the attack of her husband. She wondered why there had been an attempted robbery. Her orders to Armando were specific: to make it look like a robbery gone wrong. Mrs. Estrada was going to break out crying—something she had mastered.

She had given Armando two assignments: eliminate her husband and ensure there was nothing left behind to incriminate her. *I cannot believe that a worthless man had the fortitude to fight back.* Her main concern now was recovering his laptop and phone. Mrs. Estrada realized that in one day, she had suffered a business loss: the man she had designated to run the organization in Texas.

On Saturday, January 6, 2018, three days after two unprecedented traffic congestions, two families started to enjoy their vacation. They were unaware of their close encounter with pure evil.

On that same date, another family was going to become acquainted with the horrors of human trafficking. "Mother, I do not want to be late. Would you dress Mia? She is refusing to listen to me, and I have not finished dressing. Everyone else is ready."

"Relaxed, honey. Every bride has the jitters on her wedding date. We have plenty of time; you take care of yourself, and the girls will help you. I will have Mia ready in a few minutes."

Forty-five minutes later, an anxious bride to be, Carroll, arrived at her church. Henry was outside smoking a Cuban cigar as the men around him started rushing him into the church.

Carroll waited until Henry went inside the church. She was anxious for the ceremony to begin. Mia ran out of the car.

Henry was not suspicious. He wanted to abide by tradition. He caught a glimpse of Carroll and her sister Mia running in between the group. Mia was bouncing in, and the crowd disappeared. He kept looking back, but Mia was nowhere in sight. He found that odd.

Henry was impatient for the ceremony to start. "Has anyone seen Christian? He is late again."

They were running behind schedule when several police officers walked into the church. The men in three-piece suits were accompanied by the police officers. He did not recognize them. *They must be from my betrothed's party.* Yet they walked toward his parents.

One of the men in suits said, "Sir, do you have a son named Christian?" He then identified them as FBI agents and added, "We need to speak with you outside. Would you please follow us so that we can converse in private?"

Silvia and Warren held hands; she was becoming anxious in anticipation of what they were going to hear. Her oldest son was an alcoholic. A long time ago, she accepted that one day a police officer would notify her of Christian's death, likely in a car accident.

Warren was a snob who loved throwing names around. "Officer, you are creating a scene. Give me your business card, and I will contact you when I get around to it. Police Commissioner Madison has been invited you to the reception. Do yourself a favor and leave."

Agent McFarland was never known for being tactful, and he said in a boisterous voice, "Mr. Warren Bridgemore and Mrs. Silvia Bridgemore, you are under arrest for human trafficking and selling your daughter into human slavery."

While Agent McFarland was talking, a uniformed officer moved in to handcuff them. Other officers read them their rights in front of all their guests. FBI Agent McFarland then turned his attention to Henry. "Are you Henry Bridgemore?"

Henry nodded and feared what the officer would say next.

"You are also under arrest for human trafficking. I heard you asking about your brother Christian; he is in our office cooperating with the investigation."

Carroll wondered why they had not started playing the music. Was Henry getting cold feet at this stage? She could not wait to start walking down the aisle. Then she noticed several persons leaving the church, and they seem to be averting their eyes from her.

Carroll saw Henry and his parents were being escorted in handcuffs by the police officers.

Seven-year-old Mia ran over to Carroll and held her hand for the first time in weeks. Mia was smiling. She never liked Henry—he always gave her the creeps.

In San Antonio, five minutes before the arrest of Henry, Silvia, and Warren Bridgemore, DA Lara Fitzgerald was in her office waiting for a call from Oklahoma City. She had indicted more public officials in the last two weeks than most district attorney did during their entire careers.

Detective Fillmore was proud of the work DA Fitzgerald had accomplished but was concerned about her welfare. The way she was exposing corruption in this city was unprecedented, and she was fast becoming a target. Notoriety, fame, or having an ego had nothing to do with it; Lara Fitzgerald saw the law in black and white, and this was a way to clean the city of all corruption.

"Carl, you seem distracted these last couple of days. Is there something wrong? Have you heard anything thing from your connection in Oklahoma City? How is the classification of the movies coming along?"

"We have solved several murders because of those videos. The parents of the twin boys were buried alive under the orders of Mr. Guzman. I believe we will unearth their bodies by next week; we know the area where their bodies are."

Fillmore wanted to converse without any interruptions, so he made sure the door was closed. "I want to discuss something with you, and I want you to be truthful in your answer. Have you received any threatening calls?"

"No. Carl, you have asked the question in several different ways. You need to stop worrying."

"Lara, a reporter wrote that you are the most feared prosecutor in San Antonio. People have to be worried you may go after them next. Understand that many officers support what you have accomplished and want to see you continue. You have to be vigilant. This is the list of high-ranking officers their names and ranks, and their cell numbers." You can trust them."

"Even if someone looks at you cross-eyed, do not hesitate to call any of those numbers. And you have my number." Carl passed her the list of the officers she could trust. As they were carrying on their conversation, her cell phone rang.

"DA Lara Fitzgerald, if you try to trace this call, I will hang up. This will be my final contribution to the weak justice system we have in this country. Mr. Manuel Mendoza has a storage locker on 3440 Fredericksburg Road in San Antonio. He has incriminating evidence of the organization and persons involved. Get a search warrant, and you will hit the jackpot. Congratulations on the Bridgemore family; I just heard it on the news. And be careful about whom you trust—Mendoza's list contains heavy hitters.

"So far, you have been dealing with lower-level personnel up to this point in the organization; this is the list of judges you can trust for the search warrant." Michael gave DA Fitzgerald the locker number and the names of three judges she may be able to trust. He then hung up the phone without waiting for a response.

Two hours later, Lara Fitzgerald and Carl Fillmore had gone over all the documentation they needed for Monday. She had one case at 1:30 p.m. in court, and the warrants were a secret between them. "Let's call it a day. If this information is correct, we will be busy for quite a while. Carl, are you and Brenda coming over for dinner tonight?" Brenda was Fillmore's wife of thirty years. "I will prepare her favorite dish."

Fillmore nodded. His main concern was checking the area for any suspicious activities or characters. "I will follow you home."

Lara Fitzgerald started her pickup and had a look of dissatisfaction. "Okay."

Carl Fillmore was about to reach his car when he heard two shots ring out. He turned toward DA Lara Fitzgerald, who was slumped in the seat. He drew his weapon while running toward her. As Carl ran, he was wounded and struggled to reach her, and he called for backup and an ambulance.

"Carl, I should have taken your warnings seriously. Do not let them get you. Hide this." Lara was unaware he also was shot. Those were her last words.

A few police officers ran with their weapons drawn toward their location.

Fillmore knew what she had implied and took the key from her hand. He placed the key in his keychain before collapsing to the ground.

Two days after Michael learned DA Lara Fitzgerald had been assassinated and a detective was critically wounded, he was still feeling guilty. He though it did not make sense. Then again, Michael was the one who had started her down this road.

Michael was visiting Veronica Bishop in Huston with his fiancée, Amber. Amber was the one who had finally convinced him. Michael had not seen Veronica since he was nine years old.

Amber indicated he could have a misconception about his aunt and needed to give her a chance. "Michael, honey, when she opens the door, smile. You are not dealing with the Wicked Witch of the West, as you are fond of saying."

A servant greeted them at the door. "Miss Amber Fisher and Mr. Michael Jayden Manford, Mrs. Bioship is waiting for you. Please follow me."

Veronica Bishop wasted no time in asking Michael his plans for the future. "Michael, let me be blunt with you. The offer from New York sounds good. Your military record is spotless, with a Purple Heart, Bronze Star, and Silver Star. Moreover, it is my understanding that your commander has recommended you for the Congressional Medal of Honor for your last assignment."

"Your military record is impeccable and your meal ticket into politics. You need to take advantage of it now. I suggest you run for office in my party, and I recommend you move to Houston. With my endorsement, you would win by a landslide. However, if this area does not suit you, I can help you find a more suitable location."

Michael was stunned. His last mission had been classified Top Secret. How had she obtained that information?

"I am preparing to run for the presidency in 2020. I think I will make history as the first female president. Please keep this to yourself. Should you decide that politics is not for you, work on my campaign. Afterward, you will be able to write your ticket in Washington, DC."

Michael replied, "Amber here was one of the first female Navy SEALs. She has been in combat and decorated. The newspapers will eat up that the type of publicity. Amber knows more about politics than I do."

He wanted to see Mrs. Bishop react. From what he observed, she was only interested in him. Her focus was him running for office or work on her campaign. Michael had no way of knowing what she was up to, and it made him edgy. He wanted no part of whatever she was contriving, and he wished he had followed his instincts.

When Mrs. Bishop stepped out of the living room to answer a phone call, Amber said in a low voice, "Have you noticed there are no pictures of her husband? No photographs anywhere. I find that strange."

"We have never been closed. All I know is when her husband died, she had him cremated the next day. I think she told Auntie Jayda once that her family name carried more weight in politics than her husband, and he was only the first person in his family to attend college."

"Michael, are there more family like your aunt? Because she acts concerned for your health and career. However, she is as phony as a three-dollar bill. I am waiting for the butler to disinfect this room as soon as we leave. Thank you for renting a room downtown. I will not stay here any longer than we have to—she gives me the creeps. You are right about one thing: she is evil incarnate. Why did you bring us here?"

Michael looked at her with a surprised look. "What? You are the one who defended her!"

"Michael, you have to learn one thing, now that we are engaged to be married. This means I am always right, and you are never wrong–as long as you agree with me." Amber smiled as she kissed him.

On Friday, January 12, 2018, Michael disbanded the team. Barbara Whitmore had contacted her parents and flown to Montreal–Pierre Elliott Trudeau International Airport in Canada. Greeting Barbara at the airport were her parents and Mr. Muller. He had never given up on finding his daughters. He had hope of finding them or at least giving his daughters a proper burial. Members of the police task force had wanted to interview her.

Victor Fernandez moved to Washington State. He wanted to move his family far from his activities in the last four months. Furthermore, Jason had told him many good things about the state.

Michael and Amber were on their way to New York. Richard

Livingstone informed him the position was filled. Michael had a meeting with Richard in Manhattan because Richard was in New York on business.

On Sunday, January 14, 2018, Michael and Amber were on a flight to New York City from Houston, Texas. They were planning their future, including the number of children and where to settle down in New York. They were both college graduates from prominent colleges. Amber had several interviews lined up. Michael had two interviews set up the following week. They were going to select an affluent location to live in and raise a family.

Forty-five minutes after landing at JFK, Michael flagged down a taxi, but another taxi cut off the first on. Michael shook his head and thought, *Taxi drivers are outrageous.*

After an hour of traveling, the taxi came to an abrupt stop. Michael knew that traffic was heavy at this time of the day in the city and did not give it a second thought. Suddenly, the doors flung open, and a man was yelling at them, "Get out now!" He had an accent and aimed weapons at them.

Michael realized the driver was in on the holdup. Furthermore, this was no ordinary robbery.

"You guys can take whatever you want. I need her identification," the man in charge instructed the other two men.

Michael realized he needed to buy time and create a distraction. He grasped Amber by her hand, directing her toward him. When they stepped out of the taxi, he tossed his wallet at the driver. "We will walk away; you can have our possessions."

Michael was only concerned about protecting his fiancée. He stared at the man in charge. They were not leaving witnesses behind; the other men were also aiming their weapons. Michael tried to cover Amber with his body as the men started shooting at them. Michael was hit twice in the back and lost consciousness.

On Tuesday, January 16, 2018, Michael woke up at Saint Vincent Catholic Medical Center. Jayda was sitting by his bedside, and she looked worn-out, as if she had not moved from his side since she arrived.

"Auntie, was Amber hurt too bad?"

"Michael, we have to talk."

Michael already knew what Jayda had to say. He had seen that expression on her face twice before. He did not want to hear what came next and broke down crying.

CHAPTER 14

REVENGE IS A DOUBLE-EDGED SWORD

For the longest time, I studied revenge to the exclusion of all else. I built my first torture chamber in the dark vaults of imagination. Lying on bloody sheets in the Healing Hall, I discovered doors within my mind that I'd not found before, doors that even a child of nine knows should not be opened. Doors that never close again. I threw them wide.

—Mark Lawrence

Three months after the assault on Michael Manford and Amber, Captain Mora felt something was wrong with the case assigned to Detective Aurora. "What is bothering you about this case being classified pending? We have a good description of two criminals."

"When the police officer tried to question Michael for a physical description of the last man, in my opinion he held back, claiming the individual stayed in the background and was unable to see his face, and the man did not speak. Yet in his verbal statement at the hospital, the third man opened the door to his side of the car and ordered him out."

"What are you thinking, Detective Aurora? Mr. Manford is out for revenge?"

"Captain Mora, I have traced the two men described by Mr. Manford to the morgue. The men were tortured to death. Mr. Manford has a convenient solid alibi, yet, he is guilty as hell. Look at his military record."

Michael was in his condominium, unable to make sense of why these men had spared his life. Up to this point, no one could give him a reasonable explanation. He had moved to Guttenberg, New Jersey, where he could see the Hudson river from his co-op.

"Michael, I am here. Where are you? Oh, there you are. I do not believe you have left this prison you've created for yourself. Go clean up—you look a mess. I have not seen you look like this since you were defecating in your diapers. It time you confronted your monsters."

"Auntie, I have everything I need right here: a gym, a swimming pool, and a racetrack that's about half a mile. I have the equipment I need to recover from my injuries. I can have whatever food you want delivered. And the reason I look a mess is that I was working out at the gym."

Jayda cut off Michael. Watching him wither away in his condominium, which he had turned into a tome, broke her heart. *He has secluded himself from family and friends.* Jayda was afraid that in time, Michael would become a hermit. She knew that if he continued down this road, it could lead to attempted suicide. "Michael, I am sure you went out last week— on the twelfth of the month, to visit Amber's grave. And you scheduled a medical appointment for the same day. Michael, you have centered your life around her death. How am I doing so far?"

Her tone of voice shook Michael. Jayda had never talked to him in that manner. "Auntie, what is out there for me to look forward to? If you want to eat, I can order anything you want. There is nothing out there for me I want. Why don't you come back tomorrow and let us see how I am feeling?"

"Michael, are you throwing me out of your apartment? Yes or no?" Jayda had a look of hurt in her eyes. Their conversation was interrupted by a knock on the door. Jayda walked over to the door, concern for the mental health of Michael. "Yes, how can I help you?"

"Excuse me, I am looking for a Michael Jayden Manford. Is this where he lives?"

"Can I ask you how you got up here without a security guard at the lobby announcing you? I am calling downstairs and finding out what kind of Mickey Mouse operation they are running here."

Michael heard the conversation between his aunt and the man at the door. He had never heard the man's voice before, so he quickly grabbed his weapon. Michael was not surprised that these animals were coming after him. However, his aunt did not have anything to do with his activities in Texas or elsewhere. No one was going to hurt Jayda.

As he stepped into the hallway and concealed his weapon, Michael recognized the voice: it was a detective from San Antonio. Michael remembered reading about the detective who was wounded. *That was a fast recovery.* Michael figured the detective was here to question him about the fire, however he had been nowhere near the club. *Let me see what he wants. This man is not here to arrest me; he is out of his jurisdiction.*

"Detective, I remember you working in the DA's office in San Antonio. This is my aunt, Jayda. Come in. Can I get you something to drink?"

As Carl stepped into the apartment with a cane, he struggled to maintain his balance. "My name is Carl Fillmore. I am no longer with the police department; I retired several months back. Can I trouble you for some water?"

Jayda quickly walked over to the kitchen to retrieve a bottle of water. As she passed Michael near the kitchen, she caught a glimpse of Michael carrying an automatic weapon in a holster, covering it with his shirt. She thought, *Has Michael lost his mind? This is not normal behavior.* Jayda did not even know he owned a firearm.

She was going to talk with Michael to find out how he could draw a weapon when someone knocked on the door. *This has to do with his trip to San Antonio.* She got a glass with ice and opened the bottle of water in front of Carl Fillmore. She then excused herself and headed toward one of the spare rooms.

"Michael, you can relax. I am not here to reflect on your activities in San Antonio. As I informed you, I am retired am not wired. I have turned off my cell phone. I want to know how many people you entrusted with the information you were providing us. Whoever you trusted betrayed all of us, and that almost cost our lives." Carl pulled out his phone and showed it to Michael.

Michael was feeling guilty about people losing their lives and was tired of carrying the guilt. He was not sure what this man wanted from him, but he would play dumb. He needed to protect the members of his team and the women they had fought to liberate. "Carl, you are right: someone betrayed us. I can assure you I worked alone."

"I understand your sense of loyalty for wanting to protect the people helping you, however this is what I know. Understand I am not here in an official capacity. Nor am, I after you for any reason other than finding out who betrayed us. Let me lay my cards on the table. A club mysteriously when up in flames. You managed to help nine women escape in a van disguised as two police officers, one being a woman. At the same time, you rescue four women from the front of the Hotel Emma under the alias Christen Roberson.

"You will excuse me, but that is one hell of a trick for just one person to pull off. Harry Houdini could not have pulled off that stunt by himself, and you are no magician. Before I forget, there are cameras at the hotel that caught your image, as well as the two police officers and the chauffer. Shall we stop bullshitting each other?"

"Okay, let us have a frank conversation. Whoever killed DA Lara Fitzgerald, the information did not come from my team. The leak had to come from her office or the court, when she tried to obtain a search warrant. I apprised her not to trust anyone. The information provided to your DA was on the level. Furthermore, those were the only judges Manuel Mendoza could not bridge."

"I will buy that. However, we were never able to obtain a search warrant. Once DA Fitzgerald was out of the way, the majority of the cases were dropped. Furthermore, the evidence against DA Bolton disappeared from the police department. Let us get back to why I know the betrayal came from a member of your team or someone you trusted.

"When you started feeding us information, I began sweeping her office and even placed a camera in the office. I did find a couple of items that were not government-issued."

"I never told my team members about what information I was obtaining from Manuel Mendoza or the documents he may have in his storage locker. I never even told my aunt what I was up to. Mr. Fillmore, I need …" Michael stopped cold in his thoughts. There was something he wanted to verify before making any accusations.

"Michael, do not make that call. You will tip them off. And please, call me Carl; Lara always does—I mean, she used to. You do not have to wonder about the recording that may have an image of two people liberating women from Mr. Guzman's club or the hotel. It seems those files have disappeared."

"Carl, the way you are expressing yourself, it sounds like she is still alive. Tell me the truth. For the last six months, I have tormented myself for all of their deaths. You trust me enough to try to recruit me? I know you did not track me down to tell me I am no Houdini."

"You are correct, Michael. Although it looked like DA Lara Fitzgerald was going to pass away, she is recovering. She will still need some medical attention. Michael, I am sure you will understand we had to make it look like she had."

"Where are you hiding her?"

"I am concerned that our secret is out. They do not want the public to know she is alive because they want to eliminate her. They also learned that she has a habit of making duplicates of each case she was working on.

I would say that is making them nervous. The word on the street is that El Fantasma placed a million-dollar bounty on her head."

"Carl, has anyone attempted to recover the documentation? You have the locker number? The evidence could expose their leadership—and maybe even El Fantasma. It could place them on the run or in jail."

"Michael—do you mind if I call you by your first name?"

Michael waved his hand to indicate it was okay.

"After the shooting of DA Lara Fitzgerald and me, I had someone rent a locker on the information you gave us. I had cameras installed around the area to see if someone showed interest in the contents of Mr. Mendoza's locker. He used an alias to rent the locker. There is no legal authority to obtain a search warrant unless we know the information."

"Manuel Mendoza was vague in the information he provided; it was like pulling teeth. He believed I had evidence establishing his innocence of killing Mr. Davila Soto. I would exchange it for knowledge he had against Mr. Guzman and El Fantasma. All the information obtained, I relayed to the DA Fitzgerald. Trust me, you do not want to know how." There was a pause in his sentence; he did not want to implicate Jason in a murder plot. *Jason died a hero. Why tarnish his memory?*

"Manuel Mendoza was a wealth of knowledge on human trafficking with names, dates, and places. Let us not forget the information that is in the locker. I tried to turn Mr. Guzman; you already acknowledge the results: it turned into a dead-end. I returned home to marry my fiancée, and that is a topic I do not want to discuss."

Carl said, "You think you and your fiancée, were selected at random? Is that why you were running around the track like a Navy SEAL training for a mission two weeks after being released from the hospital? You are gearing up to go back, except you are alone and not after justice. It is vengeance you have in mind. Tell me I am wrong."

"Sir, if you are not here to investigate me or to turn me over to authorities, what do you want from me? I tried to help your DA, and it all went to hell because of the broken justice system."

"I want to help you finish what you started, legally, because whoever went after all of us is not finished with their work."

Fillmore gave Michael a newspaper clipping and commented, "The article is from the *Toronto Sun*. Miss Barbara Whitmore was killed in an automobile accident in Toronto." The article was about her life while being held by human traffickers for over ten years.

As Michael conversed with Fillmore, Jayda received a phone call. "Have you talked to my nephew? It has been six months, and I will need an answer soon. I cannot hold that position too much longer for Michael. I want to give him the opportunity he deserves. Has he told you what we talked about before?"

"Mrs. Bishop, Michael was shot several times and almost killed, and Amber was murdered. You will excuse me for saying this, but Michael did inform me that you wanted him to run for political office. Michael said he was not interested. Why are you insisting? I will have him call you back later; he has a visitor right now."

Jayda did not wait for Mrs. Veronica Bishop to respond, and she hung up the phone, she was still in a bad mood. Veronica always exacerbated her.

"Michael, I am telling you we need to work together as a team. Otherwise, they will pick us off one by one. This organization has already killed a woman you liberated. Please understand that you are not alone."

"Mr. Fillmore, you will excuse me, but in your present condition, you will slow me down, and we could both be killed. You would be exposing DA Lara Fitzgerald to further dangers."

"Maybe I did not make myself clear. I will be working in the background, protecting DA Lara Fitzgerald. Two other people are working with you."

"I want to meet these people you want me to work with, and if I don't approve, no deal. Detective Fillmore, who is guarding DA Lara Fitzgerald now?"

Chapter 15

Human Trafficking: The Never-Ending Cycle

Carl Fillmore departed the apartment two hours after his arrival. Jayda wanted answers. "Michael, are you ever going to tell me what that man wanted? He did not travel from San Antonio to wish you a speedy recovery. He needs more medical attention than you. One more thing: since when you carry a weapon in your apartment? Is that weapon registered in New Jersey? Does this have to do with your trip to San Antonio?"

After a few seconds, it was obvious Michael was stalling or was not going to answer her questions. Jayda took from her purse a booklet that seemed to be old but it in good condition.

"Let me give you what you have been looking for ever since the death of your mother."

"Auntie, what is this?"

"You have tried to break the code of the diary. This booklet contains the code. You left it on the nightstand when you took the journal. Michael, remember that you are not a vigilante. I raised you to know better than that. In San Antonio, you were looking for answers about your father? I had my doubts about the death of Jayden, however I did not want your mother to know. Catherine was adamant the death was no accident."

Michael nodded.

"Well, that booklet may give you the answers you are searching for.

However, I warn you do not do anything stupid that you will regret for the rest of your life."

"Auntie, how did you know this is the code?"

"Catherine told me she wrote in code and that the booklet has the key, because a certain nosy boy was always trying to read her diary. Furthermore, remember that your vigilante days are over. I expect you to turn over any evidence to the authorities."

"Auntie, I once overheard my mother inform you that she felt my father was killed. You dismissed the idea as without merit. You told her it was her grief speaking. Have you always believed that to be the truth, or were you frightened someone would come after us? Whom did you suspect?"

"No one in particular. It just seemed like a strange accident. Your father was an amateur racecar driver, a good one, and he could have turned pro. The driver of the dump truck steered into him on purpose."

In San Antonio, Mr. Arthur Charpentier had searched for several people. It seemed that the original reports of the demise of DA Lara Fitzgerald were premature. He was on his way to the Admirals Club because the manager may have a tip on her whereabouts. He had been in San Antonio for over three weeks and had been looking for DA Lara Fitzgerald, to place her underground.

The manager greeted him. "Mr. Arthur Charpentier, I hope that I pronounced your name correctly. Call me Esteban. If you need anything to help accomplish your work, do not hesitate to ask. Meanwhile, if you need anything, please let me know; it's on the house." Esteban looked at the woman working in the club as if saying, *Pick one.*

"After I complete my mission here. And call me Arthur. Do you have some good news for me? I could use a ride back to the hotel."

Esteban took out a white envelope from his sports jacket and handed it to Charpentier. "Angel, our chauffeur, will give you a ride when you are ready."

Early the next day, Arthur was conversing with El Fantasma. "I was under the impression that we were looking for only two collectible items. I see five relics on this list."

"Congratulation on your job in Toronto, Canada. Now, I want those items to appear to different collectors." They had learned to speak in code in case someone overheard their conversation. Furthermore, El Fantasma was a collector of the painting and artifacts, so it made sense to use that lingo. Afterward, El Fantasma would research items that could be sold in the area that she would be interested in adding to her collection.

A week earlier, Michael was having lunch with Richard. Michael, I wish you would have informed me four months ago. The position is no longer available. We had to transfer one of the most experienced men in our main office to New York. Presently, I do not have any openings."

"Richard, I have always valued your opinion. I have an opportunity in San Antonio and will be relocating there." Michael hated saying those words; he had never wanted to go down this road in his life.

"Michael, you are going into politics? I am sure you will win. Have you selected a location San Antonio where you are going to live? I have been meaning to talk to you about Amber. I feel somewhat guilty." Richard found it difficult to express himself and seemed to stumble over his words.

Michael interrupted him. He did not want him to continue—it too painful for him to bear. "I should have been paying attention to the driver. That will never happen again; I will be looking around San Antonio. Amber loved that area of Texas, and I was thinking of settling close to where she grew up."

Back at present, in San Antonio, former DA Thomas Bolton was having a conversation with his attorney. "What do you mean, I have a problem? They never had any evidence against me! DA Lara Fitzgerald tried to make a name for herself by destroying the lives of anyone who stood in her way.

I am an honest person, and she has trashed my reputations. I do not mean to speak ill of the dead; may she rest in peace."

"Sir, you will be indicted. We received the tip from a clerk at the court. Do you have any idea what they may have? Sandra Carlson has turned state's evidence to the Feds, and they have given her a plea deal."

After twenty minutes of consulting with his lawyers, Bolton walked out of the office dejected. He wondered what evidence Sandra Carlson had on him. He needed to clear his head, and walking always helped him do his best thinking. After thirty minutes of strolling around town, it came to him.

Sandra Carlson had been into criminal activities for a while, and she purposely omitted certain crimes to the feds. Bolton had known that for some time. That would void her plea deal while destroying her credibility on the stand; it may even lead to his acquittal. *I will make it look like the federal government covered up her crimes to prosecute me.*

I remember losing a similar case with more evidence, especially after the prosecution evidence disappeared. The defense attorney mounted a vigorous defense for his client with more evidence against the defendant. Tomorrow, I will consult with my attorneys to inform them how to mount our defense. Now, I need sleep.

Bolton walked into his condominium on 215 Center in San Antonio.

The headline in the newspapers the next day read that former DA Bolton, reportedly facing new criminal charges, committed suicide.

Fiona made a call to Sandra Carlson and said, "We need to talk now." Then she hang up without saying another word.

Fiona made the arrangements to meet Sandra Carlson at the office of their doctor in private. Once inside, the examination room was made available for a modest price, where they could converse without interruptions. "Have you seen the news today?"

"Fiona, you call me here to tell me the obvious? I was surprised he lived this long."

"No, it is time we vanish, or we're next. El Fantasma already put a hit on us. You know that as well as I do. We talked about taking our money and disappearing when things got hot. Well, I say we are approaching our time to bail."

"You're forgetting something, one minor detail: the ankle bracelets." Sandra was upset at Fiona as she pointed to the ankle bracelets they each had.

Fiona smiled. "Sandra, do you remember Officer McNamara? He is allergic to shellfish. No one knew how, but the officer came in contact with shrimps. McNamara was drinking coffee and got sicker than a dog. He lost the keys to the ankle bracelet temporarily, just long enough to make copies of it. You can learn a lot from dating married men."

Fiona held up two keys. "These brackets have a malfunction, sending a false message of being disconnected to the police station. The desk sergeant will not dispatch a unit unless the system is offline for over three minutes. Sandra, this will give us the time we need to remove the ankle bracelets and have them working again."

Fiona and Sandra carefully masterminded their escape plan. They would not travel together, would never contact each other, and would not inform the other of her journey. They figured it would take the police at least two weeks before discovering their escape.

A week after Fiona and Sandra carefully hatched their plan, the desk sergeant dispatch patrol car to their homes to check on them. For over a day and a half, Fiona had not moved, and Sandra had barely moved around. The police had to break into their homes after no one answered the door. The officers found a dead cat with an ankle bracelet around its body.

A search of Sandra revealed a small dog in critical condition with an ankle bracelet around its neck. Investigators concluded that the women forgot to leave food and water for the animals.

The DA believed that they escaped on the same day they had medical appointments and put out an all-points bulletin for their arrest. They concluded that because former DA Bolton had committed suicide, Fiona and Sandra absconded to circumvent longer prison sentences.

A few days after the police discovered Fiona and Sandra had absconded, Mr. Arthur Charpentier was having a conversation with El Fantasma. "A job well done once again. All the interested parties are happy with the sales. What about the other two items? I want this wrapped up as quickly as possible. There are other business ventures, and I want those artifacts before moving on to a different enterprise."

There was some hesitation in selecting his phrasing. "I have secured the artifacts you were interested in purchasing. The last commodities will be more difficult to find; we may have to shop outside of San Antonio. I will keep searching in various stores. So far, I have come up empty. Do you want the receipts for the first three items?"

"No, you can dispose of them; keep me informed. I need the whole collection." El Fantasma had to have those persons terminated.

Arthur Charpentier thought, *I will keep these receipts for my collection.*

Michael read the journal of his mother, and tears rolled down his face. It helped him understand her. He was disappointed there were no clues as to who may have killed his father. He had returned to San Antonio to help track down whoever was after DA Fitzgerald.

Michael kept a close eye on the new club. There was one completely unexpected ally. Michael had been keeping records of people visiting the club and had observed the area for weaknesses. He examined each photograph while matching them with names.

Angel Castillo had returned to work at the club under new management for the last three months. He accepted being a chauffeur while faking a limp and using a cane. Angel did not want to work for the organization, however Mr. Guzman had a hit on him and his sister. Angel had no choice until he could find a way out without jeopardizing his sister. These animals would come after both of them.

At 11:55 p.m., Michael and Carl had been studying photographs taken at the club for hours. "Carl, do you have the name to go with this picture?"

Carl looked through the notes. "I got the information here. His name is Mr. Arthur Charpentier. He is here from Toronto. Why the interest in this man?"

"That is our assassin—the man after you and DA Lara Fitzgerald, and the man who killed Barbara Whitmore."

Lara Fitzgerald cut in on their conversation. "Michael, how could you be so sure?"

Michael replied, "Barbara Whitmore informed us of her kidnapping with two friends who never forgot his name. Do you think he is here on vacation, or maybe it is coincidental? Consider the scenario we have in front of us. We need to obtain the property Manuel Mendoza has in the storage lockers."

Carl said, "Lara, will you please excuse us? I need to talk to Michael alone." Then Carl turned to Michael. "We cannot legally obtain the evidence in the locker. It wound be inadmissible in court."

Michael said, "Carl, you are right. However, this will give us other avenues with those documents we can use to confirm their actions."

Carl warned, "The fruit of the poisonous tree' is a legal term that means any evidence obtained afterward is not admissible in court."

Michael was upset. "You have to be kitting me, right? You are troubled about the legality of using the documents that may or may not be found? These animals have no respect for human rights or the law. We have been dancing outside the law since you asked for my assistance. Carl, do you have a badge tattooed on your ass? You are a retired police officer. Who are you trying to protect? Not your honest Joe Blow on the street.

"Carl, you could have been shot by a rogue cop. It is time we fight back. Let me know when you are ready to do that. Otherwise, I am wasting my time." Michael was hot under the collar and ready to walk out on them and do things his way, as he has been planning long before Carl had showed up in New Jersey.

Two hours after Michael and Carl had their discussion, a van drove down a dirt road. Arthur Charpentier was heading a three-man crew to eliminate Detective Fillmore and DA Lara Fitzgerald. He had not wanted to move against the detective until he had found the DA. Arthur had received a tip DA Fitzgerald was staying at the same residence.

Arthur Charpentier instructed the driver to keep the engine running, and he and the two other men quickly walked in the direction of the former detective's home. They were going to frame Carl Fillmore by planting drugs and money; two police officers and a detective were in on the arrangement. The police officers would wait until Arthur called 911 and then be the first on the scene.

Outside the home, Arthur Charpentier told one man, "Go around the back—and no witnesses."

The man turned and walked toward the backyard.

Arthur walked up to the front door with one man and knocked. After a while, he heard someone sounding sleepy. "Yes?"

That was their clue to ram the door hard and take out the person answering. The other man would come in through the kitchen. They both hit the door hard, but to their surprise, they flew into the home.

Carl had set himself up to ambush the intruder and was entering the backyard. Then the lights went on, surprising Carl.

Brenda was unaware of the events taking place, and she had turned on the lights in the backyard. She walked in between Carl and the intruder. She had mistaken the intruder entering through the back gate for her husband. "Honey, what are you doing out here in the dark?"

The man shot Brenda repeatedly.

Carl ran toward his wife, throwing caution to the wind. He was unable to get a clear shot and was shot twice, fatally. He caught his wife, and they both passed away in each other's arms.

Angel Castillo ran up to the intruder and shot him in the back of the head.

Meanwhile, at the front door, Michael waited until both men were on the floor. Michael shot Arthur Charpentier in the right shoulder and then turn his attention to the man who was starting to recover. There was no mercy for this man; Michael shot him in the chest.

Michael quickly turned toward Arthur Charpentier, kicking him in the stomach repeatedly, and then shot him in the left shoulder. "Arthur, do you remember me? I hope you do, because I remember you. You should have killed me. Now it is my turn to decide who lives and who dies—unless you start talking about who wanted Amber killed, and why."

Arthur Charpentier turned his head toward Bernard Gunther, a longtime partner, and closed his eyes as tears rolled down his cheeks.

Two weeks later in Dallas, Richard said, "Michael, I want to thank you for meeting me here; I know you are trying to settle down in San Antonio. Your aunt, Veronica Bishop, suggested that my firm handle your security once you announced you are running for the House. She wanted you to meet with her before you go public."

"Richard, I have a question for you. How long have you passed information about me to Mrs. Veronica Bishop?"

Richard wanted to cut him off. Michael had been secretive lately and wondered what he had learned. "What are you talking about, Michael?" Richard asked. "Have you forgotten Amber lost her life during the hold-up? You were lucky to escape with your life."

"Richard, let us stop playing games with one another. You know what I am talking about. You have been informing Mrs. Bishop of my every move, including when Amber and I were returning to New York. Why did Mrs. Bishop have Amber killed?" Michael held up the engagement ring he had bought for Amber. "No, Richard, I would have gladly traded places with Amber. Recognize this? Furthermore, you were correct: Amber loved this ring.

"You were the only one who could have informed Mrs. Bishop that I was returning to New York, and before blacking out, I heard their leader caution them not to shoot me because Amber was their target. I never told anyone that Veronica wanted me to run for political office, yet you knew. Don't ever refer to that woman as having any relationship with me."

Richard swallowed hard. He realized Michael was on to his aunt. *When I heard the news Amber was dead, it hit me hard. Now that Michael has the ring, there is only one way he could have obtained it.* Richard never knew what Veronica Bishop was up to until it was too late. Michael had to be wrong about the hit.

Richard's eyes were turning red, and his voice cracked as he continued. "Michael, I did tell––Mrs. Bishop that you and Amber were returning to New York and when you would be arriving. My father drove this company into the ground, and my medical expenses were exorbitant. When Mrs. Bishop approached me, she bought the company. I am just a figurehead, and she ordered me to help convince you to run for political office. In return, she would make my financial troubles disappear. I have no idea why she would want to kill Amber, and it is still difficult to believe. At first I thought it was a robbery. A hit never entered my mind."

"Why is Mr. Arthur Charpentier after me?"

"Michael, I do not know who he is. Mrs. Bishop would not sanction a hit again you—she is planning a campaign with you by her side, making as many appearances as possible. She feels you are vital in her run for the presidency! On several occasions, she has stipulated that your military record will help her and you.

"Michael, what are you going to do? Mrs. Bishop has dirt on the people who have to announce their intentions to run for the presidency. Mrs. Bishop is using this agency to eradicate her opponents. How can I make it up to you?"

"Richard, as long as you keep this conversation between us, I am not going to do anything. You are working for me now. I will spare your reputation, but you will have to live with the memory of Amber. Remember her? The Navy SEAL who saved your life? The information I want from you is as follows …" After Michael finished taking, he walked out.

A week later, Richard relayed all the information his former friend had requested. Later that morning, Richard was in his office, and he called his secretary on the intercom and canceled all his appointments for the week without an explanation. He hung up the phone.

Minutes later, a single shot rang out from his office.

Mrs. Bishop had a big day plan for Friday, May 3, 2019. Jayda, Michael, and her family were in a restaurant. Mrs. Bishop was making her announcement for the presidency. Michael would introduce her to the public. First, Mrs. Bishop had gathered her family together for lunch at her favorite establishment.

Mrs. Bishop was an expert at manipulating the sympathy of the media and public. She had set up a moment: when she was walking out of the restaurant, a seven-year-old girl would run up to her kiss and give her a bouquet of followers.

Jayda knew Michael was playing a dangerous game. *Veronica Bishop will destroy anyone who double-crosses her. Michael is right about one thing: that woman is pure evil, and her vengeance knows no limit.* "So, Michael, when are you moving to San Antonio and making your run for political office?"

"Do you think I would help Mrs. Bishop become president of the United States? She is not fit to be dog catcher in Afghanistan after she had my father and Amber killed."

"Michael, you should not say anything critical about her. I do not like her either, however she very vindictive. If this country is stupid enough to elect her, she will destroy you and anyone else who stands in her way. Why are we here, if you feel that way?"

Around the same time that Michael explained to Jayda what he had learned about Veronica Bishop, DA Lara Fitzgerald was returning to her office under and FBI agent escort. She obtained a search warrant for the evidence against the organization in the lockers of Manuel Mendoza.

Agent McFarland led a team of agents and police officers to arrest Veronica Bishop. The evidence the FBI received had been collaborated, and they were moving to indict Veronica Bishop. Furthermore, Arthur Charpentier was dead after his raid of Detective Fillmore's home; the rest of the details were still sketchy.

Mr. Charpentier, the number two man, and Mr. Bernard Gunther, and his lover, felt no loyalty to Veronica Bishop. Mr. Gunther was recovering from his wound and detailed her criminal activities. Bernard Gunther had additional evidence against Bishop and her lawyer, and he worked out a plea deal.

The butler was expecting many people that day as he opened the door. FBI agents pinned him against the wall, and he quickly commented, "Miss Bishop is in the master bedroom upstairs," pointing to her bedroom.

The FBI agents rushed up the stairs and into her bedroom. A few minutes later, she was arrested for multiple counts of murder. Mrs. Veronica Bishop was escorted outside of her estate in handcuffs. Reporters rushed toward the front door while she tried to cover her face.

Michael had called the photographer who was in front of the estate and informed him to take plenty of photos of Mrs. Bishop. The cameraman tried to inform Michael of the situation, stating that the FBI agents were about to escort Mrs. Bishop away in handcuffs. Michael ignored the photographer and informed him there would be a bonus if he obtained good facial shots of Mrs. Bishop.

The photographer was speechless, although the bonus sounded good. He responded, "Yes, sir."

Jayda turned. "Michael, you and I do not drink, but let us go back to New York. I have a bottle of wine I have been saving for a special occasion, and I am going to take my first drink in celebration."

Michael placed three hundred-dollar bills in the hands of the waitress meal they ordered, thank her. He wondered what to do with the copies of documents he had accumulated on the organization.

Agent McFarland led Mrs. Bishop out of her estate handcuffed. She saw the butler and informed him, "The FBI agents are being used by my political enemies to frame me. Call my lawyers!"

The butler walked to an area where he could be alone. He thought, *I do not like you and no longer work for you.* He took out a throwaway phone, called her attorney, and then made another call.

The other end of the line said, "We are watching on the television. I warned Mrs. Bishop that she should stay away from political office. She has always been greedy. Neutralize the targets she wants. Afterward, I need you to do the following …"

The butler received his orders and hung up without saying a word. He destroyed the cell phone, walked out the back, and drove off.

As Michael and Jayda walked out of the restaurant, a crowd was gathering, and a hysterical woman was screaming to a police officer. The only information the officer could obtain was a name and age, eleven years old. A paramedic had to tranquilize her. "My daughter! Someone has taken my little girl!"

Human beings are similar to onions: the deep cuts expose more layers of suffering and grief. When human beings impose their intentions on the weak and defenseless out of greed, a never-ending cycle of dysfunction is created. Society must learn to bring a halt to these people who are willing to enrich themselves at the expense of our most vulnerable, who suffer the consequences.

The End?

Lightning Source UK Ltd.
Milton Keynes UK
UKHW011836020721
386556UK00001B/23